GW01159142

# Immersed By Blood

## Angela Sanner

Copyright © 2024 Angela Sanner

All rights reserved. No part of this book may be reproduced or transmitted in any form or by any means, electronic or mechanical, including photocopying, recording, or by any information storage and retrieval system without permission in writing from the publisher.

EerieLit House of Publishing—Bridgeville, Pennsylvania

ISBN: 979-8-991-7046-1-8

Library of Congress Control Number: 2024922082

Title: *Immersed By Blood*

Author: Angela Sanner

Digital distribution | 2024

Paperback | 2024

This is a work of fiction. Names, characters, places, and incidents either are the product of the author's imagination or are used fictitiously, and any resemblance to actual persons, living or dead, events, or location is entirely coincidental.

Thank you to my family and friends who pushed me to never give up. Times have been tough, but we've made it through! We've made it through the darkness, and we've entered the light at the end of the tunnel. Without you, this book would've never been written. Thank you all for your help and support!

# ONE

During the wrong moment, that woman's beautiful brown eyes happened to glance upward toward the darkened sky. Her long black hair; clipped to the sides of her head by diamond jewels. The diamonds glinted from the sun but suddenly covered by a rain cloud. She smiled at the sprinkle of raindrops as they splashed onto her eyelids, slightly smearing her mascara. Her dark skin was radiant and smelled fresh from her new bottle of cocoa butter. She didn't like to have dry skin. And quite frankly, she loved feeling the soft breeze as it gave her a sweet chill that chiseled right through her bones. Soft breezes made her feel happy and alive.

Her freshly painted red fingernails clutched the tiny fingers of her five-year-old son. His name was unknown at the time, but his mother's name was Lilly... like the flower. She was only twenty-one years old. She had the heart of gold. She was everyone's favorite little princess.

She was a beautiful, rich, African American woman; loved by so many but hated by one. The one person she trusted and the only person who wanted her dead.

Of course, it was only about jealousy; a deep hatred in Jasmine's mind. She had no heart and absolutely no love for her loyal baby sister... the flower. The sister that EVERYONE loved.

But her death happened so fast, faster than a blink of an eye. The bullet entered Lilly's right temple and pierced her brain upon impact. At that very second, the sun peeked out from behind the rain cloud as if it were asking what had happened.

It was a tragic loss to Lilly's family and friends as they gathered around the picnic table. They served a feast of chicken breast, corn bread and mashed potatoes for lunch.

Her five-year-old son spotted the sniper rifle. He screamed bloody murder as he still clutched his dead mother's pinky. His ears were ringing from loud screaming and crying from his family just a couple of feet away. He covered his right ear with his hand as he watched the rifle glimmer in the stubborn sunshine as it quickly whisked away through a window.

The church service ended ten minutes ago but Rosary Chime stayed in her seat to pray for her sins...sins that she doesn't want anyone to ever know about. She knows that these sins will eventually drag her down and beat her senseless.

Sometimes, Rosary wishes for this to happen; always put into her place. She even hates herself for the things she has done and the lives she has ruined.

Rosary feels as though her buttocks have frozen to the pew. She can't move. She feels ill as she self-loathes while gripping her mother's rosary necklace between her shaking fingers.

Her forehead perspires as she places soft fingers onto her right temple. She slowly places the strands of her short, black, sweaty hair behind her ear. Her pale, white skin gleams from the sunlight shining through the church's side window.

At least she's dressed appropriately for this occasion. Her mother would be proud of her for wearing her own black pants suit with a red jeweled necklace. Black is Rosary's favorite color. She always used to tell her friends that it matches everything. Her combat boots are even black. They look brand new even though they're ten-years-old. She can't seem to get rid of them.

She feels accomplished but she also feels like she has run a marathon. She's tired and weak in the knees. This illness is sudden and quite unexpected. She has never felt this way before. Her stomach is a tangled web of pins and needles. She has never felt THIS sick afterward.

She's rather calm as she collects her thoughts, thinking of her next move.

One thing is for sure, she doesn't plan to leave this church anytime soon. She's thinking of laying her stiff, thin body across the pew like a cat stretching its claws during a belly rub.

She just wants to sleep. Her thirty-seven-year-old body has taken its toll. She needs to retire. Her specific career path has taken up her time since she was sixteen years old. She's ready for a change. She's ready to move on and leave this, "hell hole of a state." That is what she likes to call it, but her opinion doesn't matter to most people.

New York isn't for her anymore. She wants to move out west. Her loneliness has gotten the best of her and she's ready to start fresh. She might even meet new people. But she's a loner, someone who doesn't have any friends anymore. Her family members have died or disappeared into thin air like a ghost...a ghost that haunts her brain every day of her life.

Rosary isn't like most people. She's highly skilled and extremely intelligent. As a matter of fact, she knows that she shouldn't be sitting here in this pew inside of this church. She knows damn well that she shouldn't be thinking of sleeping at a time like this.

But her combat boots are stuck to the floor as if someone squeezed glue onto the bottom of her soles without her knowledge. Her body is deeply exhausted and numb. Her arms feel like jelly and her legs are suddenly sore from running...running away from her problems.

Running away so she doesn't get caught...

Her mind seems to not care anymore. It feels as though her body wants caught. Her body wants to rest. It NEEDS to rest. She has been running for so long that she has forgotten how to treat and take care of her body.

She doesn't eat normally. She may bite into an apple here or there, but she doesn't actually sit down to eat a home-cooked meal. She likes yogurt and pudding. She munches on graham crackers and pieces of cheese. She's so thin that when she looks at herself in the mirror, it makes her sick to her stomach.

The same sickness she has right now. She doesn't understand why she's feeling so ill. Maybe she does need to eat something. She hasn't eaten anything in two days. Her work has taken over her health. Her work stresses out her mind and body deep down into their core.

*Things really do need to change.*

As she thinks of this remarkable decision to change her life, a veteran FBI agent of thirty-seven years, Detective Anthony De Carlo, enters the church as he sets his big, brown eyes on the back of Rosary's sweaty head.

His posture is dominating and strong, a tall, African American man with broad shoulders and a bright smile upon his face. He wishes at this very moment that someone could write the word, "Gotcha," on the front of his forehead.

His clipped badge at the front of his belt gleams in that same beautiful sunlight.

His fifty-five-year-old stance immediately looks like a barbarian ready to attack Rosary from behind. He creeps like a silent tiger ready to pounce on its prey. Although he is a big man, his footsteps are quiet and steady as he makes his way toward Rosary's pew.

Rosary sighs long and hard. The noise from her mouth sounds like the wind blowing in the breeze. Although she feels defeated, she doesn't feel scared. Her heart pounds with this sudden excitement as she feels this overwhelming mix of fear and happiness.

She closes her eyes briefly as she listens to the footsteps creeping toward her. She can hear Detective De Carlo's slow breathing. It's as if he's trying to hold in his breath but can't seem to hold it long enough. He sounds tired as well. He might even feel exhausted over the amount of time it has taken him to find her.

Her luck had run out. Her time is up.

And she let it happen.

Calmly, Detective De Carlo sits down next to her. His breath puffs out of his mouth like a cloud of smoke; thankful to stop holding it in for so long.

The detective watches a pastor emerge from a side door leading to his office. The pastor looks at him and smiles, nodding his head. The detective politely nods back, slightly glancing at Rosary with a sideways look upon his face.

"Well," the detective says smugly, "if it isn't Rosary Chime."

Rosary chuckles and then pauses for a moment, "Right before your very eyes huh?"

Now, it's the detective's turn to chuckle, "My tired eyes."

Rosary smiles as her eyebrows lift in laughter, "Finally."

De Carlo sighs, nods, and then bursts into laughter, "Yes ma'am. FINALLY."

There is an awkward silence as De Carlo thinks of something to say to this beautiful woman. He's awestruck at her beauty and charm. Her lips are full, pouting with bright red lipstick.

He simply cannot believe that this woman does what she does for a living. She seems so sweet and innocent, like an angelic light casting shadows inside of his skull.

He suddenly blinks; an image of him and her in his bed. He shakes his head as the feeling of a blazing fire licks his skin. He loosens his tie as he clears his throat.

Rosary watches him with a sideways glance and chuckles once again.

Turning her attention back to her mother's rosary necklace clasped between her fingers, she says, "You know, I usually come here after a clean sweep."

De Carlo watches her red-painted fingernails intertwine with the necklace and clears his throat once again. The hotness continues to creep up his neck as he glances at the side of her beautiful face.

"I know," he finally answers after a minute of silence.

Rosary turns to him, watching the sweat drip down his forehead, "Hot in here huh?"

De Carlo nods while he chuckles once again. This isn't what he expected. This isn't how he was going to approach this situation. But he had no clue about her true beauty in-person.

He doesn't feel that sense of urgency he had upon entering the church. Deep down, he suddenly wants to let her go. He suddenly feels guilty for coming to her place of worship.

He watches her eyes sadden as she stares at the rosary necklace.

"How fitting?" he blurts out as he stares at the necklace with fiery eyes. Gripping the top of his tie, he gracefully pulls on it back and forth to feel the soft breeze between his shirt and his hot skin. It feels like a fan on his face, and he sighs in relief.

Rosary laughs, "Yes. My mother was deeply religious."

De Carlo clears his throat again, "I seem to have something stuck in my throat."

Rosary laughs, "So... what's with the Italian name, Detective Anthony De Carlo? They call you Tony, right? You are obviously a beautiful Black man."

De Carlo can't help but burst into laughter once again. *A beautiful Black man? Now she's coming onto me. I can't deal with this heat anymore;* De Carlo thinks to himself.

"Yes," De Carlo answers as he watches Rosary cross her short legs. "I was adopted into an Italian family. I was a week old in fact, lived every day with a loving family."

*Well, isn't that just a bunch of roses in a garden?* Rosary thinks to herself.

As she nods, strands of her hair come loose from behind her ear. This simple action shoots another blazing fire through De Carlo's groin area.

*Stop it!* His brain screams.

"My mother died. She was sick," Rosary admits.

Although that's a half truth, Rosary smiles as she untangles her mother's necklace from her fingers, leaving it dangling from her fingertips. "My mother was a "church hero," they used to call her. Her involvement with this specific church was her whole life."

De Carlo isn't sure how to respond. He nonchalantly glances at the time on his gold watch. His wife, Jada De Carlo, bought that watch for him for their thirtieth wedding anniversary.

It's three o'clock, time to get going and head back to the station.

However, De Carlo feels as if Rosary has this urgency to spill her guts to him. He does know that she is a very lonely person. She has NO ONE. He suddenly concludes that she might return to this church to make peace with her mother.

Rosary chuckles once again as she says, "I find my media name very amusing. I am the cleverest, "hit woman," known to man." She continues to laugh.

Although he doesn't find this to be funny, De Carlo laughs with her. He finds it to be disturbing and quite sad for her. That guilty feeling continues to creep into his heart. He wants to apologize for showing up, but he knows that he has nothing to apologize for. She did this to herself and now she must pay the consequences.

De Carlo has been chasing this woman since she was eighteen years old. He finally has her in his grip, and he suddenly wants to tell her to run.

However, De Carlo senses that Rosary has finished running. That is why he is sitting next to her at this moment. He is beside himself as he realizes that he did not quite "catch," her. She just finally gave up from this nonsense in her life.

She is tired.

And so is he.

Rosary sighs, "I would rather be the church hero," she explains.

To lighten the mood, De Carlo laughs and says, "Well, most people have called you a courageous, "serial killer." How is that for a hero?"

Rosary bursts into laughter, "Serial killer...huh? I don't think that's any better."

As she nods, she watches De Carlo glance at his watch for the third time.

*My time has come.*

It has taken twenty-one years to end this nightmare.

She was taught at the tender age of sixteen how to shoot a sniper rifle. Her then, thirty-year-old boyfriend was a professional hit man.

She thought that Daryl was sexy and charming. She ran into him one day at the grocery store. During their ten-year relationship, they used to make jokes about the way they met.

Rosary had bumped her buttocks onto his thigh while trying to nonchalantly pick up a dropped apple. Of course, it was completely done on purpose because she wanted his attention.

He was incredibly attracted by her beauty that he immediately gave her a ride home from the store and then slipped a note into a grocery bag with his number written in a faded pen.

The numbers were written extremely sloppy, causing Rosary to call three different numbers before she finally dialed the correct one.

They laughed about it for ten years until Daryl was killed by his boss for Rosary not completing a hit job. Daryl had sworn up and down that Rosary was the right one for the job. She wouldn't let them down, he promised.

But she did let them down. The poor victim was a sixteen-year-old boy that she knew from school. She didn't have the heart to splatter his brains in front of his mother and nine-month-old sister. They were at the park playing and having a good old time.

Daryl suffered the consequences, and Rosary has never forgiven herself for it.

Up until this point, she completed her jobs and did what Daryl's boss told her to do.

As the tears fill her eyes, Rosary quickly blinks them away. She doesn't want this FBI agent to sense any weakness. She's not weak and she's only cried twice in her adult life.

Looking up from her mother's necklace, Rosary watches the pastor decorating the pews for Sunday's celebration of Easter.

She smiles as she begs, "Please, don't arrest me inside of the church."

De Carlo nods in agreement as he watches tears fill her eyes once again. He surely knows that she's not crying over being arrested. She's a lot stronger than that. She's actually the strongest fugitive and killer he's ever known.

He realizes that there's something else deep inside of her heart. There's something else that has tricked her mind into thinking that this was the right time to feel sorry for herself.

He isn't sure what she feels sorry for, but he intends to find out... someday.

He glances at his watch for a fourth time. It is now three-fifteen. He needs to get a move on, or his boss will, "ring him a new one," is what he likes to threaten.

"You are so beautiful. You shouldn't have chosen this path," De Carlo blurts out.

Rosary nods in agreement. Her tears instantly wash away but she looks satisfied. She looks as though she has come to terms with the consequences for her behavior.

De Carlo's cell phone rings.

*Simply great,* he thinks to himself. His boss is ready to pounce on his prey.

De Carlo excuses himself and answers the call from his boss, forty-eight-year-old, Curtis Garcia. Rosary nods as she watches the agent step away from the pew.

Her heart pounds through her chest as she suddenly imagines herself running from the church. She's running through the parking lot with, "guns blazing." She imagines shooting off one of her rifles and watching a bullet pierce through Detective Tony De Carlo's warm heart.

But she doesn't want to do that, and she shakes the thoughts from her mind.

She could get away with it. But that means she would forever have to run, and her mind reminds her once again that she's DONE running.

"Yes boss. I am making the arrest as we speak," De Carlo lies.

"That's not why I'm calling De Carlo," Curtis fires back. "I need you to come down to the Hotel Inn...Times Square. We have an urgent crime scene."

De Carlo hesitates. He would actually like some more time with Rosary, but he knows that it's not possible now. His boss sounds urgent. He sounds angry.

"I'm on my way," De Carlo responds.

Curtis hangs up.

De Carlo slips his cell phone back into his back pocket. Rosary tangles her mother's necklace around her knuckles as if she's about to punch the agent with a brass knuckle.

His heart skips a beat. He's suddenly angry and urgent once again as he imagines her punching his gut and taking him down as if he was a weak man on his knees.

He slowly approaches the pew. She turns and looks at him with saddened but bright eyes. She's ready to go and she wants to go now. It is TIME for her to go.

He realizes this notion and reaches out for her free hand. Smiling, she places her soft fingers into his firm, strong grip. De Carlo suddenly has this tantalizing thought of kissing her fingers.

*Maybe in another lifetime,* he thinks to himself.

Stepping outside, Rosary blocks the incredibly bright and warm sunshine with the necklace-twisted hand. Under the circumstances, the day has become beautiful and inviting.

*Maybe I should've waited for a rainy day to be arrested.*

Rosary laughs at her own thoughts as they approach the steps that lead downward toward the wide sidewalk. Her blue eyes blink from the brightness of the sun.

*Damn, I should've brought my sunglasses.*

De Carlo's vehicle sits alongside four other FBI agent's vehicles. Five agents are standing like perched birds at the bottom of the steps, pointing their weapons toward Rosary. De Carlo's partner, thirty-five-year-old, Tiara Mills, stands at the opened church doors while pointing her gun at the back of Rosary's head.

De Carlo raises his left hand and motions for his fellow agents to lower their weapons. Tiara is confused as she watches Rosary grip De Carlo's right hand in fear. Rosary is suddenly scared but she's trying to be strong. Well, she knows that she's strong but she's losing that feeling.

She doesn't want to sit in a jail cell surrounded by murderers and rapists. Maybe she could convince the warden of the prison to place her somewhere away from her fellow inmates.

De Carlo lets go of Rosary's hand as he pulls out the handcuffs clipped to his back pocket.

"Rosary Chime, you are under arrest for the murder of Lilly Brown. You have the right to remain silent. Anything you say can and will be used against you in a court of law. You have the right to an attorney. If you cannot afford an attorney, one will be provided for you," De Carlo stops as he watches his fellow agents open the back door to his police vehicle.

He continues, "Do you understand the rights I have just read to you?"

Rosary smiles a devilish grin. Her insides burst with laughter as she watches the faces of the other FBI agents. They look absolutely terrified as their eyeballs open wide, staring at her as if they just witnessed her snipe one of her victims.

"I'm ready to retire anyways," Rosary answers as she closes her eyes in ecstasy.

# TWO

The Hotel Inn in Times Square has become a mad house at this very moment. Tony De Carlo enters the hotel through the revolving doors and is immediately taken aback by the number of people huddled in groups, whispering to each other as if a rumor is passing along. He watches the manager of the hotel break up a group of employees who are fidgeting with their badges, talking on their cell phones, and looking around the entryway as if they want to escape.

He spots his boss, Curtis Garcia, speaking with a fellow officer of the NYPD. Other officers are speaking with hotel guests as they write notes in their notepads. They look bored as they try to seem interested in their conversations. A couple of guests brush past De Carlo in a hurry as if they want to get out of the hotel quickly. Everyone looks solemn and scared out of their minds.

De Carlo looks around the ritzy hotel with its bright lights and stunning décor. He smiles as he remembers bringing his wife here for the first time thirty years ago. Their original fling was only supposed to be a weekend getaway. They spent most of their time inside of their hotel room eating junk food and binge watching her favorite television show, "The Fresh Prince of Bel-Air."

They enjoyed themselves so much that De Carlo proposed to her a week later. She was astonished to say the least, but she said, "Yes! Of course I'll marry you!"

Thirty years later, they're still married and kicking it as if they just met.

Curtis notices De Carlo smiling as he touches the boutique of flowers on a table next to the seating area. De Carlo's mind is reminiscing the, "good ole days," as Curtis approaches him with a sour look upon his face. De Carlo touches the delicate flowers with the tip of his finger.

"Pretty, aren't they?" Curtis asks, sarcastically.

De Carlo snaps out of his trance of making love to his wife in their hotel room.

"Uh... yeah...sure," De Carlo responds as he smiles at his wife.

Curtis grabs his arm, "What the hell is wrong with you? And what took you so long?"

Curtis is in a foul mood and would rather be spending time on his newly built deck in the backyard while barbecuing. He needs a vacation from all this chaos, and he can't seem to get out of this funk that he's in. The past couple of weeks have been hectic for their department and he needs a break from all this madness.

There's a serial killer on the loose and Curtis can't take much more. They've been after this guy for months, but yet, the killer is still on the loose, making his rounds like a Merry-Go-Round. The whole city has been spinning in turmoil and he's frustrated at their lack of ability to catch the damn killer. They have come so close but they're so far from the truth.

Curtis has felt beaten down by his own boss as well as his fellow agents. Everyone has become on edge as no one walks down the street without looking over their shoulder.

They're on victim number ten and Curtis feels downright frazzled and torn. He can't believe that this is happening inside of his city, and he's vowed to catch whoever the killer is before he takes that long awaited vacation from this entire monstrosity.

"I was working on a case," De Carlo snaps, bringing Curtis out of his thoughts of his brand-new grill sitting on his deck, waiting for the cooked burgers and hot dogs.

"Yes, Rosary Chime. Did you finally bring her in?" Curtis asks as he looks around the chaotic hotel sitting area. Officers have dispersed, leaving as quiet as a mouse.

"Yes, with cooperation."

Curtis chuckles, "Good, one less bitch on the streets."

De Carlo's blood begins to boil over after the realization that the man doesn't give a damn about Rosary or the situation that De Carlo has been going through for the past nineteen years trying to catch, "this bitch." Curtis has never encouraged a safe ending to Rosary's shooting habits. He gave up on catching her until De Carlo persuaded him that he would, "do everything in his power," to follow her at every angle.

And he fulfilled his persuasion.

"Case number ten for the current killer," Curtis says changing the subject.

De Carlo's heart is beating fast, but he desperately tries to calm himself down. He and his boss do not see eye-to-eye sometimes and this aggravates De Carlo beyond his control. His boss steps on his toes and pushes him to the limit.

De Carlo has considered retiring early just so he doesn't have to see Curtis's stupid-looking face anymore. The man has a big nose that everyone stares at daily. As a matter of fact, he has a big mouth too that irritates most agents.

Newcomers think that he's the best Latino since sliced bread, until months down the road when they get to know him better.

He means well most of the time, but he's rude and obnoxious about most situations.

De Carlo predicts that one day his eyes will get stuck from rolling them so much.

As Curtis leads the way toward the elevator, he says, "Victim is an African American woman, fifty-years-old, black hair, brown eyes and about a hundred and ten pounds."

After the elevator doors open, De Carlo and Curtis step inside.

"Wait a minute. This specific killer has been murdering white women," De Carlo says.

Curtis nods in agreement, "Yes, the first nine victims have been Caucasian. That's why this case has changed every single lead we have accomplished. Same MO, same message, same kind of torture. So, the question is..."

"Why did the killer change the description of his victim to a Black woman?" De Carlo interrupts, asking more toward himself than to Curtis.

After a brief silence, De Carlo asks, "Do we even know that it's the same serial killer on the loose? Maybe it's a copy-cat. Maybe someone else wants their fifteen minutes of fame."

Curtis nods as he ponders De Carlo's remark.

"That's not a bad assumption..." Curtis trails off.

Stepping off the elevator, they enter the fifth floor. De Carlo smiles: imagining Rosary in his arms as they hug, holding each other as they passionately kiss.

Wait a minute...

Rosary Chime in his arms?

*Stop it! You are a married man!*

De Carlo shakes his head in shame. He can't seem to get that woman out of his mind. He wonders how she's doing at this moment. He hauled her off to the station where they took her fingerprints. He watched her face change from sadness to acceptance. She knew it was her time to sit back and relax and enjoy the time away from her boyfriend's boss.

De Carlo made a mental note to quietly visit the man who helped force her into a life of extreme danger and foulness. He's known the man's name for some time. All De Carlo knows is that she blamed this man for her sorrowful life as she tried multiple times to escape from his wrath. He always found her and threatened her life.

This man even found Rosary one time hiding at her sister's house. Her sister's information exposed like skin, and she never forgave Rosary for it. Rosary's sister, thirty-eight-year-old, Agatha Chime, wanted to be left alone from her family and Rosary had to BEG for her help.

Agatha regretted it the day she agreed.

But that's water under the bridge and Rosary hasn't seen her sister in ten years.

De Carlo follows Curtis down the hallway in silence. The hotel should have been buzzing with loud televisions, music playing, people laughing or walking down the halls. They should be walking past the hotel housekeepers as they prepare for their cleaning of the empty rooms.

It's a ghost town. It's eerie and quiet. De Carlo thinks maybe everyone in the hotel left for the day so the police can conduct their investigation.

Whatever the reason is for this silence, De Carlo doesn't like it. It makes him nervous.

He suddenly feels as though he's losing his mind. He can't seem to grasp the changes surrounding his environment. He's finally caught Rosary Chime, and she will soon be sitting in a jail cell for possibly the rest of her life. He's currently chasing another serial killer who has scared the whole city into thinking that every white woman will suffer the consequences of their actions. They are scared to meet new people. And forget sex, they don't want to be touched let alone dazzled by a stranger that they just met.

Everything is changing in a bad way. The biggest accomplishment was the capture of a hit woman who is cunning and smart.

Cunning and smart since day one.

There he goes again, thinking of Rosary Chime as she settles behind bars.

De Carlo inhales a quick breath and then sighs. He's confused but he knows that he is tremendously loyal to his wife. He has never cheated on her and he doesn't plan to.

But he has never felt this way about another woman in the past thirty years. There's just something about Rosary that keeps pulling him toward her.

It might be her beauty or charm. Well... IT IS her beauty. Even though she has killed people since she was sixteen years old, she seems classy and outgoing. She didn't have one mean bone in her body during the conversation at the church.

De Carlo's mind continues to swirl in circles as he and Curtis enter room number 504.

His life is in a sudden blur. He can't focus on the task at hand. He has this urgent feeling of suddenly leaving and driving back to the station. He wants to take Rosary and hide her in a safe place. She will not make it in prison. She's too beautiful and sweet to be locked up in a cage.

*WHAT ARE YOU TALKING ABOUT? GET A GRIP DE CARLO!! YOU HAVE NO IDEA WHO THIS WOMAN IS! STOP IT!*

As they enter the room, De Carlo immediately watches forensics as they take pictures of the deceased victim. They collect evidence, placing the victim's purse and clothing inside of plastic bags. This seems like déjà vu to De Carlo. Every week they are entering this hotel room and adding another innocent woman to the list of murder victims.

He notices the word, "CHEATER", written in capital letters on the wall above the bed in bright red lipstick. Writing this word is typical of this specific killer.

Whoever it is, they are exposing a victim's infidelities.

De Carlo sighs. It kind of irks him that they've come across this many cheating women.

*Who are you kidding De Carlo? All you've thought about for the past hour is Rosary Chime. You can't get enough of her for God's sake!*

De Carlo swears under his breath as he watches fellow agents stare at him with fear in their eyes. *Do I look THAT scary? Calm down people!*

"Get to work! Why are you standing around and gawking at me?!" De Carlo scolds the agents as if they were five-year-olds stealing his toy.

Immediately realizing that his anger has gotten the best of him, he takes a deep breath as Curtis approaches him. His boss's demeanor has changed drastically. He's no longer angry and annoyed. He's no longer insensitive and bored.

De Carlo quickly glances at the deceased victim and then turns away. This is the part that he hates the most. He hates looking at the dead bodies of these poor women. He feels helpless. He feels as though he can't help save them. There's a deep sadness that overwhelms his heart.

Of course, there's the typical tying of the female's wrists to the posts of the bed, the typical strangulation by a noose around her neck. This killer doesn't seem original but that is his particular MO. De Carlo and his crew have seen this kind of death hundreds of times.

After the room falls quiet with whispered words from his fellow agent's lips, De Carlo decides to approach the bed ever so slowly. His heart beats like a drum as everything turns into slow motion. It feels as if he's the only person in the room with the victim.

He stares at the woman with confusion in his eyes as he takes a step closer. He's creeping like a tiger pouncing on its prey once again.

He suddenly imagines Rosary Chime as victim number ten.

He imagines her silky, black hair tangled in a pool of blood. He imagines her naked body covered with decomposition. He sees her wrists and ankles tied to the posts of the bed.

As he takes another step closer, he sees the victim's black hair covering her precious face and eyes. Her head resting to the left side as if she were slapped across the face with such heavy force.

As he steps closer once again, he imagines Rosary's beautiful, blue eyes staring back at him. He imagines the hit woman reaching her bloody hand out for help.

He stops as his mind spins out of control. He blinks as he stares at the victim.

Placing his giant hand onto the woman's hair, he removes it out of her face.

Curtis's words replay in De Carlo's mind, *"Victim is an African American woman, fifty-years-old, black hair, brown eyes and about a hundred and ten pounds."*

De Carlo softly places his fingertips onto the woman's left cheek. He slowly lifts her lifeless face toward his teary eyes.

His wife of thirty years, Jada De Carlo, stares back at him with those big, brown eyes that he has loved for so long.

She stares but there's nothing inside of them anymore. He's expecting her eyes to light up with happiness like they do every day when he comes home from a long day of work.

He's expecting her to say how much she loves him and that she's sorry.

Was she ever sorry? Sorry for cheating on her husband?

As an officer is bagging a note left behind from the killer, Curtis slips on a pair of latex gloves and takes the bag from the officer. He removes the note and slowly walks toward De Carlo as if the man is about to explode with anger and sorrow.

He just might. He just might scream and tear this hotel room apart. He might rip the carpet out and flip the bed over onto its side. He might punch a wall or throw someone through a window. Better yet, he just might cry like a baby in front everyone in the room.

That's what he wants to do. He wants to feel sorry for himself. He wants to feel sorry that he never caught his wife cheating. He's sorry for not paying closer attention to her. He's sorry for working long hours and not satisfying her needs.

He's sorry that she had to turn to another man for love and support.

He's sorry that she was murdered for her infidelities.

Curtis approaches De Carlo with caution as he tries to hand him a pair of gloves.

"This is addressed to you," Curtis says with sadness in his eyes. He holds up the note as he waits patiently for De Carlo's response. Curtis's sense of urgency has disappeared as he stares at not only his agent of fifteen years, but his friend that he knows and loves like a brother.

Curtis would've never thought in a million years that Jada would have cheated on Tony. She always seemed so loyal and loving. She cared for her husband deeply.

But her body is dead from strangulation because she couldn't keep her hands off another man...a man who was able to enter her body with ease. This was a man who showed jealousy and despair. This was a man who wanted Jada all to himself.

Just like her husband did. Tony De Carlo thought that he had his wife all to himself.

De Carlo takes a glove from Curtis and slips it on. As he reaches for the note, he hesitates.

*What if it is a note for the man's declaration of his love for Jada? What if he wants to torment me or make fun of me for not knowing what she was doing behind my back?*

Curtis nudges the note against De Carlo's hand. He stares at Curtis with tears spilling down his cheeks. Curtis looks down at his shoes, unable to look at his friend's sadness and tormented eyes. This is the worst case they have ever come across together as a team.

De Carlo is trying to focus on straightening out his blurry vision. The tears are blocking the words written on a single page.

That's it...just a single page with a few words.

*Read it goddamn it! Stop acting like a baby! She cheated on you! It's time to act strong.*

*It's time to read what this son of a bitch said.*
De Carlo takes the note from Curtis's shaking fingers.

The note reads:
*Beautiful woman, beautiful eyes,*
*She was not what she disguised.*
*She said she loved me, she said I'm wise,*
*But in the end... her tongue, her lips, spoke of lies.*
*She loved us both, it made her mad,*
*She was the best lover I ever had.*
*Please forgive me, because I loved her so,*
*She ended it with me, to be with her beloved Tony De Carlo...*
*They all deserved it... Jada was just like the rest of them.*

De Carlo reads the note several times before he hands it back to Curtis for evidence. Curtis nods and replaces the note back inside of the bag.

The room continues its silence. Two of the forensic investigators quietly leave.

De Carlo's partner, Tiara Mills, enters the hotel room. She suddenly stops as she sees the tears in De Carlo's eyes spill down his cheeks and into the corners of his mouth. Curtis motions for the remaining officers to exit the room so De Carlo can have a little bit of privacy.

The officers leave as Curtis softly pats him on the back.

"Call me in about an hour," he says to De Carlo as he waves goodbye to Tiara.

De Carlo doesn't answer. He's frozen in his spot, staring at his dead wife before him.

Tiara approaches Jada with caution as she covers her mouth with her hands. As she stares at the noose wrapped around her neck, Tiara turns to apologize to her partner.

But De Carlo is gone.

# THREE

## ONE YEAR LATER

An early morning breeze shifts the temperature down to fifty degrees. April has approached as fast as lightning speed. The crisp, spring air sends chills down De Carlo's spine.

As his mind spins with thoughts of Rosary Chime, he questions himself whether the chills are from the chilly rain clouds forming above his head, or if it's from finally getting the chance to see this beauty for the first time in a year.

As he speeds toward the highway in his brand-new police Suburban, he envisions Rosary wearing an orange jumpsuit and her fingernails painted black.

He chuckles as he admits to himself; he has been secretly and anonymously sending her female products through the mail. He leaves no forwarding address on any of the parcels.

If Curtis Garcia found out, he would surely become angry at his agent.

De Carlo likes to send her deodorant, nail polish, toothpaste with a toothbrush, feminine hygiene products and make-up. One time, he even sent her a revealing black dress to wear for her court hearing. He didn't get to see her wearing it, but he imagined it showcasing her body like a professional model on the runway.

Rosary's lawyer, Judd Alexander, has repeatedly appealed for her three consecutive life sentences. Technically, the only proof of death that the courts have shown was the death of Lilly Brown. Other victims of Rosary's wrath have never proved to be her. Besides, her lawyer has argued repeatedly that Rosary Chime was under the supervision of Emilio Delgado, her boyfriend, Daryl Jake's crime boss. It was proven that Delgado forced Rosary into these, "snipe jobs," and if she didn't comply, he would threaten her life and beat her to a "pulp."

The judge has never been convinced of this theory and claims that Rosary had a choice to either run and hide or go to the police for help. Running and hiding was such a mind-boggling and bold suggestion that Judd immediately felt appalled and sick to his stomach.

It has been an endless battle for Rosary but her lawyer refuses to give up on his client.

Tony De Carlo refuses to give up on her as well. He feels as though they had some sort of connection that day he arrested her in front of a church.

And the day he found his wife dead at the hands of a tough, smart, and skillful serial killer.

De Carlo shakes his head. Every day he hopes and prays that the son of a bitch gets caught. He needs closure for his wife's death. He needs to finally sleep and get some much-needed rest. He will not stop until every single woman that has lost their lives by the hands of this sick individual, receives justice. It has been a little over a year and De Carlo still hasn't had the pleasure to wrap his handcuffs around the killer's wrists.

De Carlo slightly turns the heat up. He must be getting old. This spring weather has never given him chills like this before.

Well... he has never visited such a stunning and beautiful woman at a secured prison before.

The chills must be from the thoughts of her slim and sexy –

*Stop it!*

De Carlo chuckles once again. *Oh... how some things never change!*

As he pulls up to the New York State Prison, he unclips his badge from the front of his belt.

Two guards carrying rifles approach the vehicle as De Carlo winds down the window. He flashes his badge at the guards. A tall, African American guard with a fresh hair cut snatches De Carlo's badge from his fingertips as if he has no business being there.

"Good morning to you too, sir," De Carlo responds to the guard's nasty behavior. He watches the man as he lifts the badge closer to his sunglasses to see the details.

The other tall, Caucasian guard with a red-curled mustache smirks, "Benny hasn't had his morning coffee yet. It has been a long night."

Benny hands De Carlo his badge and then punches red-mustache guard in the chest.

As Benny then presses the button for the gate to open, De Carlo presses the button for his window to slide back up. But he suddenly stops and smirks at Benny.

"Maybe next time you should take those off," De Carlo says as he nods at the sunglasses perched on Benny's nose, "Might be able to see better... asshole."

As De Carlo drives through the gate, he can hear the red-mustache guard burst with laughter.

De Carlo smiles as he drives through the parking lot searching for a decent spot to park. Well, at least he knows that he and Benny will not be best buds anytime in the future.

Upon entering the prison, the sudden loud noises slam through De Carlo's brain like a hammer pounding on a nail. He feels as though his head is about to explode like a volcano.

A fight has erupted inside of the visiting area and as he approaches the glass shield in front of the desk, he watches multiple guards trying to break up the fighting prisoners.

De Carlo shakes his head as he remembers working undercover as a prisoner guard at a state prison many years ago. It was the worst experience of his life, and he will never do it again.

Approaching the desk, De Carlo politely smiles at the receptionist as she flashes big yellow teeth with pink lipstick smeared on her crusty lips.

*Where the HELL do they find these people?* De Carlo jokes to himself.

He places his FBI badge, his driver's license, his gun, and a brown paper bag through a compartment and slides the box toward the receptionist. He reads her name printed in bold, black letters on her name tag: EVA.

"Thank you," Eva says politely as she giggles. She then glances at his license while cracking her bubble gum between her teeth.

*For Christ's Sake!*

She then places his badge and license back into the compartment and slides the box slowly toward De Carlo as if she's trying to get his full attention.

De Carlo politely smiles as he retrieves his items, watching her rummage through the female products inside of the brown paper bag. She places each item on her desk; thoroughly searching through them as she opens the box of tampons, the box of toothpaste and a new hairbrush.

Nodding, she places the items back inside of the brown bag and then aggressively shoves it inside of the compartment, pushing the box toward De Carlo.

Her demeanor suddenly changes as she asks, "Who are you here to see?"

*That took a wrong turn*, De Carlo thinks. *Must be jealous...*

"Rosary Chime," De Carlo responds politely.

Eva quietly whispers, "Ha!" before she presses a button. The giant door buzzes and clicks as it opens for him to enter the visiting area.

"Have a lovely day," De Carlo says to Eva as she waves him off. She quickly turns her attention back to the paperwork on her desk before saying, "You'll get your gun later."

De Carlo takes a seat at a table as he watches the previous fighters disperse through the opened metal door with multiple guards gripping their arms in frustration.

He glances back at Eva as she's talking on the phone while glaring at him with piercing eyes. She then suddenly smiles at him as if she were in a trance. She then replaces the phone back onto the hook as she helps a woman stepping up to the glass shield.

"Nut case," De Carlo whispers to himself.

The anticipation of seeing Rosary for the first time in a year excites De Carlo so much that he feels like a giddy ten-year-old opening a Christmas present.

He truly doesn't understand why he even feels this way about her. He doesn't really know much about her past or her childhood. He doesn't know what she likes to do for fun.

Besides, he's here for a serious conversation. He's not here to wine and dine her. He's not here to ask her out on a date. In fact, he should be completely head-strong and confident with this proposal he's about to ask.

This woman makes him act differently somehow. She makes him weak in the knees. She makes him feel like a teenager all over again as if he is asking her to be his girl-friend.

He used to be shy growing up. He was never one to be outspoken or loud in a sense. He kept to himself as he only had just a couple of friends. He was not bullied in school because of his build. He was big, just like he is now, and tall with long, muscular legs.

He joined the wrestling club and played football. He loved his sports.

De Carlo was easy to talk to and friendly with everyone. Despite his looks, his extreme intelligence with school-work, or the color of his skin, he talked to mostly everyone in school and no one ever had a problem with him. He didn't care if whether an individual was black, white, brown, female or male, he was friendly and that was what everyone adored about him.

But he can also be scary when the time is right. His anger is terrifying, and it can even scare him half the time. He is not someone to mess with in a time of crisis.

He will rip a person's head off.

De Carlo thinks of this as he chuckles. Well, not literally... but he could rip someone's head off if he were desperate enough.

As he continues to wait for Rosary's arrival, he watches the television's screen turn on and the volume turned up by one of the guards. A weather man declares that it will be a bright and sunny day despite the rainy clouds hovering above as he speaks.

De Carlo checks his gold watch. He doesn't have time to sit and wait much longer but he doesn't want to leave until he's seen this beauty from inside of this beast of a cave.

*She doesn't belong here.*

A woman guard suddenly steps through the hallway while clutching Rosary's arm with her sweaty fingers. They approach the metal gate, and the guard buzzes the door open.

Rosary is clutching her mother's rosary necklace between her fingers as she looks up from her feet and stares directly at Tony De Carlo.

Her eyes light up like Christmas lights on a tree. De Carlo smiles as the feeling of butterflies tickle the insides of his stomach.

Rosary steps inside of the visiting area. The woman guard with a name tag of: TAMMY shoves her prisoner into the seat across from De Carlo.

Rosary glares at her with those piercing blue eyes. Tammy leaves as she slams the gate closed and locks it with her set of keys.

"Beautiful, isn't she?" Rosary asks sarcastically as De Carlo watches the guard disappear through the hallway. He feels his cheeks burn with embarrassment.

"Not as much as you," De Carlo blurts out the words before he can stop himself.

Rosary smiles as she looks around the visiting area, "Very true," she agrees, laughing.

De Carlo slides the brown paper bag across the table. Rosary grins as she slowly takes it from his fingers, touching the tip of his thumb.

An electric shock strikes the inside of his body and into his groin.

"So that was you sending me all these pretty little gifts," Rosary says as she rummages through the bag. "Yes, I do need more toothpaste," she continues, laughing at the tampon box.

"I can just imagine the look on the cashier's face with this prized possession," Rosary shakes the box of tampons and then places them back inside of the bag.

De Carlo laughs. He loves the ease of her friendliness and joking personality. She's like a ray of sunshine on a cloudy day. She makes him feel warm and fuzzy inside.

"So?" she asks as De Carlo glances at the television. He suddenly feels shy and awkward. He looks at her with a puzzled expression on his face.

"What brings you here Detective Anthony De Carlo?"

De Carlo laughs, "You can just call me Tony."

"Okay... Tony. I'm sure you're not here to eat eggs and pancakes with me."

De Carlo nods in agreement, "No, no I'm not here for that. However, that wouldn't be a bad idea." Rosary laughs as she plays with the strands of her black hair.

De Carlo notices that she has painted her fingernails a light purple color. She's wearing the brown eye shadow and black eye liner that the agent sent to her three weeks ago. Her hair is the same length as when he last saw her exactly one year ago; combed and held back with purple hair clips attached to both sides of her head.

She is wearing an orange jumpsuit with her prison number written in black marker across her chest. Her favorite combat boots are tapping the floor with impatience.

"You just want to get down to business I guess?" De Carlo asks.

Rosary looks around the visiting area, "Well, it's not like I have all day huh?"

"Fair enough," De Carlo agrees as he glances at his watch.

Rosary watches him with a sudden feeling of sadness through her veins. The last time she watched this man glance at his watch with impatience was when she was finally arrested.

At that time, she was ready to go. She was ready to relax and finally get away from Emilio Delgado. She wanted to feel secure inside a safe place.

The warden of this prison, Adeline Montana, agreed to place her in a cell far away from mass murderers and rapists. Rosary hasn't gotten the chance to meet the warden face-to-face, as of yet. She wants to thank her and shake her hand. It appears as if Rosary is living a life of luxury here at this prison and she is actually enjoying every minute of it.

She thinks about her apartment quite often. Sometimes she wishes for her belongings.

She also thinks about her next move if her lawyer ever gets her out of this place. However, she knows that she has a long way to go before she can step into her apartment and pack up her stuff. She wants to get, "the hell out of dodge," her mother used to say when she was younger.

That saying used to make Rosary laugh. Now, it makes her sad.

"Well," De Carlo says, interrupting Rosary's thoughts of relaxing in a soap-bubbled bath. "I have a job for you... unless of course you decline."

De Carlo piqued her interest at this point.

"And that is?" Rosary asks with a sly smirk to her lips.

De Carlo clears his throat. His face flushes with heat, and he unbuttons the top button to his collared shirt. He knew not to wear a tie this time. He didn't want to choke to death from the intense heat that this woman burns into his skin.

He stares at her intense but curious eyes. Her long eyelashes blink at him with a flirtatious smile. The small, round birthmark on her left cheek crinkles as she continues to smirk, intensifying the heat that licks through the inside of De Carlo's chest and into his heart.

"I would like to hire you," De Carlo answers as he fumbles with the top button to his collar.

Rosary raises her eyebrows as she tightens her grip on her necklace.

"For what exactly?" she asks as she watches De Carlo's forehead perspire.

After a brief pause, De Carlo responds, "To find the serial killer who killed my wife."

Rosary looks at the agent with sadness. This information takes her by surprise. She had no idea that his wife was murdered, let alone by a maniac running the streets.

"Easy enough," Rosary says as she listens to the news reporter on the television screen.

"The latest news... another body has been found at a hotel in downtown New York..."

De Carlo slowly glances at the screen and sighs as he thinks of his wife's dead body tied to the bedposts. The word, "CHEATER," flashes inside of his brain like a neon sign.

He feels this anger as he thinks about a killer running around and torturing poor women.

"I want you to kill him," De Carlo cuts the silence with a knife.

Rosary ponders his statement. She isn't sure how to react to an FBI agent who is demanding that she, a "hit woman" and a "serial killer," herself, commit murder while sitting in prison.

For a moment, Rosary slightly thinks that this man isn't well. He must be ill like her mother was. Her mother was shipped to a mental institution long ago for being ill.

Before Rosary can respond, De Carlo continues, "My wife's case is cold... as many other cheating wives' cases have been cold." Rosary's eyebrows lift in surprise once again.

"It has been a little over a year. He was on the loose about a month before you were arrested," De Carlo says as he glances at his watch for a third time.

Rosary is shocked and quite sad that she has had no idea about what has been going on. She suddenly realizes that if she didn't make that choice to get caught, she could've gone after this wild man a while ago. She could've saved many lives.

She feels angry at herself. Her heart feels hurt.

"I need your help," De Carlo begs, "I need you as my hit woman."

De Carlo suddenly feels this rush of anger flow through his veins like a waterfall. He feels angry at himself, he's angry at his wife and he's angry at Rosary for letting him catch her. He isn't sure why this angry feeling pulsates throughout his whole entire body.

There's a long silence between them as the reporter on the television screen changes the subject to social media posts. Rosary isn't sure how to proceed with this situation.

Sure, she would like to get her hands on her sniper rifles once again, but she isn't sure if she wants to kill anyone ever again. Her mind is confused as she imagines herself looking through the scope and shooting a bullet through this killer's brain. She's confused because she decided to be completely done with this type of career path.

De Carlo once told her she shouldn't have chosen this way of life... and he was right.

"I need closure," De Carlo suddenly continues as he watches Rosary's painted fingertips wrap her mother's necklace around her fingers.

De Carlo is quite puzzled and intrigued that the necklace hasn't snapped in half from how hard she actually pulls on the jewels when she becomes uncomfortable.

Rosary notices his puzzled look of confusion and snaps, "It keeps me from holding my rifles," which is the God's honest truth. She must keep her fingers busy.

Killing had become her addiction. When she wasn't perched high up in a building somewhere gawking through an open window, she had to find another way to keep her hands free from harm... harm toward other people.

"Even though my wife is a victim," De Carlo says, changing the subject, "she made her bed and had to suffer the consequences."

"I'm sorry to hear that," Rosary says as she untangles the jewels to her necklace. "I've given your request a lot of thought."

De Carlo takes a deep breath. *Here it is! She's going to stop this madness!*

"And I will think about it some more," Rosary answers as her combat boots tap with impatience. She's ready to go back to her cell. She has had enough conversation for the day.

His request has become quite stressful for the past several minutes. Her mind is on lock down and she no longer wants to think about killing another human being. That is why she is here. She chose to stop murdering people for payment.

"I will pay you well," De Carlo begs, "No one will have to know. This is between me and you. You will not get into any trouble."

Rosary nods as she listens to the desperation in his voice. "I'll think about it," she says again as she looks around the visiting area for a guard, gripping the brown paper bag in her other hand.

Suddenly, De Carlo's anger rushes through his body and he's unable to control it. Reaching forward across the table with his massive fist, De Carlo grabs Rosary's throat, and squeezes with his bare hand. As she chokes, she happens to smile at his angry eyes as she grips her necklace inside of her fist. She doesn't scream. She doesn't even cry. She watches De Carlo's brown eyes fill with tears.

An alarm sounds off and red lights flash throughout the visiting area. Rosary continues to stare at De Carlo as he chokes her. In some way, she wished for this to happen. She has wished that someone would kill her for her sins.

Three guards rush down the hallway and quickly buzz the metal door. Before it opens fully, the woman guard from earlier pushes her way through it and then pulls out her gun from its holster. She points it at De Carlo's head.

The other two guards grab his arms as he lets go of Rosary's throat.

De Carlo watches her plump lips smile at him as the guards escort him out of the metal doors and next to the desk with the glass shield. Rosary watches him through the Plexiglas windows and then suddenly blows him a kiss.

De Carlo is quiet as the guards push him through the metal detectors and then out of the front doors of the prison. The bright sun blocks his view for a couple of seconds, and he loses his balance. His feet stumble but he catches himself using a pillar next to the front doors.

"Get the hell out of here!" one of the guards' yells in his face.

As De Carlo takes some time to catch his breath, the guards enter the prison and slam the doors shut.

*What have I done?* De Carlo thinks to himself as he sits down on the top step of the stone staircase leading up to the prison doors.

He's too old for this. He can barely breathe. Those guards knocked the wind out of him, and he has become quite dizzy. The sun beams down on his forehead as the sweat drips onto his temples and then slowly creeps its way onto his cheeks.

He needs a drink... an alcoholic drink.

As he imagines the taste and sharp bitterness of whiskey on his tongue, the front gate guards, Benny and red-mustache, come running toward him with their weapons drawn.

"I knew you were trouble... asshole," Benny says as he points his gun at De Carlo's head.

Red-mustache happens to glance past De Carlo and then he suddenly backs up, lowering his weapon. He suddenly seems nervous and anxious to go back to his post.

Benny takes a step backward as he continues to point his gun at De Carlo.

De Carlo hears the sound of high heels hitting the pavement as the front doors of the prison close shut. De Carlo turns around, suddenly aroused at the sight of this gorgeous woman standing before him.

"I suggest you lower your weapon," the woman says to Benny.

Benny begins to respond but the woman holds up her hand to shush him, "Go back to the main gate," she orders with a smile on her full lips.

Red-mustache quickly turns and runs down the steps two at a time. Benny lowers his weapon but glares at his boss with hatred in his eyes.

"NOW!" the woman shouts as Benny continues to ignore her request.

The woman takes a step closer toward Benny as he takes a step backward, "Or do I have to make you leave?" the woman asks as she stands nose-to-nose with Benny.

Benny chuckles and then quickly glares at De Carlo. Without another word, he turns and leaves, following red-mustache to the front gates.

De Carlo takes a deep breath as the woman approaches him. He quickly stands up and holds out his hand. The woman kindly shakes it and then softly touches the strands of her long, brown hair as if she has become suddenly entranced in De Carlo's beauty.

"Beautiful and bold," the woman says.

De Carlo chuckles, "That's the second time I've been called beautiful."

The woman smiles and laughs as if he said a humorous joke. Her piercing blue eyes seem to have put De Carlo in a spell.

"So..." the woman says, "Did Rosary's attitude get to you too?"

De Carlo clears his throat, "Something like that," he answers.

The woman nods, "My name is Adeline Montana. I am the warden here. This is my home away from home...a place that I cherish very much."

De Carlo nods in agreement. He suddenly feels awkward. He feels as though she's about to scold him like a Kindergarten student. He knows he messed up in there and he doesn't want, nor does he need anyone to tell him how badly he reacted to Rosary.

Adeline chuckles after she waits for De Carlo's response. He doesn't give her one and this makes her feel disrespected.

"I know Rosary can be a smart ass. That's why I'll let this incident go," Adeline says as she glares at De Carlo with those fiery eyes. "BUT... if this ever happens again on my property, then I will have you arrested for attempted murder... FBI agent or not. This is MY home."

De Carlo nods. He's perfectly capable of escorting himself out of this hell hole. AND he doesn't need some hoity-toity, powerful witch, telling him what to do.

Before De Carlo can stalk off toward the parking lot, Adeline hands him his gun. Without saying another word, he takes it, walking away.

As he opens his Suburban's driver-side door, Adeline waves goodbye. De Carlo waves back and then suddenly flicks her off with the middle finger.

"Charming," Adeline says with a smile as De Carlo speeds off toward the front gate, "Asshole."

# FOUR

The past month has been incredible, erotic, and wild. She has done things that she has never done before. This experience has given her this sense of tranquility, she feels free from her narcissism of a husband. She's tired of his controlling behavior and she was tired of him accusing her of cheating.

She was not.... at first.

She was honest and faithful. She never even looked at another soul.

But now, she has felt this rush of excitement and sweet butterflies fluttering inside of her stomach. She has fallen in love all over again.

Of course, she didn't expect this to happen this soon. Her life has been a blur for four weeks and she can't believe that she has these types of feelings for her new lover.

At least, this is what thirty-year-old Amelia Dickinson thinks and feels now as she stares at herself in her hotel room's bathroom mirror.

Her cherry-brown hair is a mess from making love all night. Her blue eyes sparkle with happiness. Her cheeks have a rosy glow as she dabs fresh powder onto her face.

She smiles as she thinks about her body touched with tickling fingers and soft lips covering her hard nipples.

She feels the heat rise into her chest, up into her neck as she grips the collar of her red, satin bathrobe. She closes her eyes as she imagines those tickling fingers caressing her breasts.

She should stop. She's getting herself worked up again.

Her husband's face suddenly pops into her mind as if he's scolding her for her behavior.

That blonde-hair of his slicked back with hair gel is his favorite style. His piercing blue eyes crinkle in the corners as he stares at her with his infamous angry expression upon his beautiful face. His plump lips are stern and motionless.

Amelia doesn't want her husband of ten years to ruin this moment. She doesn't want him to pick inside of her brain without even stepping foot into this hotel room.

This moment has nothing to do with him. It is just her and her new lover.

Maybe...

She's completely confused on how to proceed with her life. Her husband means the world to her, and he has been there through thick and thin. But he has anger issues and becomes abusive at times. She doesn't like his jealousy and constant nagging of her party lifestyle.

They have no children. He doesn't want any. Sometimes she imagines a little boy running around their house while laughing and playing. These thoughts make her sad because she knows that it will never happen with her husband.

She suddenly feels ashamed. She's ashamed for playing him for a fool.

But she can't help it when she thinks about her newfound love. Her lover makes her feel warm and tingly inside. She feels loved and cared for all over again. It's like a new beginning.

As Amelia brushes her long hair, she ponders on her next move. She wants to tell her husband the truth. That's the right thing to do. She must tell him so she can move on and start her next journey in life...whatever THAT is.

"Hey babe! I have a confession to make," Amelia shouts. As she waits for a response, she continues to brush her hair, admiring her own physique.

She's happy and ecstatic that she's found, "the one." She never imagined feeling this way toward her new lover. It happened so fast. It feels surreal, like she's floating on a white cloud. She feels relaxed and open with expressing her feelings and thoughts.

She feels alive. She feels loved as a sudden tingling feeling takes over her body. Her heart is filled with joy, and she senses that it might burst into tiny pieces.

"Did you hear me?!" Amelia continues as she waits for a response.

Confused, she places her brush onto the sink but then smiles as she glances at her new bottle of perfume. Her lover had given it to her as a gift last night and it feels amazing to finally have someone who shows love and affection. She finally has someone who cares and wants her to bring out the best in herself. She finally has someone who isn't jealous of her every move.

"These past four weeks have been amazing," Amelia continues as she lifts the nozzle from inside of the glass bottle. "I have to be honest though, I've been thinking a lot about Richard." She sniffs the perfume and closes her eyes in ecstasy, "I must say...I think I should tell him the truth. I feel bad for what I've been doing lately."

Amelia dabs a small drop of perfume on both sides of her neck. She then giggles as she dabs a drop in between her breasts.

"I didn't have the heart to end things with him yet. I know that sounds crazy but I'm not sure what direction to take from here. I can't seem to leave him behind. I hope you understand."

There is still no response from her lover.

Amelia continues as she replaces the nozzle back inside of the bottle, "This perfume smells wonderful. You have amazing taste!" she shouts, waiting for some sort of response.

Amelia becomes puzzled but excited at the same time. Her lover likes to leave her in suspense sometimes and this excites her to the core of her belly. She receives thoughtful gifts, amazing hugs, and endless kisses as an appreciation of her love and tenderness.

"I hope you didn't leave," Amelia continues as she runs her fingers through her hair one last time. She then freshens up with a swipe of her deodorant under her armpits.

Leaving the bathroom, she enters the bedroom and realizes that the hotel room is empty.

The room is huge with soaring ceilings and golden pillars. The living area is empty as well as it holds a light-gray couch and a fluffy, white plush chair. A furry, gray rug lies underneath a glass coffee table that holds two cups of fresh brewed coffee.

Amelia glances at the unkempt bed with its blue, satin sheets and freshly washed white comforter. She smiles as she presses her fingertips to her neck once again. Her face flushes with happiness as she imagines her lover kissing her soft lips.

Curious, she glides past the furniture like a model and makes her way toward the door. Opening it, she peeks her head out into the hotel hallway and glances to the right. She sees a housekeeper entering another room. The housekeeper smiles with such happiness. She waves as Amelia waves back, nodding her head in acknowledgment.

Amelia turns and looks to the left. She watches another couple enter their room. They're laughing and kissing as they close their door.

Amelia sighs. *What the hell? Did I do something wrong?*

Closing the door, she's immediately faced with someone wearing a black ski-mask, a black coat with a hood and green, suede gloves.

Suddenly, a rope grips Amelia's neck, tightening. While being strangled, she's dragged to the bed. She grips the rope with her green-painted fingernails and struggles to remove it, choking as her attacker ties her wrists and ankles to the bed posts.

Amelia tries to scream for help, but her attacker covers her mouth with his hand as he then whispers, "Ssshhhhh," with a finger to his lips.

Amelia's eyes are wide and shocked. She continues to struggle with the rope wrapped around her neck. Amelia bursts into tears as she tries to shake her head no. Her attacker then pulls harder on the rope as it's twirled around the killer's fist.

Amelia is choking to death as she makes loud gurgling noises. Her attacker then ties the ends of the rope to the bed posts.

The killer stands at the end of the bed as he pulls out a tube of red lipstick from his back pocket. He then steps onto the bed with black combat boots and writes the word, "CHEATER," in capital letters on the wall above the bed.

Stepping back onto the floor, the killer stares in admiration at his artwork.

Amelia's tears stream down the sides of her temples and drips into her ears. She desperately tugs onto the rope, almost loosening it. She can feel her heart race with a sudden tinge of happiness that she will escape this wrath from her attacker.

The killer realizes that the rope isn't tight enough and hurries to the bed posts. He pulls even harder this time, choking Amelia to death.

Her sudden movements stop, and her body becomes still.

Tony De Carlo has decided to never forgive himself for his wife's death. He blames himself for not being that wonderful husband that she fell in love with all those years ago.

He hasn't forgiven himself either for not finding her killer for the past year.

These issues have crawled inside of his heart like maggots eating his organs. He hasn't slept properly, and he doesn't eat like he used to. He loved to eat steak and shrimp with Jada because those foods were her favorite. But now, he just makes a sandwich here or there, so he doesn't die from starvation. He knows that it isn't healthy, but he can't help feeling sick to his stomach thinking about his wife lying six feet under the ground.

He knows that he needs to get himself together. He must pick up the pieces of his shattered life and finally come to terms with these saddening changes. He needs to move on and find some happiness during these dark times. A killer is on the loose and he needs to protect his city once more. He needs to step up and save lives like he always loved to do.

He can't seem to step out of this funk and into the fresh sunshine. It has been beautiful outside for the past week with no rain in sight. He has been moping around his garage day after day, hoping and praying that he will have a lead into this serial killer's location and whereabouts.

As he stands alone inside of his dingy garage, he stares at the corkboard nailed to a wooden wall. He taps his finger to his lips as he sadly glances at the picture of his wife pinned to the left side of the board. She's smiling with bright, white teeth and a yellow sun hat tied to her head. The waves of the ocean are behind her as she poses in a red bikini. Her hands nestled onto her hips with her head tilted backward, laughing up at the bright sun.

De Carlo remembers that day like it was yesterday. Jada was full of love and innocence.

It was their trip to the Bahamas four years ago. De Carlo had taken two weeks off. He needed a long break at that time as well. Rosary Chime had been giving him a run for his money. She had shot and killed four people in one month. Unfortunately, he didn't quite have the proof that it was her, but the eyewitness's sightings of the killer matched her description.

Rosary had gotten sloppy with her work as if she wanted caught several years ago. Multiple people have seen her in action, but they never completely saw her face. She apparently liked to wear mask coverings, but she often left her hair exposed.

Well... she did this up until a year ago when she walked around mask-less and didn't give a damn about who saw her smiling face.

As she mentioned, she was exhausted and done with her excessive, unruly behavior.

De Carlo shakes his mind from the beauty of Rosary Chime. She is currently on his, "shit list," as she has become stubborn and selfish.

*Stubborn and selfish?* He thinks as he chuckles at this nonsense. He knows deep down in his heart that, "thinking about," his proposal isn't stubborn or selfish. She's looking out for her best interest, and he respects that. He just had a moment of anger that he regrets deeply.

She will not accept his calls. The two letters that he has sent in the past week and a half returned to the mail. She refuses to talk to him, and he doesn't blame her.

He nearly choked her to death.

De Carlo sighs in frustration as he remembers the smug look upon Rosary's face while he gripped her neck. It appears as if she wanted De Carlo to kill her. She was pleading... begging with her sharp and clear eyes.

He will never forget that look as long as he lives.

Approaching a large, wooden work bench, De Carlo picks up a picture of Rosary, staring at it as if she will burst through the photo and shoot him in the head.

He often thinks about her setting revenge on him. He imagines her sitting on a stool behind a window while setting up her sniper rifles. He watches her look through the scope of her favorite rifle as she adjusts it to her vision.

She once described her favorite weapon. This rifle is a dark shade of red. It is rare and given to her by her boyfriend, Daryl. He had admitted to stealing it from his old boss who he killed for that weapon. His old boss hunted him for three months like a predator in the woods. He wouldn't give up until he received his rifle back. Daryl was a lousy, good-for-nothing thief and scoundrel who lied to everyone and anyone, including Rosary.

De Carlo suddenly becomes angry once again as he glares at the picture of this beautiful woman gripped in between his fingertips. He crushes the picture into a ball with his angry fist and then throws it to the ground.

With a swift shove with his arm, he angrily pushes the contents of his work bench onto the ground as well. He yells up into the air with frustration as if he's becoming a "hulk." He raises his fists into the air as he screams with madness.

Suddenly startled, he hears the pounding footsteps climbing down his basement steps. As he draws his gun, he points it at his partner, Tiara, as she quickly enters the doorway to his garage. She has her gun drawn as well, pointing it at De Carlo's head.

Tiara surrenders as she backs away from the doorway.

"Your back door is unlocked. I tried knocking but you didn't answer. I heard screaming," Tiara says as she places her gun back inside its holster on her hip. She continues to hold up her hand as she watches De Carlo's frightened expression, gripping his gun with both hands as he continues to point it at Tiara.

After a moment of silence, De Carlo realizes who the intruder is and lowers his gun. He takes a deep breath as he places his gun onto a clip at the front of his belt.

"I've been busy!" De Carlo snaps as he sweats profusely.

"What the hell is wrong with you?!" Tiara shouts. "Get yourself together agent or I will report you to Curtis!"

"You think that will hurt me?!" De Carlo shouts back.

Tiara falls silent. She knows that will not hurt this man. He has been through hell and back. As a matter of fact, if Curtis approached him about his anger, De Carlo might even quit on the spot. His behavior has been out of control and unusual.

Tiara looks at the corkboard hung up on the wall. She glances at the beautiful picture of Jada De Carlo until her eyes notice other pieces of evidence pinned to the board.

Tiara sighs in sadness. She had no idea that De Carlo is THIS fixated on finding his wife's killer. He told Tiara five months ago that he had given up hope and was, "done with this bullshit." He promised that he would put this case on the back burner and focus on the other issues that have been forming in his city.

Tiara shakes her head as she watches De Carlo pick up the crinkled picture of Rosary Chime. Using his hand to smooth out the crinkles, he pins it to the right side of the board.

"This has become too much for you," Tiara says as she steps into the garage.

Approaching the board, she notices red lipstick smeared onto a tissue. She then reads that infamous note that the killer wrote to De Carlo. It's pinned in the middle of the board with the word, "WHO?" written in blue ink above the note. His wife's panties, her nightgown, and a blood-stained necklace dangle from a pin to the board.

Tiara turns from the corkboard and watches De Carlo sit down in a recliner chair.

*He's getting too old for this. He needs rest.*

Tiara tiptoes toward De Carlo as if he's a shark out of the water, ready to bite her head off. She softly places a hand on his shoulder in comfort. He looks up at her with blood-shot eyes and whiskey in his breath. His hair is disheveled, and he reeks of body odor.

"I was under the impression that you were taking a break," Tiara scolds as she takes a seat onto another re-cliner chair across from De Carlo.

"I did," De Carlo replies sharply.

Tiara nods so as not to make him angry more than he al-ready is. She feels uncomfortable and nauseous. His behav-ior is quite frightening, and she isn't sure how to approach this situation. He has never acted this way toward her and she's shocked and hurt that he's chosen to turn against her when all she's wanted to do is help.

He has become a dear friend to her, and she doesn't want to see him crawl down the wrong path. His obsession with finding the whereabouts to the current killer has not only strained his relationship with Tiara, but it has strained his friendships with their boss and fellow agents. Everyone is concerned for his health and safety, and no one seems to be getting through to him.

De Carlo is annoyed and tired. "What do you want from me?" he asks Tiara as he places his head in his hands with exhaustion.

"I need you to stay focused. People are worried about you."

"Well, no one needs to worry about me! I can manage anything."

Tiara chuckles as if he just spewed a joke, "You can't manage yourself," Tiara says, nodding toward the empty bottle of whiskey in the trash can.

De Carlo shakes his head, "I'm fine," he answers as he calms down, "Look, I'm sorry. Everything is eating me alive. I can't sleep. I can't eat knowing that someone continues to kill innocent women in my city." De Carlo rubs his tired eyes, "It is too much."

Tiara smiles as she grabs De Carlo's hand and squeezes.

"I'm here for you Tony... always. I'm still your friend no matter how hard you push me away. I feel your sympathy. I just need you to stay focused. Don't let this killer get into your head. That's what he wants..." Tiara trails off as she watches De Carlo smile with a wide grin.

"And by the looks of it," she continues, "it HAS worked."

De Carlo laughs, "Yes it has."

Tiara squeezes his hand once again. "I stopped by to ask if you would like to go to dinner with me. We could relax and enjoy tasty food."

As he's about to decline the dinner date, De Carlo's cell phone rings. It's a call from Curtis Garcia. As he answers, his heart pounds with anger once again. He listens to Curtis talk as he nods his head in agreement.

As he hangs up with Curtis, De Carlo says, "Another case, maybe some other time."

# FIVE

As De Carlo and Tiara step inside of the hotel, the gloomy atmosphere slaps the agents in the face upon entering. It feels like déjà vu as De Carlo watches FBI agents and police officers continue conversations at the reception desk. The hotel is a bustle of hurried guests and quiet whispers of the current victim of infidelities.

Only this time, no one stares at him with sadness in their eyes and quiet words of prayers. No one even acknowledges that the agents have arrived. It's as if this has become the norm. There are victims upon victims who have no clue that spending time with a certain serial killer...would cost them their lives. There are several missing pieces to this puzzle and De Carlo suspects that the killer will slip up soon.

*He has to,* De Carlo thinks as he watches Curtis Garcia step away from a fellow agent and head toward him and Tiara. Curtis looks exhausted and drained. There are dark circles under his eyes, and he has lost weight.

De Carlo's mind lights up as if someone just flicked on a light-switch inside of his brain. His boss is angry and tired of not finding this killer as well. He's sick and tired of seeing dead women tied to bed posts with their necks strangled. He's tired of seeing the same messages splattered across walls as if the killer was acting like a child.

*Because he is,* De Carlo acknowledges as his boss approaches him, stopping to rub his tired eyes. *This killer is a crybaby. I need to figure out WHY!!*

"Amelia Dickinson. Thirty-years-old, cherry-brown hair and blue eyes..." Curtis trails off as if he had forgotten his next sentence.

De Carlo is a little bit shocked by his boss's bluntness. No, "Hi, how are you guys?" No, "Hello, how is your night going?" No exchange of pleasantries. He just wants to get down to business. This situation that they are all in doesn't even feel real to Curtis. He seems to just want to get this over with so he can go home and sit on his couch to drink his sorrows away.

"Cut to the chase, right?" De Carlo asks, "Same MO?"

Curtis stares at De Carlo with a puzzled expression, "What else would you like me to say agent? This isn't the time to talk about football or cars. We're not here to make friends."

Tiara watches both men as if a fight is about to break out.

"Calm down the both of you. This situation isn't ideal for anyone. Put your big boy panties on and let us capture this son of a bitch," Tiara says as the frustration glows on her light-skinned face. Her piercing blue eyes spit fire like an angry dragon.

De Carlo became Tiara's partner ten years ago. He requested a male partner at first but when Tiara showed up, he was like a kid in a candy store. He loved the change of pace that she offered. She was hell bent on catching the "bad guys" and making a name for herself. Most of the agents in their department respect her and love her as a person. She's sweet and kind but when she's angry, people say, "Here comes Tiara!"

She has wanted to be an FBI agent since she was ten years old. Her parents would watch those "cop shows" and she absolutely loved the thought of chasing criminals and arresting them.

However, her friends didn't agree with her career choice and would constantly beg her to change her mind. They would always say, "An African American woman has no business being an FBI agent." She would then try to convince them of the positivity of this job.

No one ever agreed with her explanations and theories. Let's just say, she isn't friends with them anymore and she's happy about the decisions that she's made in her life. She became an FBI agent to make a change. She stepped up to make her goals worth living for and her dreams come true. She wouldn't change her decision for the world.

And she sure as hell will not let these two ding-dongs ruin her focus on what's at hand.

"I am calm," De Carlo snaps without making any eye contact toward Tiara. He glares at Curtis like a bull ready to attack his picador.

"We will catch this son of a bitch," Curtis answers Tiara as he glares back at De Carlo as if he's wishing that his agent would charge toward him. "We haven't given up."

De Carlo mumbles under his breath as he chuckles, "Like you haven't given up on Jada, right?" He can't stop himself from spewing those hateful words out of his mouth. He instantly regrets it as he watches Curtis's expression change from anger to sorrow.

"You know damn well that isn't true," Curtis says as his mind races. His feelings are actually quite hurt. He suddenly feels this sense of depression take over his heart. "I'll ignore that statement this one time. If you EVER say anything like that to me again, I will personally kick you off this case and force you to take time off. You need it. Your anger is out of control. You blame everyone for your wife's death."

De Carlo falls silent as his boss's words float in his brain on top of a rainy cloud. He suddenly imagines his wife scolding him for his hateful words and childish behavior.

She would never want him to act this way. He can't seem to focus and get back to the way he used to be. He used to joke and laugh. He used to have fun with his co-workers.

The past year has been hell for everyone. His co-workers, "walk on eggshells," around De Carlo as if he will burst like a volcano at any minute. His bad attitude has given him nothing but losses in friendships and dinner dates. He has tunnel vision and only looks for the negative aspects to people in general. He doesn't talk to many people nowadays.

"Let's go and assess the situation," De Carlo says to Tiara, changing the subject.

Curtis watches the agents as they step inside of an elevator. De Carlo continues to glare at him but subconsciously feels awful for putting the blame on his boss. He knows that it's not Curtis's fault, everyone in the department has tried to help in some way. De Carlo just has to find someone to blame... besides himself.

His head suddenly pulsates with a migraine. He needs to sleep. He needs to eat. His body is in pain. He can't quite explain to his fellow agents why he has these sudden mood swings. He can't seem to control his own body. He feels frozen as the elevator lifts into the air and stops on the fifth floor. *This killer must have a fascination about this particular floor level.*

The elevator dings and the doors open. De Carlo's shoes feel glued to the elevator floor, and he can't seem to step out. His heart is racing, and his forehead is perspiring with beads of sweat.

Tiara stops just outside of the elevator doors and almost immediately shoves her arm in between them as they begin to close. Her puzzled expression is written all over her face like a scene in a book. She's worried for her partner. He hasn't acted like himself in a long time.

"Get your shit together De Carlo," Tiara snaps as she grabs her partner's hand and pulls him out of the elevator with such force that De Carlo trips over his own feet.

As he lands on his right knee, he closes his eyes; a feeling of warmth overwhelms his heart.

He smiles at his soon-to-be wife as she cries happy tears. He bends down on one knee as he proposes on the sand of the beach. Jada is ecstatic as she laughs; tears spill down her cheeks as De Carlo slides the ring onto her left ring finger. Her yellow sun hat falls to the sand as she tilts her head backward, laughing up into the bright sky.

"Get up!" He hears Tiara scold him like a child. "NOW!" She yells after a brief pause.

De Carlo blinks as if he isn't sure where he is. The image of his wife splashes into his brain like droplets of paint from a paint brush. He sees beautiful colors of reds and blues. He picks up Jada's yellow sun hat and places it back onto her head as her hair blows in the soft breeze.

Jada's favorite color was yellow. She loved sunflowers. Every summer she would lie on her back in their bed of sunflowers in the backyard almost every night and stare up at the stars in the night sky. She would giggle like a schoolgirl as she plucked one of her flowers out of the ground and she would place it onto her chest. She would fall asleep, dreaming of different shades of yellows and gold. Her flowers made her feel warm inside and the sun was always inviting.

"Earth to Tony De Carlo. Where have you gone?" Tiara asks as she tries to help De Carlo stand up on his feet. "Knock it off. You look drunk," she continues.

De Carlo looks around the empty hotel hallway as he snaps out of his visions of the waves of the ocean splashing Jada's beautiful face.

The images of her dead eyes haunt his brain like a ghost spinning in circles inside of a whirlpool. Her cold skin is something he will never forget the feeling of.

He takes a deep breath. Each case gets harder and harder and the killer refuses to slip up.

*When he does, I'll be ready,* De Carlo thinks to himself as he and Tiara reach Room 504.

Two forensic evidence employees are snapping pictures of the deceased as De Carlo closes the door. The word, "CHEATER," written in red lipstick above the bed immediately hits the agent in the face. That word seems to cut deep into De Carlo's soul with a sharpened knife, leaving scars too powerful to disappear.

*This killer is extremely powerful and cunning. He seems to be a smooth talker, someone incredibly handsome because he wouldn't be claiming all these beautiful women if he looked like a hit-and-run skunk.*

De Carlo chuckles inside as he slips on a pair of gloves. *It's time to find something out of the ordinary... hopefully.*

Tiara searches through Amelia's suitcase as she pulls out lingerie and socks. She finds pallets of make-up and brushes. She unzips a pocket and places her hand inside. As she feels around for any contents, she suddenly grips an envelope filled with cash.

De Carlo enters the bathroom and sniffs the air. The fragrance is overwhelming and takes him by surprise. It smells so good that he feels a tingling feeling inside of his groin. He knows that this is not the time or the place to think and feel like this. His senses have shot like a rocket just like the red liquid inside of a temperature gauge. Sometimes, he smells fire and smoke from the flames licking the inside of his brain.

A fire is raging inside of his body, and he can't control it.

As he sniffs the air a second time, he spots the perfume bottle on the sink next to a hairbrush. Opening a plastic bag, he slips the hairbrush inside. Slowly, he picks up the glass perfume bottle and places it next to his nostril, inhaling the sweet scent.

He hears Curtis Garcia enter the hotel room. His boss asks Tiara, "Where the hell is Tony?"

Tiara points toward the bathroom door as she bags the evidence of cash.

De Carlo is frantic as he hears the heavy footsteps of his boss. He blinks quizzically as he sniffs the perfume bottle once again. He then hurriedly slips it into the inside of his jacket pocket just as Curtis steps inside of the bathroom doorway. De Carlo scratches his head as if he's trying to figure out a clue. Curtis eyes him suspiciously as he glances at the Zip-lock bag.

"Find anything useful?" Curtis asks.

De Carlo shrugs his shoulders as he lifts the woman's hairbrush, "Not much," the agent mumbles as sweat pours down the sides of his temples.

"Keep looking," Curtis orders as he leaves the bathroom in a huff.

De Carlo's cell phone rings.

"Oh, and by the way," Curtis yells from the living area of the hotel room, "talk to the victim's family tomorrow. It's late and you need some sleep."

De Carlo hears the hotel room door slam shut as he reads the words, "private number," on his cell phone's screen. He quickly answers.

"Would you like to accept a call from.... New York State Prison?" the automated voice on the other line asks as if she's a robot calling.

De Carlo's heart pounds with sudden excitement and fear. He wants to hear her voice, but he isn't willing to accept her dismissal of his offer once and for all.

"Yes," De Carlo answers as he grips the phone in his fist.

"Will you accept the charges from...Rosary Chime?"

De Carlo suddenly feels nauseated. His head is spinning with dizziness. He feels as though he might pass out onto the floor of this hotel room that he has become accustomed to. He has learned every square inch of this room, victim after victim.

"Yes," De Carlo answers, swallowing hard.

He hears a clicking sound and then a moment of silence. He closes his eyes, an image of Rosary Chime smiling with her bright, white teeth and red lipstick. Her short, black hair blows in a soft breeze at the beach. Her head tilts up into the air as she laughs hysterically. Her yellow sun hat falls onto the sand.

He hears heavy breathing on the other end of the line. De Carlo clears his throat.

"You ready to talk?" Rosary asks.

De Carlo is nervous and shaking with fear. He can't seem to understand why Rosary Chime has this "spell" on him. This woman has him shook to his core. He's afraid that she spilled the beans to someone inside of that prison. He's afraid that she confided in someone and told them about his wild offer of killing this veteran serial killer for money.... and lots of it. He will pay whatever he has to pay to get this lunatic off the streets.

He wipes the sweat off his forehead with a paper napkin as he pulls into the entryway of the prison. As he pulls up to the front gates, his window slides down to a frustrated Benny and the smiling red-mustache guard.

"Get the hell inside," Benny snaps before De Carlo can speak. Benny quickly and angrily nods his head toward the parking lot as he glances at the beautiful figure of Adeline Montana.

She stands at the top of the stone steps, grinning from ear to ear. She's wearing a revealing, purple, skin-tight dress with purple high heels. Her long, brown hair flows with the sunny breeze. Her eye make-up is dark gray, and her lipstick is dark purple.

De Carlo gets this sudden urge to call her a grape as he slams his car door and makes his way toward the steps. She poses like a statue with her slender legs and curvy hips.

De Carlo licks his lips. They're not dry; he's just imagining ripping the dress right off her body and slamming his tongue down her throat.

"I hope you're in a better mood today," the warden says as she straightens her back, pushing her breasts forward, teasing his groin once again.

De Carlo smiles as he reaches the top of the steps. As he inches closer, nose-to-nose with the warden, he licks his lips a second time. He stares at her beauty, her bright blue eyes, and her crooked smile. He then glances at her neck as he imagines planting kisses on it. His imagination runs wild as he kisses her shoulders.

De Carlo leans slightly forward and smells her sweet, vanilla-sugar, perfume. He's in ecstasy as he takes in her scent. Her hair smells of some kind of fruit. He can't put his finger on it, but it smells amazing. Her whole posture and demeanor screams, TAKE ME!

Adeline slowly gropes the agent's arm muscles and then makes her way down to his waist. She feels his gun clipped to his belt. As she continues to frisk him, she runs her fingers onto the back pockets of his jeans. She then bends down, feeling for any weapons strapped to his legs. She feels the top of his boots and then inside near his ankles.

As she slowly stands up, the tip of her thumb slides against his groin area.

De Carlo panics, wanting to kiss her mouth. He feels his soul igniting a flame deep inside his belly. He closes his eyes for a moment as he tries to catch his breath. His heart pounds wildly as his body shakes with this sense of urgency...an urgency for this woman to be in his bed.

"Just one more thing," Adeline says, breaking De Carlo's concentration. "Keep your hands off my prisoner. If you touch a strand of her hair, one of those beds in there will have your name on it," she threatens as she leans into his ear. "You understand?" she whispers.

De Carlo slightly nods as the warden slowly licks the tip of his ear.

"Now," Adeline shouts as she watches Benny and red-mustache eyeing the two of them, "what brings you here this fine morning?"

De Carlo thinks for a moment, "An old case. It would be nice to have Rosary's input."

Adeline nods in agreement as she thinks about his answer.

"Here for advice? Isn't that kind? Do you care about a criminal's input? Interesting..."

"Only this criminal," De Carlo answers with a fake smile upon his lips.

Adeline smiles, "I would have to agree. I've gotten to know the ins and outs of her mind. She's very smart."

De Carlo politely nods as he glances at the time on his watch.

"Well, you must have a million things to figure out. Don't let me hold you back."

Adeline steps aside. De Carlo brushes past her as he takes in her erotic scent. It smells like a love potion, and he seems to be drowning in it.

Adeline smiles as he steps inside of the doorway to the prison. Her beauty hits him like a ton of bricks. His mind whirls with the possibilities. *Maybe she could give me a chance?*

As he slowly closes the door with his hand on the handle, De Carlo watches the warden through the crack. She winks as he then completely shuts the door in his own face.

He laughs, *I don't stand a chance.*

De Carlo approaches Eva as she's sitting at the desk. Her eyes light up with fear. A woman guard, who has her buttocks perched onto the corner of Eva's desk, immediately stands up and points her fat finger at him.

"Don't come any closer," the guard orders as she approaches him, smelling like goat cheese and cigarette breath. Her muffin top jiggles as if it's singing a tune.

She frisks him roughly, sliding his gun out of its clip.

"The warden already told me. Now, go get her," De Carlo snaps.

The guard glares at him but doesn't say another word. She places his gun into a bin and then hands it over to Eva. She then leaves through the metal gates, still glaring at De Carlo as if she's inclined to suddenly eat him as prey.

De Carlo lets out the breath that he had been holding as Eva opens the gate for him. He steps inside of the waiting area once again and sits down at the same table he sat at a brief time ago.

The waiting area is quiet this time. De Carlo feels self-conscious as he thinks that everyone in the prison was warned about his return. There are no other visitors in the waiting room and two guards are watching television. He watches Eva hang up the phone.

He has this weird feeling that someone is about to beat his ass. Maybe Benny will bust through the prison doors with his rifle while pointing it at De Carlo as red-mustache man laughs his ass off. Maybe he has put himself inside of a trap.

*They're going to let Rosary Chime kill me.*

De Carlo shakes his head at his own thoughts. *They would never let her get that satisfaction.*

The guards are watching a comedy show. They burst into laughter, breaking the silence.

The agent glances at his watch once again. He isn't sure why he's becoming impatient. He's off duty today. He needed a break from Curtis and Tiara. They've done nothing but hound him about his odd behavior and temper tantrums.

They think he has taken a short trip to the beach.

What they don't know won't hurt them.

De Carlo suddenly hears whispers as the "Big Bertha," guard shushes Rosary. The beast stomps down the hallway with her prisoner in her grip. De Carlo envisions bruises alongside Rosary's arm from the guard's nails digging into her flesh.

Rosary enters through the metal gates as the guard uncuffs her wrists. She then slams the gates closed as she glares at the both of them.

Rosary sits across from De Carlo. She looks tired and weak. Her skin is pale, and she isn't wearing any make-up. Her nail polish on her nails is chipped and unkempt.

"Sweet and kind, isn't she?" Rosary asks.

De Carlo laughs. Rosary smiles politely as she grips her rosary necklace in between her fingers. Her skin has become raw from the indentations of the necklace.

"You don't look well," De Carlo says.

Rosary shrugs her shoulders, "I think the warden has a vendetta against me."

"She has one against everyone," De Carlo says, turning to look toward the prison doors.

De Carlo thinks for a moment as Rosary falls silent, "I thought you said she was taking care of you in here," he asks.

"Key word: WAS. She moved me into a different cell. I am harassed by inmates and groped by the guards. I haven't misbehaved at all..." Rosary trails off.

De Carlo is concerned. He doesn't like her sudden disheveled appearance and her lack of happiness. She was full of life the last time he saw her.

His heart suddenly drops. *Maybe I'm the cause of this change!*

"I still haven't met her," Rosary says, interrupting De Carlo's thoughts. "Maybe she's afraid of me. Maybe fear will push her into letting me out," Rosary chuckles. "Some guard told me that the warden didn't like talking about me at first. He said she did seem scared to have me in this prison. I don't know if that's true or not. People like to start rumors."

De Carlo glances at her with a confused expression on his face. He was under the impression that the warden was protective of Rosary. She mentioned being ecstatic to have this popular hit woman inside of her walls. It made Adeline famous for locking up such a notorious killer in HER prison. Rosary Chime is extremely popular, and she doesn't even realize it.

De Carlo shrugs his shoulders, "Let's get back to basics."

Rosary laughs, her dimples smiling. "Murdering a hot-headed killer is basic, huh?"

De Carlo bursts into laughter, "Something like that."

Rosary is silent once again. De Carlo takes her shaking hand into his clutch. "I'm so sorry for what I did. I have no idea what came over me. You've become very special to me."

Rosary's eyes fill with tears, and she isn't sure why. She doesn't cry at the drop of a hat.

She looks defeated and exhausted from being cooped up inside of these walls. It has only been one year, but she feels as though it's been a lifetime already. She misses her apartment, her favorite foods, going to her mother's church, and...

Killing. She misses looking through the scope of her favorite red rifle.

She never knew she would come to terms with missing her old life. She wanted out of it so bad that she gave herself up. She gave herself up to an FBI agent who now has feelings for her.

She knows this. Deep down, she realized that Detective Anthony De Carlo had fallen in love with her. This notion has destroyed her mind. It's all she ever thinks about.

How could someone who doesn't even know her that well, have those kinds of feelings for her? She's no one special. She's just a lonely criminal who gets paid to kill people.

"You are forgiven... for now," Rosary says, smiling from ear to ear.

"That's a relief... I think," De Carlo chuckles as he looks back at Eva. "Well, we might not have much more time. Eva is on her phone looking at us already," De Carlo is urgent as he turns back to Rosary. "You called me. Let's talk."

"Alright," Rosary nods but pauses for a moment, thinking. "I'll do it. But then I'm free. I also collect one hundred thousand dollars."

"Kind of steep don't you think?"

"Not at all. Take it or leave it."

De Carlo thinks for a minute...two minutes...then three minutes.

Rosary points to De Carlo's watch, "Time's a wasting."

De Carlo smiles as he nods, "Deal."

"Besides," Rosary says as she untangles the necklace around her fingers. "I miss it. It has been a miserable, long year. But now..."

De Carlo cuts her off, "We need to get past Adeline Montana. Don't you worry about your pretty little head. I will take care of her."

He suddenly motions toward Eva to approach the glass window. She looks around for a guard, fear in her eyes. De Carlo gets up and points to the window a second time. Eva is frantic as she picks up the phone. De Carlo knocks on the glass, pleading.

Eva reluctantly hangs up the phone, tip toeing her high heels, she approaches the glass.

"I need the warden," De Carlo says.

"Sure thing," Eva answers nervously.

De Carlo suddenly feels butterflies inside of his stomach. The warden has really gotten into his mind. He isn't sure if it's a good thing or bad thing. He suddenly wants to see her beauty and smell her fresh scent. He wants to run his fingers through her hair and pull with all his might.

He sits, watching Eva make a phone call. The woman should glue her hand to the damn thing because all she ever does is talk on that phone.

He watches her nod. She then looks at him, waving him over to the window.

They both approach it as if a snake will pop out and bite their faces off. Eva seems tense and tired. She doesn't have that bubbly personality that she had the last time he was here. This place seems incredibly solemn and gloomy. The waiting area is dark and lifeless.

He just needs and wants to get Rosary Chime the hell out of here. She has been stuck here long enough. She has paid for her sins. She knows what she did was wrong.

De Carlo chuckles inside. *It's ironic that I'm trying to get her out of here to KILL someone.*

"She needs to go back to her cell. Adeline will see you outside," Eva says, glancing past De Carlo at one of the television-watching guards as he approaches the metal doors.

"I'll see you soon," De Carlo promises as Rosary drags her feet down the hallway.

De Carlo steps outside into the bright sun. He quickly blocks it with his hand as he sees Adeline Montana approach him with a smirk on her face.

"Couldn't stay away from me, I see?" Adeline says, laughing into the sunlight.

"I need Rosary's help," De Carlo answers, trying to ignore her sexual passes as she licks her lips this time. His heart races a mile a minute. He isn't sure if it's from his bluntness or from watching her tongue wiggle.

"With what may I ask?"

"I mentioned earlier...an old case. She knows more than I do. Like you said, she's very smart." De Carlo continues a small prayer inside of his mind. All she needs to do is let Rosary out for a brief time. He will bring her back.

Maybe...

"And you'll bring her back in one piece?" Adeline asks suspiciously. She looks at him up and down with those big, beautiful, blue eyes.

"Of course," De Carlo answers sweetly. Rosary Chime will be a free woman.

Adeline looks around the building and then spots Benny standing at the bottom of the steps.

"Go take a break," she orders, pointing to the front door to the prison.

Benny hears her and chuckles as he slowly climbs the steps.

"Hurry up. Get out of here," she says as Benny brushes past her.

"Always barking orders," he mumbles as he enters the prison, slamming the doors.

"Kind of rough, aren't you?" De Carlo asks of her behavior.

"Let's just say... Benny and I have history," she smiles. "So! How much?" She changes the subject quickly.

"How much...what?" De Carlo asks confused.

"Well sir, you didn't expect me to release my prisoner into your hands for free now, did you? This is in fact, illegal. I can't just let you walk out of here with Rosary Chime unless I am compensated. Am I clear?"

De Carlo thinks for a minute. He does have his wife's savings set aside for a rainy day. He could pay her a little of something.

"Crystal," De Carlo answers. "How much?" he asks, exasperated from all this drama. If only he could catch the killer himself, he wouldn't need their help. He wouldn't need a criminal or a manipulative bitch on his side. If this damn serial killer would slip up, he would be fine.

"How much you got?" Adeline asks.

De Carlo thinks once again. His brain is burning from all this thinking and making deals. These women are ruthless. It's all about the money. It's never about catching the bad guys and saving the community. *Someone always wants paid.*

"Fifty thousand," De Carlo lies. He knows damn well that he has a million dollars "waiting in the wings" for his retirement. Between his wife's riches and his savings from the department, he has the life of luxury right now.

But he knows that the money will soon come to an end. Not only is that an issue, but these deals are cutting into his life of retirement and a peaceful transition to living off the grid.

*Ruthless.*

"That will do...for now," Adeline agrees as she places the tip of her finger on De Carlo's cheek. "I want more if she ends up getting caught. She escaped with your help...right?"

De Carlo's heart pounds with fear. Now, this woman is toying with him. She's toying with his money, his emotions, his mind, and now his body.

Adeline slowly places her finger near his waist. A surge of lightning strikes throughout his whole entire body.

"Maybe this tension between us will escape in the near future as well," Adeline says as she slowly kisses his cheek.

"I'll have the check sent to you tomorrow morning," De Carlo says.

"Good boy," the warden teases. She suddenly turns, clicking her heels as she makes her way toward the front doors. Waving, she then blows a kiss. "Wait right here. I'll have a guard fetch her. He will bring her from the back door."

As she enters, De Carlo hears her shout at Eva to give him his belongings.

Eva rushes out of the door with a bin in her hand. De Carlo reaches for his gun as Eva becomes suddenly saddened. "Be careful," she warns, smiling as she runs back inside.

It was such a quick gesture that De Carlo doesn't have time to process her warning as two guards appear from behind the building, gripping onto Rosary's arms.

As they approach De Carlo, one of the guards takes the handcuffs off her wrists.

The other guard pushes her forward. She almost falls to the ground, but De Carlo reaches for her, grabbing her shoulders. The guards laugh it off as they walk away, leaving them alone.

Still in his grip, De Carlo looks down at Rosary Chime's blushing face, "You ready?"

Her face lights up with happiness, "More than you know."

As De Carlo and Rosary strut toward the parking lot, Adeline Montana watches them leave through the cracked, open front doors to the prison.

She smiles.

# SIX

Rosary is completely silent during the drive toward De Carlo's house. She isn't sure what to say or how to thank him. She never thought in a million years that the warden would let her escape so easily. She never knew that she could have this much luck in her life... EVER.

She isn't one to have any luck. Her life has always been in turmoil, and she has struggled for the most part. Her mother, Sherry Thomas, was manipulative and completely insane. She didn't properly take care of her and her older sister, Agatha Chime, at any time in their lives. She liked to play the "damsel in distress," and made the public think that she was a constant victim.

Sherry was a constant narcissist. Rosary was the constant warrior.

She picked up the slack that her sister yielded from. Agatha was weak-minded and her ideas were sloppy. She never thought of the consequences of their actions. She didn't see the "big picture." She never thought about the future of their repercussions.

Agatha was too quick to turn a negative situation into something much worse.

And she did... with their mother.

Rosary has worked hard into forgetting her childhood and moving on from Agatha's terrible actions that has caused Rosary's mind to crumble into shambles.

She hasn't felt happiness in years.

Except for today...today is a new day and a new chance at life. She wants to find and kill this ruthless serial killer and move on to bigger and better things. She has plans to live the rest of her life successfully and she wants the drama to end.

She wants to live off the grid.

That is something she has wanted for many years. It could finally happen; all because of this caring and loyal FBI agent she had the pleasure of meeting.

Meeting under very cruel circumstances.

Rosary glances out of the vehicle window as they pass luxurious homes and trees swaying in the spring breeze. These homes look more like mansions than anything else. She can't imagine the maintenance of these homes and the people who live in them. She wonders if the owners are snobby or nice. She wonders if a rich wife sits at home while her husband makes all the money. She wonders if she will leave the house to get her nails and hair done on a weekly basis.

Rosary has wanted that kind of life as well.

She has wanted a rich husband. She has wanted to be a stay-at-home mother.

Rosary sighs. She can't have at least one of those things and it has tormented her mind since the day she found out the terrible news almost fifteen years ago.

She has longed for a child. She wants to be that courageous and adored mother who totes toddlers on her hips. She wouldn't mind changing diapers and waking up in the middle of the night to feed her sweet baby.

But...she can't. She can't have children because of her stubborn body. She doesn't have that luxury of carrying a baby in the womb. She longs for it. She craves it.

And she cries about it inside of her mind... especially when she witnesses mothers taking strolls through the park while pushing a baby stroller.

One incident had her body shake and her mind racing. She couldn't believe that her mind would stoop so low...

One day, she was perched like a bird at a building across the street from the park. Her latest mission was to shoot and kill twenty-five-year-old, Rebecca Sloan. Rebecca had been on Emilio's radar for many years because she had stolen a massive amount of cash from his secret stash under the floorboards.

One morning, Rebecca had witnessed Emilio counting his cash. He thought she was sound asleep in his bed. She was, but then she heard strange noises and jumped out of bed. She was a light sleeper, and Emilio wasn't quiet with his endeavors.

She snuck upon him, memorizing the secret code he pounded into the keypad to his safe.

The next day, Emilio left for a meeting and Rebecca became money hungry. She stole five hundred thousand dollars...just like that. In the snap of a finger, she felt rich.

Rosary watched Rebecca push the stroller while her baby was inside. She sat on a bench and lifted her five-month-old up into the air. The baby laughed and giggled.

Rosary stared through the scope to her rifle with tears in her eyes. She couldn't shoot and kill a mother while playing with her child.

Could she?

She pointed the red dot onto the baby's forehead. Her heart pounded with sadness. There was no way she could shoot this poor, innocent child.

Rosary closed her eyes for a split second, but it was enough time for Rebecca to notice the red dot placed onto her child's head.

Rebecca placed her baby onto her lap and quickly turned around to search for the shooter. After a moment of silence, she hurriedly placed her child back into the stroller.

She stood up and looked toward the abandoned building.

The bullet pierced straight through the top of her head.

Rosary will never forget that incident as long as she lives. She was so jealous of a mother that she had the slightest thought of killing an innocent baby.

Rosary has felt ashamed ever since. In one swoop, that baby could have had his life taken from him from a simple act of jealousy.

Rosary blinks back tears. De Carlo sneaks a glance toward her way but then immediately places his eyes back to the road. He isn't sure why she's crying, but right now, he thinks that she needs some time to herself. He doesn't blame her though; he needs it too.

They pull up to his driveway. Rosary's eyes light up like a lit candle.

The house is painted a light-blue color with black shudders. The door is painted white and contains a "Happy Easter," sign with a bunny holding a carrot. The curtains covering all the windows are white lace.

Rosary can't contain her excitement. She has never stepped foot into a house looking like this. She's used to crack houses with dingy furniture and cigarette smoke floating through the air. She's used to yellow-stained walls with holes punched through them.

As she exits the vehicle, she chuckles at the rest of the Easter decorations. De Carlo has hung up colorful eggs on the windows and funny Easter bunnies sticking out their tongues.

"Let's walk through the garage. That's where I hang out the most," De Carlo says as he presses the button to his remote garage opener.

As they enter, De Carlo continues, "I will pack some of my wife's clothing for you."

He watches as Rosary quietly tiptoes around the freshly painted garage. She glances toward his corkboard of evidence but then quickly turns away as he shuts the garage door.

"I will also ensure that Adeline thinks that you are staying here. I've already booked a hotel room for you. I will make sure that you have everything that you need."

Rosary is silent. She wants to thank him, but she feels strange, almost distant. She feels weird as if she's intruding in his space just by being there.

"I'll be right back, make yourself at home," De Carlo continues as he steps through the doorway to the basement and then climbs the stairs toward the first floor.

Once out of earshot, Rosary slowly makes her way toward the corkboard. She sees every picture of every victim, including his beautiful wife.

Rosary smiles as she places the tip of her finger onto the picture of Jada De Carlo. She suddenly wonders what kind of woman she was. She wonders if De Carlo was happy with her.

It was quite obvious that Jada wasn't happy, or she wouldn't have been killed the way she was. This thought saddens Rosary. She would never cheat on her husband if she ever had one.

That thought immediately leaves her mind as she spots a picture of herself pinned to the board. It's a black and white photo of her looking through the scope of her rifle. She can't see her entire face, but she knows that it's hers.

She suddenly wonders if De Carlo is obsessed with her. She does know that she was his "hot case" for many years, and he loathed the hell out of her.

But, seeing this reminds her of how close he came to catching her earlier on in her game of hide-and-seek. This suddenly makes her feel vulnerable and weak.

She was not... perhaps... as good as she thought.

This notion doesn't surprise her though. She was hot-headed and stubborn. She was stuck-up in a sense, always laughing at FBI agents while they searched for her day and night.

She knew that she would never be caught. This thought makes her sigh once again.

While sitting alone in her jail cell, she questioned her actions time and time again. She wondered why she let herself give up. She left a trail that the police couldn't find. She was cunning and slick. She always got away from the crime scene. She hid for days, for weeks on end until she felt it was safe to come back out into the world.

But that was the problem. She knows that she was sick and tired of hiding. She wanted to live a normal life and if getting caught would change things, then she had to make it happen.

Sitting on her bed day after day in her cell made her wish that she wasn't so stupid. She called herself stupid every night before she would lie down in bed.

She felt stupid for giving up. She felt stupid for wanting to get away from Emilio. She should have just taken him out whenever she felt threatened. She was a professional sniper. She knew that she could pull off killing one of the most wanted men in the area.

But she just had to get away and she knew that Emilio wouldn't let her live if she decided to just, "run away," from him. She had many choices and going to prison might have actually become the best decision of her life.

She smiles. *Look at you now; one hundred thousand dollars richer and out of prison after just one year. AND you have an FBI agent who is madly in love with you.*

Rosary laughs, *if only he admits it and finally acts upon it!*

But she questions whether she WANTS him to act upon it. What if he does? What should she do? She has only been with one man her whole entire life, Daryl Jake.

Rosary suddenly feels self-conscious about her looks and hygiene. She let herself go for the past few weeks and hasn't felt comfortable about her appearance. She felt cornered deep inside a rabbit hole, and she couldn't seem to dig herself out. She was depressed and saddened.

She missed being out in the world. She missed seeing and laughing with normal human beings. She missed eating ice cream and playing with her cat, Berry.

She can hear the footsteps of De Carlo climbing down the basement stairs. She doesn't move though; she wants him to know what's on her mind.

He enters the garage with a suitcase filled with his wife's items. He stops, watching Rosary touch every piece of evidence placed on his corkboard.

Without looking at De Carlo, Rosary asks, "I want my cat back. Where is he?"

De Carlo places the suitcase onto the floor and then stands next to Rosary. Rosary nonchalantly sniffs her armpit, hoping for it not to smell like bad body odor.

It doesn't and this makes her feel relieved.

"He's with Tiara, my partner. I'll get him back for you."

Rosary nods. She feels this sense of awkwardness and hears silence in the air. She isn't sure what to say to him now. She knows she's being silly about all of this, but she isn't sure what he is thinking and feeling about her being inside of his house.

She is a cold-blooded killer.

She wipes her face with her hands and then quickly brushes her hair with her fingers.

"I do see a pattern with the victims' appearances...except for your wife," Rosary says as she points to every single victim with the tip of her finger, "Seems to be the outcast."

De Carlo nods, agreeing. "All white women, a shade of blonde hair, some dark, mostly blue or green eyes."

"But...not Jada. Why? It's not part of his MO."

"That my dear... is the million-dollar question," De Carlo answers as he stares at his wife.

"It's quite confusing," Rosary continues. "Are the women having an affair with other men and the killer is catching them in the act? OR are these women having an affair with the killer and then he's killing them? And why?"

De Carlo glances at the pinned note written by the killer. Rosary spots it and reads it to herself. She then watches De Carlo's eyes read the note repeatedly.

She isn't sure what to say. She feels awkward and numb that his wife would do something like this to him. She isn't sure what Jada had been thinking, and quite frankly, she wishes that she had. She wishes that she had met Jada and was able to talk to her somehow.

Something is missing from the puzzle. Something doesn't feel right about this whole situation. Rosary is suddenly feeling exasperated and unsure if she can go through with her next mission.

She curses at herself. She does this all the time. She gets excited about a new kill, but then the longer she sits and thinks about it, the more she hates the idea.

But she knows that this killer needs to be brought to justice... and not just sitting in a jail cell somewhere. This ruthless killer needs taken out. He's killed too many women.

"This has been a constant battle," De Carlo blurts.

Rosary looks at his tired and tearful eyes. He's exhausted and feels defeated.

She places a soft hand on his shoulder and squeezes for comfort. De Carlo closes his eyes as he feels the electric chills jolt his body. He wants this woman in the worst way, but he can't tell her that at the moment. He doesn't want her to break her concentration on her new task. He wants her to stay focused and alert. She needs sleep and food to keep her energized.

De Carlo softly removes her hand and smiles. Rosary suddenly feels foolish and is clearly upset about the rejection.

"I have something for you," De Carlo says, trying to avoid the tension rising between them. He doesn't want her mad or upset with him. He wants her to feel wanted and appreciated. He just can't give that kind of commitment right now. He wants this case off his conscience.

He hands her a red folder containing every piece of evidence for this serial killer.

"It will keep you up to date while you're cooped up in the hotel room," De Carlo chuckles.

Rosary isn't laughing but she does take the folder from his clenched fist.

De Carlo watches her place the folder under her armpit and then turns her attention back to the corkboard. De Carlo is sad. He doesn't like to see her this way.

"So, why did you kill? What made you decide to do that in life?" De Carlo asks, curious.

Rosary doesn't know how to answer those questions. Five minutes pass as she stares at the victims pinned to the corkboard. De Carlo eventually picks up the suitcase and then grabs the remote for the garage door. He isn't sure why he asked her those things. She is obviously not ready to answer them. He feels like a fool.

He feels like an asshole.

Rosary's tears spill down her cheeks.

He didn't mean to make her cry. She seems extremely sensitive today and he isn't sure if her mind is all the way there. Prison must have changed her in a drastic way, and he isn't sure if he likes it. He loved her sense of humor and protective demeanor.

He isn't sure what to do or say as he watches her wipe the tears onto her orange jumpsuit. He quickly realizes that she hasn't changed her clothes. She can't walk into a hotel looking like this. People will clearly see who she is.

"Because I'm crazy like my mother," Rosary finally says after two more minutes pass.

De Carlo feels helpless as he places the suitcase back onto the floor. He still doesn't know what to say or do. He isn't sure if he should comfort her. Hell, he isn't sure if she would suddenly stab him or kill him somehow right inside of his garage.

He suddenly feels like a fool once again. He should've handled this case on his own. He should have put some more faith into Curtis and Tiara. They are the professionals.

What has he gotten himself into?

She seems vulnerable and weak. She seems quite sad and unable to focus on what is going on around her. She seems fixated on past situations.

He nearly chuckles aloud at his own thoughts.

*I am fixated on my past situations.*

He suddenly feels like a major ASSHOLE for thinking all these negative thoughts about this woman. She is beautiful and strong and is willing to step up into finding and killing this piece of garbage in this city.

She wants to get rid of what has been terrorizing these streets once and for all.

"My mother was a pimp. She sacrificed me...my sister too," Rosary blurts out.

She suddenly feels relieved, like something has lifted off her chest. She hasn't been able to share this information about her past to anyone...EVER. The only person who had any idea as to what was going on was Daryl. But he didn't know everything.

"My sister stopped it. I was too frightened because I felt like a coward," Rosary continues with tears in her eyes. Being a coward was never her personality.

She isn't even sure why she is so emotional. This has been water under the bridge. Their mother was taken care of...sort of.

She was dealt with.

"My sister left, and I haven't seen her in ten years," Rosary continues as she wipes her tears.

*Chin up! Get over it,* she yells to herself.

Calmly, she smiles.

"Let's go and get me settled. I need a nice, warm bath."

# SEVEN

De Carlo isn't quite sure if he completely trusts Rosary Chime just yet. He doesn't know everything about her, and he isn't sure if or when that will happen. After this past year, he has come to terms with learning that a person truly doesn't know EVERYTHING about someone, including someone very close to the heart. This revelation has crushed his heart into tiny pieces, and he contemplates on never becoming part of the "dating scene," ever again.

However, this beautiful woman may change his mind someday. He has realized that deep down he doesn't want to involve himself in a committed relationship. He confuses his own mind when he suddenly desires this erotic and tantalizing creature sitting quietly next to him. One day, he wants to cuddle her body into his hulk-like arms. Then the next day, he wants to be alone.

The torment of his wife's death haunts his brain every single day. This case holds him back from the happiness that he could possibly find from being with another woman.

Somehow, he feels as though he's cheating on Jada. He feels as though he's going through his own infidelities. Of course, he knows that this is nonsense, but still, it feels like Jada is still in his life as though she's going to walk through the front door to their home and say he was being pranked.

He would love for her to wrap her arms around his neck and kiss him passionately.

But those days are over, and he needs to move on. He needs to stop feeling as though the message written on the walls in red lipstick are directed toward him.

He can't move on, not yet. Once the killer is relieved of his duties, then, he can move on with the feeling of pride and ever-lasting accomplishment.

De Carlo has hope for the future and he wants Rosary in it.

As they exit his vehicle, Rosary stares at the hotel as if it's a giant insect waiting to chomp on their heads. She doesn't seem like herself once again. She seems frightened. She needs to try to get out of this depressing attitude that she has been displaying ever since she escaped the prison.

She used to be fearless and heartless. She didn't give a damn about most people. She's suddenly feeling as though she can't accomplish this mission. She feels trapped and stuck inside of a dark tunnel with absolutely no light. She feels hopeless.

She suddenly thinks of Emilio Delgado as she watches a man enter the hotel. He looks just like him, but she knows that he's not. He's most likely in hiding. He knows that she was arrested.

He called one day to try to speak to her in prison. She refused that phone call, and it was the only time he tried to reach her.

He knows and maybe he's waiting for her departure.

Rosary contemplates her thoughts for a moment.

A switch ignites inside of her mind.

*The killer must be...Emilio Delgado. Yes of course! It has to be. He's handsome, he sleeps with many women at a time, he's rich and successful, and he's charming...*

Suddenly, Rosary's face is pale as a ghost. She can't believe that she was involved with a serial killer who manipulates women, uses them for sex, tortures them, and then kills them...for what? Pleasure...for a few laughs...for the hell of it?

He's heartless, sick and demented.

Rosary thinks for another moment as De Carlo shuts the trunk door with her suitcase clutched inside of his fist.

*Just like me... heartless, sick, and demented.*

*A sniper. A hater. A killer among the living.*

De Carlo softly touches her arm, spooking her insides and jolting her thoughts inside of her brain. She needs to get a grip on reality and stop fantasizing about what if's and why's.

"I need to wake up," Rosary admits. She shakes her head as if her trance is over. She suddenly feels like her normal self. She no longer feels that fear deep inside of her gut.

No words can describe the pressure that she has been feeling since the age of sixteen. She wishes that she would've never met Daryl Jake and Emilio Delgado.

But who knows? Maybe she would've been one those women tortured for the simple fact that they fell in love with the wrong guy. Maybe she would've been strangled to death.

She will never trust a man ever again.

"You are awake," De Carlo answers as they walk across the street and head toward the front doors to the hotel. "You just need time alone."

Rosary chuckles, "I've been alone my whole life."

After they enter, De Carlo places the suitcase onto the floor next to a plush chair.

"Have a seat while I check you in," he orders.

As he walks away, he glances over his shoulder at Rosary, making sure that she doesn't run. She catches a glimpse of his fiery, brown eyes and realizes that he still doesn't trust her.

What does he think she's going to do? Run and hide again? She specifically mentioned that she is done with running. She is done with hiding.

She's suddenly angry at him. How could he not trust her?

He's the one who came to her asking for help. If he didn't trust her, why would he involve her in this important situation? Why would he ask her to do this?

*He's selfish, that's why. He doesn't care about me or what happens to me in this dangerous situation. Emilio could end up killing me instead of me killing him.*

Instead of sitting down in the chair like De Carlo ordered her to, she quietly and slowly walks around the hotel while peeking at the paintings on the wall and watching De Carlo flirt with the receptionist. She's annoyed to say the least. She's aggravated about his cocky demeanor and bad attitude. She's done with being told what to do by overbearing men.

Rosary rolls her eyes as she hears the receptionist giggle at one of De Carlo's dumb ass jokes. He tries to pull that humorous crap with Rosary, and she normally laughs like an idiot too.

Well, not anymore. She's so angry with him right now.

As she watches a couple enter the elevator, she quickly realizes that her emotional well-being is following the pattern of her mental health. She was in denial, in pain while suffering from sadness, depression and now she's completely angry. She knows that she's angry for the wrong reasons. She knows that she shouldn't be angry with De

Carlo right this minute. He has been nothing but nice and inviting.

She needs to get some sleep. She feels delusional and out right crazy. She needs to snap out of these mixed feelings and emotions. She needs to be herself again...full of life with a quirky personality. She wants to laugh again.

The elevator doors are stuck open as the couple kiss passionately. Their baggage blocks the doors from closing and the elevator makes a dinging noise.

Rosary watches the woman laugh hysterically as she tilts her head back, her brown hair almost touching the floor. She's wearing a skin-tight pink dress with pink high heels. Her lover plants soft kisses onto the side of her neck.

Rosary can't see her lover's face but he's wearing a black baseball hat, a black jean jacket and blue jeans. The woman looks over-dressed for the occasion.

As the elevator dings for the third time, the woman removes the suitcase out of the way and pushes a button. As the elevator doors close, Rosary listens to the woman laugh once again as her lover kisses her on the lips.

Rosary watches the numbered buttons above the elevator as it climbs each floor, blinking its bright, white light onto floor one, then two, then three... De Carlo looks back at Rosary, making sure that she hasn't left.

Rosary notices this gesture and glares at him. Her eyes then quickly watch the lights blink for floor number four, then five.

The elevator stops.

De Carlo leaves the reception desk with pamphlets in his hand and her suitcase dragging onto the freshly shampooed carpet. He's smiling from ear to ear.

Rosary feels nauseated. She's hungry, tired and she needs some space.

"Let's head on up," De Carlo says, cheerfully.

As they approach the elevator, Rosary asks, "Did you get her number?"

De Carlo laughs, "No, should I?"

"I don't know. You two seemed awfully chummy."

De Carlo doesn't answer as they enter the elevator. He senses jealousy and anger. He quickly frowns from the thought of her becoming mad at him for being flirtatious with the receptionist. What he does with other women is his business. They are not a couple. She's here to complete a mission. She's here to stop this menacing killer.

He's quite shocked that she's acting this way. She didn't seem the jealous type.

*You did it now,* he thinks to himself. *What have I gotten myself into?*

He doesn't want to regret his decision to send Rosary to lead the pack of wolves, but, that thought is creeping at the back of his mind. He suddenly realizes that breaking a criminal out of prison for his own benefit will have severe consequences in the near future.

*No one will find out,* he thinks. *Adeline stated that she would stick to her word.*

But he doesn't know Adeline at all. He doesn't know what she is capable of. He placed his life into a stranger's hands. Stupidly, he placed his life into TWO stranger's hands.

Hopefully, he can learn the positives in Rosary. He wants to learn what makes her tick, what makes her happy and how he can get her out of this funk that she's in.

As Rosary and De Carlo exit the elevator, they hear high pitch laughter coming from another room. De Carlo stops in front of the door to room number 503 and pulls the key card out of his jacket pocket. As he opens the door, he looks back at Rosary and smiles.

"Don't get any ideas," Rosary says, chuckling.

De Carlo bursts with laughter.

"I would never," he responds as he turns on the lights.

Rosary smells the fresh cut flowers sitting beautifully inside of a glass vase.

De Carlo checks each closet as if someone is planning to jump out and stab them to death. He points his gun while holding his breath. He doesn't understand why he's checking the room like this, but he would rather be safe than sorry.

He doesn't trust anyone right now.

"You don't have to babysit me," Rosary says as she sits on the end of the bed. "I'm not a child." She runs her fingers through her hair. She's in desperate need of a shower.

De Carlo nods in agreement. He absolutely knows that Rosary Chime is not a child. He just wants to make sure that she is safe and comfortable. This was his plan. This was his idea.

"You're absolutely right. I just want to make sure that things are okay for you."

"I'm more than okay," Rosary says, smiling. "I'm out of prison. I'm fantastic!"

There it is. There's her full-of-life personality that De Carlo has been missing. There's that beautiful smile that makes his heart race and the goose bumps stand on the back of his neck.

He suddenly wants to see that smile for the rest of life. He suddenly wants to take care of her and nurture her as much as he can.

But he knows that she doesn't need to be taken care of and nurtured. She is an independent woman with strong ethics and a smart mind. She can take care of herself. She has for many years. He knows that he can't change her independence and way of thinking.

Deep down, he wants her to lean on him and embrace his comfort and love.

*We have plenty of time for that,* he thinks, *lots of time to figure things out.*

"I'm going downstairs to the waiting area for a few hours to keep an eye out on the hotel. If you need me, don't hesitate," De Carlo answers, smiling from ear to ear.

Rosary nods, giggling. De Carlo leaves.

As soon as the door closes, Rosary frowns. She doesn't know what to do with herself. She needs to get some sleep. She needs to eat. BUT, she has so much to do.

As she glances over at the silver tray filled with different cheeses and fruits, Rosary's stomach growls loudly. She laughs, making her way over to the platter of meats and crackers.

She suddenly stuffs food into her mouth, chewing fast and hard. She swallows cheddar cheese and grapes. She grabs a piece of ham and two crackers, shoving them down her throat.

She then chugs a bottle of water, choking. The water dribbles down her chin and onto Jada De Carlo's fancy sweater. Rosary suddenly wants to get out of these fancy pieces of clothing. This is not her. This is not who she is. She does not wear cashmere sweaters and skirts. She feels silly. She feels exposed to the world. She likes her tight jeans, her pant suits and combat boots.

She had De Carlo pack her items into the suitcase as well. Those are her sacred items that she will never give up.

De Carlo refused to have her wear her clothes to the hotel because he doesn't want anyone to recognize her and call the police.

She completely understands that, however, she feels as though De Carlo wants her to become his wife, Jada. He wants her to dress like her and act like her.

That isn't going to happen. *Over my dead body.*

Rosary's stomach continues to growl but she feels full and satisfied, for now. She wants to eat more a little later. But first, she needs a shower.

And a...pit stop.

Who knows what else?

After showering, Rosary slips on tight black jeans, a red hoodie, her black leather jacket, and her favorite black combat boots. *Detective Anthony De Carlo will never change me.*

She suddenly feels alone. She desperately needs the company of her belongings, her apartment, and her damn cat! She misses Berry with his cute meows and soft purrs.

As she smiles, thinking about Berry chasing a toy mouse, she notices the folder filled with evidence that De Carlo gave her to look at. She suddenly feels like a jerk for not even looking over pieces of information that could shed some light on all this madness.

Opening the folder, she pulls out photos of each victim, their background and history, any suspects in mind, De Carlo's note from the killer and photos of the messages written in red lipstick.

Rosary self-consciously places the tips of her fingers onto her lips covered in red lipstick. This color happens to be the same shade that Rosary is currently wearing.

She finds this to be creepy and shocking at the same time.

*I'm surprised that De Carlo hasn't accused me of these murders... YET.*

Only time will tell. But how the hell could she murder all these women while in prison?

And why would she? She wouldn't do it for free...

After reading the evidence for an hour, Rosary glances at the clock on the wall placed neatly above the living area. It's just after eleven o'clock.

Rosary looks around her fancy hotel room. The plush couch is bright blue. A white armchair faces the television that hangs against a wall. A black, coffee table sits neatly in the middle of a furry, white rug. Another silver tray containing two empty coffee mugs, and a small coffee container lies in the middle of the coffee table.

She has never stayed inside of a hotel room this extravagant. De Carlo REALLY wanted her to feel comfortable. He REALLY wanted her to feel like she belonged.

But sadly, she still doesn't.

She doesn't feel like a normal human-being quite yet. She was once again hired to kill someone. Even though she knows that it's different this time, she still feels like an alien inside of a spaceship watching humans destroy the planet.

This time, she is serving her community. This time, she is SAVING lives.

As she thinks of this notion, she chuckles, picking up the hotel telephone. She places a call with the cab company. She needs some fresh air for a little while.

As she sneaks out of the hotel room, she feels like a Ninja with a sword. She skillfully places her pocketknife into the back pocket of her jeans and tiptoes through the hallway as she listens to a couple next door making love.

She chuckles. She hasn't done that type of thing in many years. She seems to forget how.

As she laughs at her own joke, she presses the button to the elevator.

She suddenly has this feeling of dread and fear. *What if De Carlo is waiting behind the doors just as they open?*

There's no way he's still here. He needs to get home and relax himself. He needs sleep. He's cranky and old.

Rosary giggles.

The elevator stops on the main floor and the doors open.

De Carlo is there.

Fast asleep on a chair, snoring.

Rosary glances at the reception desk. No one is there either.

She breathes out a sigh of relief and hurries through the hotel as if her ass is on fire. She scurries out of the hotel doors just as she spots her cab parking into a metered parking space.

She waves and the driver immediately smiles.

Climbing out of the cab, she tosses a couple of dollars toward the driver and says, "Wait right here, please. I'll just be a few minutes."

The cab driver smiles at the money and nods, watching her stare at her mother's church for a couple of minutes.

It's a breathtaking view. The church has been freshly painted a beige color with red shudders. The roof has been repaired with a large cross sitting snuggly in front of the chimney. A crystal mirror reflecting different shades of purples and blues placed in the middle of its double doors. The handles have been painted red, the same shade as the shudders.

She is overwhelmed at this beautiful sight. She is so proud that the church was able to repair the damage and make it look more inviting.

She enters the church; the smell of fresh paint slaps her nose. She notices candles lit at the altar. A small light built into the wall shines on top of the grand piano.

She feels a slight chill but being inside of her mother's church makes her feel alive again.

Rosary smiles as she slowly walks down the aisle, slightly touching the pink bunny decorations pinned at every pew, with the tips of her fingers.

She then sits, whispering a quiet prayer:

*"Lord, keep me safe. Safe from harm, safe from De Carlo, safe from Emilio and safe from death. Lord, help me through this. Help me escape my past, escape my future, and escape my present. One more time is all. Lord, I will never do this again, I promise. Amen."*

The pastor quietly exits the office doorway and watches Rosary with a smile.

"I've missed you so," he says, startling her. She hurriedly stands up from the pew, looking frightened and drained of tiredness.

"Pastor Nicholas. I apologize. I didn't realize anyone was here," Rosary says, exasperated.

"It's okay my child. You've always been welcome. Even after..." he trails off.

Pastor Nicholas knows what Rosary has done. He knew her mother very well and secretly promised Sherry Thomas that he would always keep an eye out for her daughter. He welcomed this family with open arms and never questioned Rosary's sins.

He knows.

He knows that she can be a monster. But he also knows how sweet and kind she truly is.

"I appreciate you, Pastor Nicholas. I just wanted to stop by quickly. I can't stay long. I'm on the clock."

Pastor Nicholas nods. He understands that she's not here for pleasantries. "You are free to come and go as you please. I will always be here for you."

Rosary rushes toward the pastor and gives him an incredible, huge hug.

"My Lord and Savior," Rosary says as she plants a kiss on the pastor's cheek. "I'll see you soon, Pastor Nicholas. You take care."

The pastor smiles from ear to ear as he keeps his arms behind his back.

He then slowly gestures the "Criss-Cross," pattern of an imaginary cross with his right hand. With his left, he hands Rosary a shovel.

Rosary's smile is wide. Her eyes light up like a child on Christmas morning.

After kissing the pastor's cheek one last time, Rosary leaves the church, but not before looking back at Pastor Nicholas with saddened eyes.

She has no idea if she will ever see him again. He has been a part of her life since the day she was born. He loved Sherry Thomas, but the feelings weren't mutual. She was too busy with her scumbag boyfriends to notice a good man right in front of her eyes.

Pastor Nicholas loved Rosary and Agatha as if they were his children. He secretly wished that they were. The girls' father, Daniel Chime, had passed away when Rosary was a newborn and Nicholas was there for Sherry through thick and thin. He was her shoulder to cry on.

But that's all she wanted.

You see, Nicholas and Daniel were best friends.

Sherry believed it to be a sin.

Pastor Nicholas waves at Rosary as the double doors quietly close. Rosary stands staring at the doors as if the pastor slammed them in her face.

Tears are in her eyes as she suddenly remembers the cab driver. She quickly looks back toward the cab but immediately sighs a breath of relief.

She watches the man's chest slowly rise in relaxation. The back of his head sits at the top of the seat. He snores away; oblivious that a hit woman could take him out in a blink of an eye.

She contemplates this thought for a moment. He is a witness to her late-night rendezvous.

She quickly shakes her head, disagreeing with her own argument.

*You can't do that,* she tells herself. *NO MORE KILLING!*

*Well... one more Rosary. One more time and you are on your own.*

As she leaves the front steps, she creeps toward the back of the church. She listens to the trees sway in the soft breeze. Her skin crawls with goose bumps; the thought of someone jumping out from behind the trees suddenly scares the shit out of her.

She isn't used to being this jumpy.

Well, she isn't used to escaping prison with the help of an overbearing FBI agent either.

Quickly, she digs the dirt inside of a flower garden with the pastor's shovel. The cold breeze feels good on her sweaty forehead. She makes grunting noises as she digs deeper, hoping to quickly reach what she has come for.

The shovel suddenly slams something solid. Rosary smiles a devilish grin.

After spotting the blue strap to her duffel bag, she tosses the shovel and then falls to her knees. She swipes the remaining dirt with her hand and then pulls the strap. Opening the zipper, her eyes become a fiery glow as she stares at her two sniper rifles, extra ammo, a gun stand and binoculars. The excitement that pumps through her veins makes her heart pound like a drum.

Returning to the cab with the bag over her shoulder, she slams the door, awakening the cab driver. His nose snorts like a pig before he asks, "You ready sweetness?"

# EIGHT

Leaving Emilio Delgado's wrath was like lifting bricks off Rosary's shoulders. The man is a heartless killer. He's someone that you never want to cross. He's someone that would put a bullet through a newborn baby's head without feeling any sense of empathy.

The man is quite small and short with wide shoulders and a fat stomach. His Italian roots make him lethal and incredibly stubborn. He was born into the Mafia and never cherished the love and support from either one of his parents.

They left him at the age of two. Social services made him live with his mother's sister and first husband at the time. His aunt, Lucia Dominick, wasn't loving or affectionate. Instead, she hated the fact that she had to take care of her sister's bratty-ass son and made his life a living hell. She hated him with every bone in her body.

At the age of five, he was placed into a foster home. His aunt couldn't handle his excessively bad behavior. She called him a weak bastard before slapping him across the face for calling her a "pig bitch." She tried to spit in his face, but her husband stopped her, telling her that he wanted a divorce because she was completely out of control.

Lucia blamed Emilio for ruining her life. She blamed him for her husband leaving.

At the age of six, Emilio's uncle, Ale Delgado, adopted Emilio and treated him like his own son. He loved having his nephew home with him and vowed to take great care of him.

And he did.

Ale was the Mafia boss, and he showed Emilio how their world was quite different from others. He taught Emilio to never take anyone's shit...including his own uncle's.

Ale died when Emilio turned twenty-five-years-old. He was shot like a dog in the streets.

By his own nephew...

Emilio had to face the facts; Ale Delgado was stealing money from him. Emilio couldn't let that continue. He couldn't let his uncle get away with it.

Emilio became ruthless and vowed to never trust a living soul ever again.

His big stomach jiggles like a bowl full of jelly as Rosary watches him through the scope of her red rifle. He's sitting on his recliner chair inside of his fancy living room with diamond vases and a crystal chandelier. He's laughing while watching a cartoon television show.

Rosary is perched on top of a homeowner's roof as she points the rifle across the street. Emilio's windows are open, and the chilly air blows the curtains wide as if it's inviting Rosary to take the shot. It's as if the curtains are speaking to her...

*Take the shot...COWARD!*

The sweat on her forehead slides downward and onto her cheeks. She closes her eyes as she whispers a silent prayer, "Please Lord forgive me for I have sinned."

*Take the damn shot!*

As she opens her eyes, she holds in her breath, pointing the red dot onto the front of Emilio's forehead.

IMMERSED BY BLOOD  –  105

At this point, she knows he saw it. She watches Emilio jump up from his recliner in fear, grabbing a young boy, around the age of ten, and telling him to, "Get down!"

Another young child, a girl with long black hair, jumps to the floor as she covers her head with her arms.

"Damn you Emilio Delgado," Rosary whispers as one of Emilio's bodyguards point his finger at Rosary, shoving his pistol through the opened window.

He suddenly opens fire as Rosary lowers her head just in time. The bullet ricochets off the stone chimney of the house she's vacating.

"That's my cue," she says loudly, grabbing her duffel bag and placing her rifle securely inside. She knew that this would be a bad idea. She knew that something would hold her back.

*Who the hell are those kids?*

The neighborhood becomes a chaotic mess. Neighbors from every direction begin flicking on their lights and stepping out onto their porches. Dogs are barking as people scream, "What the hell is going on?!"

Rosary climbs down a ladder and jumps into the backyard of the homeowner she just violated. Luckily, they're not home. She curses at herself for telling the cab driver to leave.

She can hear Emilio yelling obscenities as she runs into the woods behind the house. His bodyguard begins chasing her but then stops at the edge of the woods, watching her escape.

The duffel bag is heavy, hanging off her shoulders like a sack of bricks. Her forehead perspires with sweat, and she smells like the Earth from the ground. Her hands are covered in dirt, and she feels self-conscious about this fact as she hurriedly struts through the hotel doors.

As she passes the empty reception desk, she glances at the clock above the wall. She has been gone for two hours. She should be tucked under the covers and fast asleep. She's exhausted as her mind becomes delusional and her eyesight becomes blurry.

She has finally realized that she absolutely needs sleep in order to keep pushing forward. But she thinks that there's too much to do still and she just doesn't have the time.

There's no time to sleep. There's no time to eat. There's no time to lollygag or play games.

There's a serial killer on the loose and she won't stop until she finds him. It will finally end once she puts a bullet through his brain. That is exactly what she plans to do.

And no one will stop her...not even Emilio Delgado.

For a split second, Rosary forgets that Tony De Carlo was sound asleep when she left.

Snapping out of her images of looking through her blood red rifle at Emilio, she quickly glances toward the plush chair that was sunken into by De Carlo's weight.

He is gone.

Rosary blows out a long, sigh of relief. She can't explain where she was thirty minutes ago.

Now, she needs to hurry. She feels exposed and vulnerable with a heavy sack gnawing through her shoulder blade like a chainsaw.

She enters the elevator, relieved that the receptionist misses her by three seconds.

After approaching the desk once again, the woman quickly glances toward the elevator doors as they quietly close. She shrugs her shoulders, typing information into the computer.

Rosary's heart pounds as she watches each number of each floor light up as the elevator climbs toward floor number five.

She imagines De Carlo waiting for her as the doors open. Her stomach flutters with fear. Her eyes are bloodshot from tiredness, and she suddenly feels as though she's about to faint.

The last thing she needs is Tony De Carlo waiting for her in the hallway.

She needs a drink of water. Her throat feels raw from dryness and she suddenly coughs. She hopes she's not getting a cold or a sore throat. That's the last thing she wants or needs in her life.

Her plans would be delayed. Hell, they would be ruined. She would have to wait until she felt better. She can't concentrate on missions when she isn't feeling well.

Daryl used to say, "You're such a whiny bitch. Just because you're sick, doesn't mean you can't fulfill your mission. Suck it up buttercup."

Rosary had come down with the flu during a special mission personally attached to Emilio. Go figure. Rosary was the "Ginny pig," when it came to killing people that Emilio was associated with. He didn't take "no" for an answer and he sure as hell didn't give two shits if she was severely sick. She was forced to get her ass up and guns ready if she wanted to live any longer. This used to make Rosary chuckle deep down inside when Emilio threatened violence toward her well-being.

After many years, she wanted him to. She no longer feared his threats.

She once told him, "Do it loser. You won't though. You're nothing but a bitch."

Emilio had slapped her across the face so hard that her brand-new sunglasses flew off her face and onto his plush, red carpet. The blood from her mouth seeped through the corners and dripped onto that red carpet, blending in like puzzle pieces.

Those times were hard for her. Those times were hard on her. She killed someone almost every day for two weeks straight. She didn't have the energy any longer. She hadn't slept for days, missing meals, staying at Emilio's house for refuge. It was one of the worst experiences of her life. She wished to be arrested without delay.

The man used to lock her up inside of a glass cage that was built inside of his basement so she couldn't be found by the feds. He provided her with food and water, but it was scarce.

He treated her like a helpless dog, locked up and beaten.

Daryl would sit outside of the cage every night and hold her hand through the tray opening. Emilio had threatened to mutilate Daryl's private area if he ever let Rosary escape.

That is what the police officers didn't know, and they never found out. Rosary never talked specifically to them about the torture and abuse. She didn't want to re-live the horrific details.

Years later, she wishes she had.

The elevator doors open wide, and Rosary faces an empty hallway. She quickly jogs toward her room and slides the key card through the slot. Her heart pounds with excitement.

Her rifles are sacred to her heart. They are her, "babies." She has finally gotten her hands on them after a year; a long, terrible, exhausting year.

As she enters the room, the smell of cheese and meats hits her in the face. Her stomach suddenly growls, making her laugh. It isn't giving up. It wants fed.

Tossing the duffel bag onto the floor, she suddenly thinks about De Carlo.

*Slow your roll, he might be "waiting in the wings."*

This thought makes her mind reel with bloody images of her shooting De Carlo with one of her rifles. He surely wouldn't allow her to keep her babies. He wouldn't want her to jeopardize the investigation. De Carlo specifically told her that he has a rifle for the job.

But she wants to use HERS. Her red rifle will complete the job in a heartbeat. Nothing will change her mind. She doesn't need De Carlo's weapons.

Quickly, she pulls out the pocketknife from the back pocket of her tight jeans. She presses the small button, and the knife pops out of its liner.

She slowly searches the hotel room; opening closets, checking underneath the bed, checking behind the curtain in the bathtub, any place that a human his size could hide.

The room is empty.

Rosary sighs once again, placing her knife onto the coffee table.

Her mind is screaming for sleep and her stomach for food.

The cheese has become hard, and she crinkles her nose in disgust. She then shoves two pieces of ham and a cracker into her mouth, chewing like a cow.

Her mother would have slapped her face for making those awful noises. Sherry Thomas was a stickler for people chewing with their mouths open.

When Rosary was just six years old, she used to chew her gum like a cow at a farm. She and her mother were at the park during a family picnic. Her mother asked her politely, at first, if Rosary could stop making those chomping noises.

Rosary thought it was a joke, slapping her teeth against her cheeks while the piece of gum slipped in and out of her mouth.

Without hesitation, Sherry slapped Rosary across the face. Of course, it was done in private so none of the family members could witness the ordeal.

But Pastor Nicholas did.

He saw it.

And he had wished that he didn't.

He then watched little Rosary cry a waterfall of tears as Sherry then apologized for the abuse. She reminded the child that her mother kindly asked her to stop, and she wouldn't listen.

Sherry then said, "That's what happens when you don't listen to your mother."

Rosary remembers that incident like it was yesterday.

Smiling, she chomps on her food and chews like a pig in a trough. There's no one here to slap her. There's no one here to scold her like a six-year-old at a family function.

Her exhaustion suddenly takes over her body and she feels completely drained. However, she wants to do one last thing before she goes to bed.

As she kneels onto the floor by her knees, she opens her duffel bag. Her rifles glow with an unmistakable bright light from Heaven. She feels like she has found gold inside of a treasure box. Her eyes light up with happiness as she giggles like that six-year-old child she used to be.

She carefully takes them out of the bag and then slips extra ammo into her favorite red rifle.

THIS is what makes her happy. THIS is what makes her who she is.

A cunning killer. A skillful hit woman.

The best one she had ever known.

She's smart and funny, she's smooth with her words and a quick thinker. She will have this serial killer hanging by his balls.

If it's the last thing she does, so be it.

She will go down in a blaze of glory if she has to. As long as the son of bitch dies, she will live in Hell quite satisfied and unashamed of her wrongdoing.

She will pay for her sins.

She hears the wind blowing, violently rattling the windows. This excites her deeply. It's like a calling to the night sky above. The wind whispers to her. It wants her to come outside and play.

As she opens the sliding glass door to the outside balcony, she breathes in the fresh, chilly air and then exhales through her lungs. She feels the pressure on her throat and suddenly coughs.

She sincerely hopes that she's not getting sick. She will have to hide this dilemma from De Carlo. He would surely become upset with her. He might even blame her if he ever found out about her aggressively digging through the dirt in the cold, night air.

Not to mention hiding behind a chimney to suck the life out of Emilio Delgado.

She should've waited until tomorrow to dig for her rifles. She knows this but she doesn't care at this moment. She finally has her babies back in her arms.

She hugs her rifles as if her mother is about to take them from her grip. Sometimes, she wants to go back to that six-year-old Rosary Chime. All she had to worry about was dolls and cleaning her room. All she had to worry about was her grades and friends.

Rosary shrugs. *No, you had to worry about getting your ass beat by your psychotic mother.*

As she listens to her neighbors have wild sex, she snaps out of the clouds that her mind was temporarily stuck in. She laughs at the moaning sounds, suddenly remembering the gun stand that she brought with her.

After fetching the gun stand, she places it onto the balcony, placing the rifle in its spot.

She then peeks through the scope, pointing it at the street below. She watches pedestrians walking up and down the street. She can't believe people are still out and about at this hour. She wants to scream at them and tell them to go to bed.

She witnesses two prostitutes calmly taking each step with high heels and skimpy, tight dresses. One prostitute is wearing a pink boa wrapped around her neck.

Rosary shakes her head in disbelief. She's glad that her life never veered toward that way of getting paid for sex. She suddenly chuckles.

*No, you just get paid for killing people, hypocrite.*

As she looks through the scope once again, she can't seem to concentrate as the loud moaning becomes like a giant bullhorn being blown inside of her ears.

*You're just jealous, bitch.*

Rosary laughs to herself. *Maybe... maybe not.*

Smiling, she decides to go back inside her room.

She definitely needs a bottle of champagne, some decent food, and a man in her bed. She can't remember the last time the cobwebs were dusted off her private area.

Giggling, Rosary then places her ear up against the combining wall of both rooms. She listens to the moans, the bed banging up against the wall, and the woman shouting, "Uh yeah!"

Rosary closes her tired eyes. She then slides her fingertips, like a slow-crawling spider, inside of the front of her hoodie. She pinches her nipple in between her shaking fingers.

After a moment of such pleasure, she bites her lip, listening to the couple moan louder.

She unbuckles her belt. However, she suddenly stops, listening to quiet laughter.

She suddenly thinks that they are laughing at her.

*That's impossible you idiot, they have no idea what you are doing!*

As she quickly buckles her belt, she listens to the woman say, "What? Are you mad?"

Rosary suddenly wishes that she would have minded her own business. That is another part of her problem. She can't seem to ignore others and focus her attention on what she should be doing. It has been a problem that everyone in her life has complained about.

Both Emilio and Daryl scolded her for not paying attention to them multiple times.

They were sitting inside Emilio's nightclub one night. Daryl and Rosary were VIP guests. Emilio was ecstatic that they attended the grand opening of his beloved club.

They were gathered at a table, waiting on the server for their drinks. Another server had just brought their appetizers of pretzels and cheese. Rosary was famished and couldn't wait to eat. Emilio laughed at her as she shoved a pretzel into her mouth.

He then said, "Is that all you can shove into that mouth?"

Daryl coughed, choking on the pretzel that he inhaled himself.

"Not yours," Rosary answered, smiling with cheese stuck in between her teeth.

Emilio laughed. He must have been in a good mood that night because normally, he would have hit her for the obnoxious comment.

The server with the drinks began making her way toward their table. One of Emilio's men, who was the boyfriend of the server, suddenly gripped her arm and pulled her back so hard that she dropped all their drinks to the floor. Glass shattered and champagne splashed onto the legs of each chair.

Emilio laughed it off like it was no big deal.

The boyfriend screamed into the woman's face, splashing spit as it dribbled down his chin. Rosary felt so bad for the server that she couldn't take it any longer.

She felt her face flush. She felt rage inside of her body. She wanted her hands on her rifle so she could blow his brain into tiny pieces.

Daryl looked at Rosary with anger in eyes, "Drop it," he demanded.

As Emilio chewed his pretzel like a cow, he said, "Mind your business, Rosary."

Those chewing noises suddenly pissed her off. It wasn't funny and she finally understood why her mother hated it her whole entire life. That sound is like nails on a chalkboard.

"So," Emilio continues, "Business talk as usual. Rosary, I want you to..." he trails off, watching Rosary slowly stand up from her seat. "I said to mind your own goddamn business!"

Rosary lunged forward toward the waitress's boyfriend.

She suddenly hears choking as if the scene of choking that man to death has become real to her again. She gripped his neck and strangled him until his face turned blue.

The choking noises distract the images of that man lying dead on Emilio's club floor.

It was the only time she ever strangled someone to death.

She then listens to a lamp crashing to the floor, a struggle of the woman next door pleading for her life. Rosary doesn't want to believe that what she's hearing is real.

She can't distinguish what is real and what's not, at this moment. Her mind is delusional. The sleep deprivation has seriously gotten out of control and is playing with her brain.

Then suddenly...everything is quiet.

The only thing she hears is the ticking of the clock above the couch. *Tick, tick, tick, tick, tick, tick, tick, tick.*

No whispers of sweet nothings.

Pressing her ear against the wall, she can hear quiet movement. She raises her fist to knock on the wall, but she suddenly stops.

Emilio's words are in her brain, "Mind your own goddamn business!"

*But someone is dead. They were just murdered.*

*Weren't they?*

*You don't even know what the hell you just heard! Go to sleep!*

Rosary's mind is in shambles. She's so tired that all she sees through her eyes are bright lights and shadows on the walls.

There's absolutely no sound at all. Did she just imagine someone being strangled to death? The image of the waitress's boyfriend flashes inside of Rosary's skull like a flash of lightning.

That man deserved it. He deserved to die. He shouldn't have put his hands on his girlfriend like that. He embarrassed her right in front of everyone. It was her first night of work.

He was too angry and selfish to even care about her feelings.

As Rosary waits another minute to hear any sign of movement, she glances back toward the balcony at her rifle, "waiting in the wings." It's as if a light-switch flicked on in her brain.

She hurries toward the balcony, takes the rifle off the stand, and then hurries toward the door to her hotel room. She wants to make sure that what she heard was real.

Assuming can get her killed and right now, she absolutely must live another day.

Hiding the sniper rifle behind her back, she enters the hallway. She looks up and down at emptiness as she listens to the echoic sounds of her harsh breathing.

Stepping in front of the neighbor's hotel door, she knocks on it, holding in her breath.

Of course, there's no answer. This makes Rosary nervous. Quite frankly, she's suddenly scared. She's feeling vulnerable and weak. Her tiredness is not helping her to think straight.

"Hello," she calls out.

The hallway echoes her voice, "Hello, hello, hello."

After standing in the hallway for a full five minutes, Rosary decides to give up. She's being silly and acting like a fool. She doesn't know why she acts so interested in everyone's life. She doesn't understand why she worries about other people's business.

She always has to know what is going on. Anything that seems out of the ordinary makes her ears perk up like a dog. She has become suspicious of every little detail in a situation. It doesn't matter what it's about, she must take part in either helping, saving, or figuring out information so she can deal with the situation on her own.

Rosary enters her room and slams the door. She has become frustrated with herself. She can't seem to ignore what she thinks she heard. She doesn't even know what she heard.

As she dials De Carlo's number with the hotel phone, she impatiently waits. She glances at the clock once again. It's two o'clock in the morning.

And she wonders why she's extremely tired.

De Carlo doesn't answer.

She slams the phone in frustration. She then glances toward her bed and suddenly dreams of drowning herself in the comfortable sheets and blankets.

"One more thing to do then you're all mine, "she says to her bed.

Rosary heads back out onto the balcony to collect the second rifle and the gun stand.

She's feeling nauseous as she brings everything back inside, leaving the sliding glass doors wide open for a cold breeze to calm her nerves.

Her skin feels raging hot, cold, and clammy. Her insides want to vomit, and her mind wants to sleep. Her stomach wants to eat, and her body wants to lie in comfort.

She's all over the place. She feels like she's stuck inside of a labyrinth. She doesn't know which way to turn or who to trust.

She can't even trust herself. She doesn't know what is going on right now.

*Oh yes,* she remembers. *Prepare for the worst and plan for the best...*

Setting up the gun stand once again, she places the red rifle into its spot, pointing the scope toward the hotel door. She moves the armchair from the living area and places it next to the gun stand, plopping her skinny butt into it. She suddenly feels like she's floating on a cloud.

As Rosary patiently waits, her eyes slowly begin to drift closed.

She falls fast asleep.

# NINE

Rosary can see splashes of red paint all over the walls. Well, it might be red paint. It might be blood. She isn't one hundred percent sure. She can also see the word, "KILLER," written in capital letters with red lipstick. That simple word makes her skin crawl.

She doesn't want to be a killer any longer.

But is that message directed toward her at all?

She contemplates the answer to her own question as she slowly tiptoes through the living area of her hotel room with her black combat boots. She sees the gun stand with her red rifle perched toward the hotel door.

She sees herself, sound asleep in the armchair.

*What the hell?*

She must be dreaming. The deep subconscious of knowing that she is watching herself in the middle of the night is completely terrifying.

*Am I dead?*

Confused, she stares with wide eyes as the letters, "KILLER," suddenly change to, "CHEATER." The letters are written in blood this time, not red lipstick.

She's not a cheater. She is loyal and loving.

*Snap out of it!*

She must be losing her mind. She never thought that she would go completely insane like her mother. She has avoided that conflict her whole entire life.

She vowed to never become her mother. But it might be too late.

Suddenly, the room begins to spin in circles like a tornado. She becomes dizzy, falling to the floor on her hands and knees. All that ham meat, cheese, and crackers that she shoved into her gobbler slowly creeps up her throat and into her mouth.

She vomits, closing her eyes as the room spins faster.

*Make it stop,* she pleads. *Make this madness STOP!*

The room suddenly stops spinning, shifting the walls and the placement of the rooms. She feels like she's stuck inside of a puzzle.

Rosary is lying on her stomach, vomit suffocating her airways. She wipes chunks of ham and cheese away from her face with her hand, spreading the vomit all over the bathroom floor.

In a daze, she groggily stands up and goes to the bathroom sink. She washes her hands and face with a cucumber-melon scented soap. She then runs her wet fingers through her hair.

Looking at herself in the mirror, she stares at those big, beautiful, blue eyes.

"Get your shit together."

She takes a deep breath and exhales, smelling the foul odor of vomited-crusted cheese. She then searches for a toothbrush but there aren't any.

She unexpectedly hears the sliding glass door as the clasp closes quietly.

She definitely heard it. She can hear things a mile away. Her sister used to laugh at her when she would listen to the most off-the-wall sounds in the distance.

Agatha used to say, "You're not normal. I'm telling you. Your mind is so far out there."

They would laugh and laugh until Rosary's nose would snort like a pig. Their belly laughter would echo across the meadow and into the neighbor's property.

Those were the good times. That was when Agatha loved her little sister to death. She admitted that she would take a bullet for Rosary in a heartbeat.

But now, any bullet that flies toward Rosary's way would seep directly into her heart, crushing every emotion that she has ever felt for her big sister.

Rosary silently creeps out of the bathroom and into the living area of her hotel room. The shift in the placement of the rooms has her immediately confused. The bed is across the room instead of right in front of her. She watches as her chest rises and falls with each snore that vibrates through her nose like a chainsaw slicing a tree trunk.

She isn't sure what she should do. How can she wake herself up? What kind of nightmare is this? She has to be dead. There's no other explanation as to why she can watch herself sleep.

As she moves her lips to speak to herself, green suede, gloved hands, slowly appear behind her head, reaching toward the loose ends of her hair. Rosary can see a figure wearing a black coat with a black ski-mask through a sudden mirror that appears in front of her.

The figure suddenly has a clump of her hair clenched into his gloved fist. As he pulls forcefully, Rosary screams, "WAKE UP!"

Rosary's eyes pop open like a bottle of champagne. Tears are flowing down her cheeks as she becomes startled by a pulling sensation coming from the back of her head.

*I got this.*

In combat mode, she angrily grips her attacker's wrist and twists, trying to loosen the tightness between his fingers. She will bite this son of a bitch if she has to. She can't be afraid anymore. This is her life that she needs to save... NOW!

Rosary's attacker yelps in pain like a dog and then swings his other fist, punching Rosary directly in the face. She can feel a sudden burning sensation on her nose and cheeks, loosening her grip on the attacker's wrist.

Rosary refuses to scream. That's not what she does. She likes to handle any threat that comes her way with precision and quietness with a focus on eliminating the competition altogether. She will crush this killer like a bug. She's not dying today.

Not today. Not tomorrow. Not ever if she has her way. She would live forever if she could.

The killer is strong, pulling Rosary backward by both of her armpits. The back of the armchair suddenly leans backward like a seesaw. As it tips, it falls to the floor with a loud thud, slamming the back of Rosary's head and causing it to bounce like a football.

She sees beautiful stars float above her eyelids. They sparkle like the brightness of the sun. She's light-headed and dizzy. It feels as though her brain has cracked in half. The immediate headache makes her head feel as if it is about to explode.

She doesn't want to die like this. She doesn't even know who is after her. It has to be the killer. Maybe he knows that she's getting closer to him. Maybe he is trying to eliminate her before she blows his cover... it has to be Emilio!

She hasn't had any secret rendezvous with any men. She has been stuck in prison, living a life of pure hell. She didn't talk to anyone inside of those walls, let alone a man. At first, she wasn't allowed to be near inmates in general. Her cell was never near men in fear of rape and torture.

She begged two women guards to ask the warden to spare her this horrific act because her beauty could very well have gotten her into a heap of trouble.

The warden agreed.

She thinks about this as the killer continues to slam her head onto the floor. She hasn't snuggled into the arms of a man in years.

*Get up!*

Because of Rosary's flexibility, she's able to suddenly swing her right leg upward and kick the killer on the side of his face with her combat boot.

He struggles for a few seconds, only to recover quickly by gripping onto her left leg as she swings it into the air. He grabs her ankle and twists. Rosary cries out in pain but then suddenly swings her right fist and punches him on the side of his head.

She will not give up. She can't. She has worked too hard for too long to end up dying in a silly fist fight. But, if she must bash his head somehow, she will do it quickly and quietly.

She can't be afraid of this monster. He has taken too many lives away from this Earth. She will not be his next victim.

She refuses. It is not in her DNA to die by the hands of a brutal and ruthless man.

She has survived too many of them.

She has this sudden urge to rip the ski-mask off. She wants to know who this low life is. She wants to know who is causing havoc in this city.

Rosary suddenly pulls on the mask, but the killer grabs her hand and squeezes tightly. With his left hand, he then grips onto Rosary's throat, choking her.

Rosary swings her fists but misses his face with every attempt. The killer then grabs both of her wrists while still tightening his grip on her throat.

He then pushes her toward the bed.

She doesn't feel the floor with the bottom of her boots anymore. She seems to be gliding across the room like a witch on her broomstick.

*This son of a bitch is strong.*

The killer throws Rosary on top of the bed and manages to keep his fingers wrapped around her neck. He continues to squeeze as her head buries deep into her pillow.

*This is what it feels like to die. It's finally going to happen. I deserve it.*

Rosary feels this sudden urge to quit this battle. She doesn't understand why. She doesn't give up easily. She fights hard and strong, but right now, she doesn't feel strong enough.

She's losing oxygen and is fighting to breathe. She digs her sharp nails into the side of her attacker's neck, drawing blood.

The killer weakens, turning his head in pain and loosening his grip at the same time.

Rosary finds this moment to attack.

In a split second, she uses both hands to dig her nails into both sides of the killer's neck, feeling the puncture of blood oozing. The killer struggles, pushing his arms toward Rosary's face. The killer's arm brushes past her pulsating nose.

Then, Rosary lifts her right knee and slams it into her attacker's stomach. He begins to fall backward, but quickly sits up and scurries off the bed. He then pulls out a rope from his coat pocket, hurriedly tying it into a lasso.

"Is that all you got?" Rosary asks, taunting the killer.

He then swings the rope high into the air like a cowboy waiting to trap his prey. The lasso quickly wraps around Rosary's neck and then the killer pulls, hard and fast. Rosary digs her nails into the rope as she tries to avoid choking.

But it doesn't work. The rope is strangling her to death as the killer then tries to tie the ends of the rope to the bed post.

Suddenly, Tony De Carlo is pounding his hulk-fists onto the hotel room door.

"Rosary! Open the door!" he pleads.

The killer turns toward the door, immediately panicking at the sound of the FBI agent.

Rosary is light-headed, losing breath. De Carlo tries pushing the door open with the force of his weight, but his plan isn't working either. As De Carlo hears a gasp in the hallway, he looks up to the maintenance person frozen to the floor, watching him like a deer caught in the headlights.

De Carlo quickly flashes his badge. The maintenance person jogs down the hallway and pulls out a set of keys.

The killer continues to panic as he watches Rosary struggle with loosening the rope. He leans forward; his eyes are sad and staring directly into Rosary's teary blues.

*Those eyes...* Rosary thinks.

Rosary suddenly feels as though she's floating on a cloud. Maybe she will be sent to Heaven after all. Maybe HELL isn't the place for her. She is warm and gentle. She loves taking care of others, whoever deserves it. They must deserve it. She will not help any other way.

*Those eyes...*

The killer suddenly loosens the rope around Rosary's neck.

The hotel door swings wide open as Rosary takes in deep breaths, sounding as if she's having an asthma attack.

The killer is fast, hopping off the bed and then opening the sliding glass door toward the balcony as De Carlo pulls his gun from its holster. The killer runs, slamming the door closed as De Carlo presses the trigger with his sweaty fingers.

The bullet shatters the glass, making Rosary cry out with fear. She wasn't expecting that. Her eyes are blurry with tears as she can barely see what's in front of her. She's feeling nauseous but she quickly beats it into her head that she must... *GET UP!*

Rosary scoots off the bed as quickly as she can as she watches De Carlo continue to point his gun toward the balcony. De Carlo watches with piercing eyes as the killer hesitates, staring at the agent as if he's waiting to be shot at a second time.

*He's toying with me,* De Carlo thinks as his right eye squints, positioning the barrel of the gun toward the killer's head.

Rosary snatches her sniper rifle. As she quickly steps through the broken glass door, the killer runs, escaping through the emergency exit ladder that leads to the alleyway.

Rosary is on the balcony, looking through the scope of the rifle as she points it toward the killer. It's too dark to see anything but she likes to take chances. That's what she does.

Rosary shoots, missing her target.

She can hear screams from a woman standing in the alleyway. Rosary hadn't even noticed anyone else. *Why the hell are these people out so late?*

Rosary carelessly shoots her rifle a second time, missing the killer's head by an inch.

The killer is running extremely fast down the alleyway. As Rosary is about to shoot for a third time, she loses sight of him as he turns the corner.

She panics. This can't be happening. Rosary Chime very rarely misses her target. She can't believe she's lost her chance to end this madness. She had one job! She could've ended it all right here, right now.

But she didn't.

And she will feel this disheartening pain in her body until the day that that son of a bitch dies by the hands of the best sniper, "hit woman," that has ever lived.

*And that's a fact...*

*Those eyes...*

Rosary continues to stare through the scope of her rifle. She's awestruck right now. She's feeling a pain in her gut that she's never felt before. Her insides are tightening with fear. Her brain is jumbled with cords of electricity.

She feels defeated, worthless.

*How could I let this happen?*

Rosary suddenly feels De Carlo's warmth on her back as he slowly takes the rifle out of her hands. Her knuckles are sore, and her hands feel tight from squeezing the rifle in such a death-defying grip. She desperately wanted to end this. She wanted to end that killer's life, right here, in her hotel room. She wanted to be the, "hit woman hero."

A hero like the church made her mother out to be.

*That's it! The police department can deem me as a hero!*

Rosary suddenly doesn't want to let go of her precious red rifle. She nonchalantly touches it as De Carlo whispers, "Ssshhhhh..." slowly taking the weapon away from her.

Rosary is angry.

*No one will take what is rightfully mine!*

This sudden madness that escapes her mind makes her feel weak.

*Anger can get you killed. It can get you into trouble.*

But she can't help feeling this way. She's angry at herself. She's angry at the killer. She's even angry at De Carlo. He didn't answer her desperate call. He came too late.

*Or did he come just in time?*

He did save her. The killer would've finished her off if De Carlo hadn't showed up when he did. The killer was ready to end Rosary's life.

*BUT the killer saved me. He loosened the rope.*
*Why?*

Why would such a cunning and thoughtless killer spare Rosary her life? She was walking through a white tunnel, reaching toward a light when she was pulled from behind.

The killer is selfish. *Maybe I wanted to die, you asshole!*

She needs some serious sleep, maybe even some medication.

*That's it! I need to see a doctor.*

Rosary watches the woman in the alleyway as she plays with her cell phone. The bright screen light seems to be piercing through Rosary's tired eyes.

She just wants to forget about this night.

"Are you okay?" De Carlo asks as he also watches the woman scroll through photos on her cell phone screen.

Rosary feels completely out of it. As a matter of fact, she doesn't feel a thing. Her body is numb, and her mind is spinning like a tornado.

The nauseous feeling is back. She can feel the vomit slowly creeping up through her throat.

She doesn't want to puke again. That wouldn't be, "lady like." She would feel completely embarrassed if she vomited all over De Carlo.

*He's too close. He needs to back away.*

She can smell his sweet cologne and sweaty armpits. His breathing is rapid, and she swears that she can hear his heart racing with pleasure.

*At a time like this?*

"I'm okay," Rosary answers after waiting a full minute.

She doesn't know what to do or how to feel about Tony De Carlo. One minute he seems upset with her and then the next minute he wants to crawl in her bed. He seems to be all over the place just like her. One day he wants more, the next day he wants to be alone.

Neither one can make up their minds.

Rosary doesn't know if that's a good thing or a bad thing. Would that complicate their relationship even further? Would they constantly fight as a couple because they wouldn't be able to agree on anything?

That is not something that Rosary would ever look forward to. She would rather be alone than have to deal with Tony De Carlo's anger issues.

"By the way," De Carlo says as Rosary brushes past him, making her way back into the hotel room, "Where did you stash your weapons?"

Rosary turns quite suddenly and grabs her precious red rifle. She glares deep into De Carlo's exhausted eyes and growls, "None of your damn business!"

She snatches the rifle right out of De Carlo's grasp.

"Leave me alone!" she yells as she steps over the broken glass on the balcony floor. "Go do something useful. I can hear your friends coming down the hallway."

# TEN

Rosary Chime is angry, and Detective Anthony De Carlo doesn't like it one bit. He doesn't like the look on her face with dipped eyebrows, a scrunched forehead and piercing eyes that could chisel right through his veins.

He also doesn't like the pain in her eyes. She looks defeated, sorrowful, hurt and just plain exhausted from it all. She seems to be taking her anger out on him, and he doesn't understand why. *I saved her life for Christ's Sake!*

But she doesn't seem like she appreciates that gesture. She seems distant and unwilling to see things from his point of view. She doesn't seem interested in talking to him anymore for the night. She does need sleep, maybe even a few Valiums to calm her down.

He thinks about mentioning this to her, but immediately declines as he watches her sit on the bed as she stares into space. Her back hunches as she loosely holds the rifle just an inch above the floor. At any minute, she might fall asleep and drop it by accident.

That's a horrible thought that spins in his brain like a washing machine.

He feels a migraine as it pulsates his skull like the beat of a bongo. The rhythm is slow... *bong...bong...bong...bong.*

He needs a good night's rest as well. He's starting to feel groggy. His feet are too tired to walk toward the hotel room door as he listens to the pounding fists from his fellow officers.

"Open up!" One of the officers' yells from the hallway.

"I am. It's Detective Tony De Carlo. Back away from the door," he replies.

De Carlo turns to look at Rosary one last time before he places his hand on the door handle.

*Her rifle, shit!*

Quickly, De Carlo scurries over toward Rosary like a mouse sniffing a lone piece of cheese. As soon as he places his fingers on her rifle, she pulls back, glaring up at De Carlo as if she's about to murder him on the spot.

The same officer out in the hallway decides to pound on the door once again.

"Snap out of it!" De Carlo whispers at Rosary, "Put it away!"

Rosary blinks, snapping out of her trance. She looks down at her rifle and then back up at De Carlo. She instantly understands what he's saying and jumps up from the bed.

She pulls her duffel bag out from underneath the bed and gently places the rifle back inside. She nods her head toward the gun stand and De Carlo jogs to it, hurriedly picking it up.

He brings it to her, and she snatches it out of his hand. She didn't mean to act so rough, and this realization is written all over her face.

"Sorry," she whispers as she quickly places the gun stand inside of the duffel bag.

"You owe me," he has the balls to say.

Rosary chuckles as she zips the duffel bag shut, "I don't owe you shit. You owe me. Remember? You're the one who begged for me to do this!"

She slides the duffel bag back underneath the bed and then plops her butt on the soft mattress. She covers herself with a blanket while placing her legs in front of the bottom of the bed, blocking any sight of the bag.

De Carlo hurries to the door once again and whispers, "You ready?"

Rosary nods.

No, she isn't ready. She isn't ready for what might happen. They might find her precious belongings. They might take them from her. It's all she has at the moment. She will not let them take a piece of her heart. She will not let them ruin her.

Rosary absolutely feels sick to her stomach. The thought of being surrounded by police officers once again is making her want to vomit.

De Carlo swings the door open. He nonchalantly pushes four fellow officers farther back into the hallway as he turns to look at Rosary.

She's gone.

*Dammit!* His brain is screaming obscenities. He takes a deep breath as the head officer asks, "What's going on? Let us in!"

"There's nothing to see here. All the action is outside, you moron. I took a huge shit, and it stinks in there," De Carlo waits thirty seconds for one of the officers to respond. The farthest officer in the back, chuckles.

"Let's go to the alleyway," De Carlo continues as he slams the door shut.

He's so angry with Rosary right now that he has the smallest inclination to take her back to the prison; let the warden handle her bad behavior.

His brain is seething with smoke as he grinds the front of his teeth.

Rosary is in the shower tub, gripping onto her duffel bag and shaking with fear.

She doesn't feel like herself. She doesn't feel rested or relaxed. Her heart is racing, and her mind can't focus on what to do next.

But her eyes suddenly close and her mind dips into a heavy, deep sleep.

As De Carlo steps outside into the alleyway of the hotel, he is shocked to find at least fifteen police vehicles parked alongside the street. He didn't expect this many officers to respond. It finally seems as though this city is taking these murders seriously.

Other FBI agents huddle in groups, speaking about the possibility of the murderer being identified. He can't believe this nonsense. No one was in the vicinity to even see or hear anything. He didn't notice any witnesses.

*Were there?*

De Carlo thinks for a minute. He stares at the ground as the recent events play back into his mind. He then looks around the alleyway, hoping for some kind of memory to kick in.

He spots it.

*Son of a bitch, the prostitute with the cell phone...*

The woman is wearing a skimpy, lace, black pants suit with a black coat. She's speaking to an officer as she shows him photos on the screen of her phone.

De Carlo's heart is racing. He isn't sure if it's from a possible break-through of identifying the killer or if it's from this beautiful woman standing in front of him.

He recognizes her. He knows her. Her name is Steamy Heart, her old stripper name. She refuses to let anyone know what her real name is. She ran away from home at the age of sixteen. She is now twenty-six-years-old and living with a pimp.

Her pimp had been arrested multiple times, but it doesn't stop her from leaving him. The man takes loving care of her and doesn't treat her like the other prostitutes. He beats the other women, but not Steamy. She takes him on wild rides, and he loves it. She's adventurous and outspoken. She makes him weak in the knees.

She makes her pimp happy and content.

De Carlo sees why. She's voluptuous and drop dead gorgeous. Her friends have tried getting her into modeling, but her pimp will have none of that. He doesn't want other men swooning over his woman. He doesn't want anyone having nasty thoughts about her.

De Carlo imagines ripping her clothes off. The officer speaking to her points directly at him. Steamy turns to De Carlo, smiling with bright white teeth.

De Carlo's heart skips a beat. He knows that she is unavailable but that smile just cuts deep into his soul while exploding his heart into tiny little pieces.

Steamy thanks the officer and then struts toward De Carlo like a model on a runway. His heart is pounding through his chest. He isn't sure what has come over him lately.

He might just miss his wife. He might just miss having a woman in his arms.

He has become perplexed over his behavior in the last year. He needs closure to his wife's death. He needs love.

And he needs to move on and be happy in his life.

But he continues to chase the wrong women.

Steamy approaches him with a sly smile. That smile could get her into trouble.

De Carlo politely smiles back.

"Agent Tony De Carlo?" Steamy asks. She then presses a code onto the screen of her phone.

De Carlo nods, unable to move his lips.

Steamy continues, "That kind officer over there told me to show you these photos. They're of that person who was running from the emergency exit a little bit ago. I thought they might help the case."

"Thank you Steamy. May I have a look?" De Carlo finally answers.

Steamy is impressed that he remembers her name.

"Not a dull moment when someone remembers you," Steamy says, a flirtatious grin upon her face. A strand of her blonde hair falls forward from behind her ear.

De Carlo wishes to pull on that hair and make her scream.

"How could anyone ever forget you?" De Carlo asks, flirting back.

Steamy laughs as she hands De Carlo her phone. De Carlo smiles as he takes it, scrolling through the blurry photos. All he sees is a person wearing a black ski-mask, a black coat, and green gloves. He can't see the killer's face at all.

He then scrolls to the last photo with the killer looking directly at the camera. He is unsure of the person's identity, but he would like to get a second opinion from Rosary.

"Could you possibly send me these photos?" De Carlo asks politely.

"Sure detective," Steamy answers as she takes her phone out of his fingers. Her thumb rubs against his pointer finger, sending a surge of lightning zapping his groin area.

"These are extremely useful. I can print them up. Thank you for your help."

"No problem," Steamy replies, "May I have your number please?"

De Carlo knows damn well that it's not protocol to give his personal number out to witnesses. But with this woman, he will take his chances.

He gives Steamy his number and she begins sending him the photos.

"I truly appreciate this," De Carlo says as he looks at them once again. Most of the photos are blurry as if Steamy was in a hurry to take them. The only solid picture is the last one. They might be able to use that as evidence.

Another police vehicle arrives, and it is Tiara, De Carlo's partner. She had been trying to call him for the past thirty minutes, but he completely ignored her. He doesn't want to deal with her harsh attitude and complicated questions at the moment.

"You're welcome detective. Let me know if you need anything else," she leaves without waiting for a reply as Tiara approaches De Carlo with a scowl on her face.

"What happened?" Tiara immediately asks, "What's going on?"

"It's complicated," De Carlo answers as he stares at the last photo of the killer.

"Why haven't you been answering my calls? What are you up to?"

"Nothing!" De Carlo snaps. "I'm not a child. Stop treating me like one."

Tiara heavily sighs as she looks around the alleyway, "You're right. I apologize. I've just been worried about you."

"Don't be. I'm perfectly capable of taking care of myself," De Carlo answers as he hands Tiara his cell phone. "Some photos of the killer. I thought I could relax at the hotel for the night, and I had a surprise waiting for me."

Tiara's eyebrows lift into the air with a questionable look upon her face.

"And?" she asks as she scrolls through the photos.

"That's the killer, another victim right next door to my room. I could've saved her."

De Carlo feels genuinely heartbroken. The thought of Rosary listening to an actual murder sends chills down his spine. Rosary could've stopped it had she known what was truly going on inside of that room.

"Who took these photos?" Tiara asks as she reaches the last one.

"The neighborhood hooker...Steamy Heart. She was in the alleyway as I chased the killer from the balcony. He escaped from the emergency exit ladder."

"Well," Tiara says as she hands De Carlo his phone, "those photos are useless. Nice try."

De Carlo nods in frustration. He loves his partner to death, but he doesn't like her negativity.

"They will be analyzed and then we will go from there."

Tiara nods. She feels awkward at this moment. De Carlo isn't acting himself and she has a suspicious feeling that he isn't being honest with her.

She knows when he's lying. He looks around as if he's trying to find an answer. The vein in his neck also protrudes as it pulsates like a beating heart.

Curtis Garcia pulls up in his police vehicle. A look of tiredness and anger flushes his face as if he had just been sitting in the sun for too long.

He slams the car door and then makes his way toward De Carlo and Tiara.

"So, what's the run down?" he asks, waiting for an answer as he pulls out a cigarette from his pocket. A look of confusion is upon Tiara's face.

"I thought you quit," she scolds.

"I did," Curtis answers as he lights it up with his grand-father's antique lighter.

"Everything is under control. You can go home and get some sleep," De Carlo encourages.

Curtis laughs as the cigarette is stuck between his lips.

"What's sleep exactly? None of us get any of that," Curtis says as he looks around the alleyway, uninterested.

"Like I said, everything is under control. The killer was here once again. There's another poor soul about to be buried into the ground," De Carlo says, annoyed.

Tiara senses the tension. "HOWEVER," she says, "There was a witness this time. We have a few photos to analyze. Hopefully, it will work out."

She sincerely sounds positive, and this makes De Carlo quite happy inside. This woman is very rarely in a positive mood when it comes to murder cases and De Carlo isn't sure of what this change is stemming from.

"I will have a full report for you on your desk in the morning," De Carlo says, smiling.

Curtis is slightly taken aback by his agent's positivity, but he shrugs his shoulders and nods his head in agreement. He just wants to get the hell out of here and back into bed with his late-night hussy waiting for him.

"Sounds great. I'll see you in the morning," Curtis answers, flicking his cigarette to the ground and crushing it with his boot.

As he leaves, both De Carlo and Tiara stare at him with confused expressions.

"He was quick to get out of here," Tiara says.

"He's gotta get back to his hot date," De Carlo says.

Tiara slyly looks at her partner. They both howl with laughter.

De Carlo suddenly feels ashamed for lying to them.

But they absolutely cannot know about Rosary's involvement. He would get into so much trouble. He might even be hauled off to jail for his actions. Curtis will not be pleased to say the least.

De Carlo smiles as he watches Tiara continue to laugh.

He feels like such an asshole.


Rosary slowly opens her eyes to the bright sun shining through the bathroom window. She has a headache the size of Earth. Her mouth is dry, and her breath smells like old cheese and expired meat.

Her neck is sore from it being perched onto the edge of the tub. Her arms wrap around her duffel bag for extra protection.

She needs a shower, and her teeth and hair brushed. She feels disgusted and extremely sore. Her body feels as though she ran a marathon last night. As a matter of fact, she feels as though she fell from the window of her hotel room.

She knows that's not true, but she suddenly imagines her body flying through the cold air as it splats onto the wet and rainy ground below.

She peeks at the clock on the wall. It's nine o'clock. It's time to get the day started.

After finding unopened soap, shampoo, an unopened toothbrush and toothpaste inside of the bathroom sink cabinet; she takes a shower and cleans her vomit mouth.

She didn't even feel this disgusting in prison. She was always clean and smelled nice and fresh. She felt self-conscious about being gross at that hell hole of a place. It already smelled of death and decay, so she didn't want to make matters worse.

As she exits the bathroom, feeling refreshed and slightly happy that the stench is gone, she drags her duffel bag through the living area and then lifts it onto the bed.

She doesn't feel like doing anything today, but she knows that things need to get done in order for this madness to stop. She just wants to sleep all day, but she knows that De Carlo will not allow that to happen. He didn't hire her to sleep and sit on her ass all day long.

She calls room service for a plate of eggs, toast, and bacon. She is famished. She needs to find a little energy back into her life before she dies of boredom.

Rosary unzips the duffel bag and then pulls out cleaning supplies from the back pocket. It's time to make her prized possessions shine like a diamond once again.

She smiles, remembering Daryl as he taught her how to clean their guns.

At first, Rosary was nervous. She didn't want to accidently shoot her rifle and kill someone in the room. There was always someone staying over their house. Most of them were drug dealers, strippers, and coke heads. Rosary was constantly annoyed that she and Daryl never got the chance to spend time alone in their own place of residence.

Rosary was suspicious that they had nowhere to go so Daryl was always their knight in shining armor and she was always the witch of the wicked west.

Daryl didn't like her to complain. She kept her emotions bottled up inside. Sometimes, she wanted that bottle to explode but she forever kept that finger at the top of the cap to make sure that nothing ever spilled out.

Rosary places her two rifles onto the sheets of her mattress. She checks for bullets in the chamber and then takes them out.

As she dumps the solution onto a rag, there's a knock on the door.

Her heart is racing. She isn't sure who the hell is bothering her so early in the morning. There's no way that her food is cooked already.

She contemplates answering it, cleaning the red rifle as the person on the other side of the door pounds on it harder the second time.

This person must be desperate.

"Rosary," she can hear Tony De Carlo say as he tries to open the door with the locked handle. "It's me. Open the door."

Rosary feels happy inside, but she also doesn't want to let her guard down, at least for now. De Carlo hasn't shown any signs of turning her in and she wants to keep it that way.

They both seem to trust each other for this moment.

Rosary gets up from the bed just as De Carlo knocks for a third time. She opens the door to a smiling Tony De Carlo. His smile lights up the room as it lights up her heart.

"Hold your horses," Rosary says, laughing.

"I don't have any horses," De Carlo says, laughing with her.

He steps into the room, slightly pushing her. "Sorry," he apologizes, "I didn't want caught. Too many people in the hotel this morning. Lots of reporters and police officers."

As he approaches her bed, he notices the rifles out in full display. But then he notices the cleaning supplies next to the duffel bag.

"Busy morning?"

"Clearly," Rosary answers as she sits onto the bed once again.

"Well, I have something else for you to take a look at whenever you're free," he says sarcastically.

She glares at him.

"Sorry," he says, chuckling. "Remember that woman you almost blew to pieces last night?"

Rosary chuckles as she continues to clean her rifle with precision.

*The slut in the alleyway?*

"Of course. That prostitute. I can smell one a mile away."

De Carlo laughs. She's full of jokes this morning. She must have gotten some sleep.

"Well," De Carlo answers, handing over a yellow envelope, "she was lucky enough to take some photos of the killer as he escaped from the alleyway."

Rosary looks at the envelope suspiciously, "Really? Give me a break. It was dark out."

De Carlo shrugs, agreeing with this statement. But he doesn't like her negativity either.

"Check them out, would you? Maybe you can see something that I haven't."

Rosary nods, taking the envelope.

"I don't have much time. I have a report from last night that I have to drop off to my pushy boss. He's already called me three times in the last hour. I have to go," he says, glancing at his gold watch. "I'll check on you later."

"Thanks father," Rosary says smugly.

De Carlo chuckles as he heads toward the door. He suddenly turns, "Oh, by the way, did you happen to get a good look at the killer yourself?"

Rosary feels as though she's sitting inside of an interrogation room.

"No," she snaps. *Those eyes...*

She didn't get a good look and that's the God's honest truth. BUT she seems to have some sort of recognition about the person's height and stamina as she thinks about it some more.

Once again, she thinks it could possibly be...Emilio Delgado.

Rosary keeps shooting down that angle, but something keeps pulling her back to it.

De Carlo looks at her suspiciously. Rosary knows that he doesn't believe her but at this particular moment, she doesn't think that it's anyone else.

Emilio Delgado is small for a man. He's short and full of curves himself. She saw that and felt it when the killer's hands were around her neck.

"Are you sure?" De Carlo asks again.

Rosary is angry now, "You calling me a liar, agent?"

De Carlo can see the fire in her eyes. Her brain must be boiling like a pot of water. It looks like it's about to spill over.

"Have you ever felt what it's like to be shot by a sniper rifle?" Rosary continues as De Carlo refuses to give her an answer.

"Not at all," he says, smiling. "See you later."

He leaves, calmly closing the door behind him.

Rosary skims through the blurry, printed pictures and tosses each one onto the bed. When she reaches the very last one, she suddenly leans in closer.

"Son of a bitch."

# ELEVEN

The rearview mirror can be an essential part of an investigation, if and when a driver looks through it. Understanding who is crossing the street at that exact time is certainly essential as well. This moment could have ended the investigation as De Carlo's exhausted eyes peek through this rearview mirror as he sits sulking in front of the police station.

The killer is also oblivious, crossing the street wearing blue jeans, a long black trench coat with a hood, black winter gloves and a black ski-mask covering his face.

The spring air has turned into winter once again. The beautiful weather has taken a turn for the worst, forming wet crystals and icicles on plants and trees.

The petals on De Carlo's roses in his backyard have fallen off like the rose in, "Beauty and the Beast." Each petal had delicately fallen to the ground and had frozen from the cold like a stray animal out in the streets.

As De Carlo thinks about his beautiful rose bush planted years ago by his precious wife, the killer crosses the street and can be seen by De Carlo's star-gazing eyes.

He's staring into the abyss as he dreams about Jada trotting toward the rose bush and placing a gentle hand onto a petal. She smiles, lighting up the dark and cloudy sky.

The killer nonchalantly walks past De Carlo's SUV as the wind blows the cold morning air.

De Carlo snaps out of his dream as he quickly glances at his gold watch.

"Shit," he whispers and opens the vehicle door.

As De Carlo steps out of the driver's side with a yellow envelope in his hand, he slams the door shut and quickly jogs toward the front door to the station.

The killer looks over his shoulder, his looming eyes shocked at this revelation. He picks up his pace as he turns the corner and enters a side street, disappearing with the chilly wind.

De Carlo's heart is racing as he steps in front of Curtis Garcia's office door. He can see his boss with his arms crossed and his head down as he glances at his watch.

Curtis seems irritated and angry. His eyebrows furrow and his lips twitch as he suddenly looks up, seeing De Carlo stand in front of his door with a sorrowful expression.

Curtis doesn't say a word. He waits a full minute before tapping his watch with his finger. The two men stare at each other through the glass door. De Carlo suddenly wants to give up. He knows that his boss is angry with him. Not only is he late for their meeting, but he continues to hide valuable information from his boss. That could get him into big trouble.

He's already in trouble and he knows this. He knows that his ass is grass.

"Get in here now," Curtis orders.

De Carlo takes a deep breath. He then suddenly envisions himself walking away. He throws the envelope to the floor and walks toward the receptionist desk, tossing his badge and gun onto the desk as if these years put into this department doesn't matter anymore.

*They don't.*

De Carlo is quite relieved to finally come to terms with this negative thought that has been haunting him for years. He was ready to retire years ago but he wanted to hang on in order to catch Rosary Chime. He wanted to stop her. He wanted to see her rot in jail.

And he did.

Curtis swings the office door open and glares at De Carlo as if he just called him a bad name. He wants to scold him like a child, but he doesn't. He is a grown ass man who needs to come to terms with facing the consequences for his recent actions.

"Are you just going to stand there all day and stare at me like a loony?"

De Carlo clears his throat.

His mouth is dry, and he suddenly becomes self-conscious about his coffee breath. He should've popped a mint into his mouth before he exited his vehicle.

He was completely focused on his dead wife; her beautiful hair blowing in the chilly wind. The rain pouring onto her sun dress decorated with yellow sunflowers. Her yellow hat falling to the ground as her head tilts backward, swallowing the raindrops like water from a bottle.

She was unique like that, very playful and energetic.

As De Carlo watches his wife pluck a rose from its stem, Curtis grabs De Carlo's arm and pulls him inside of the office. He slams the door, awakening the agent from his peaceful dream.

"What the hell has gotten into you De Carlo?" Curtis asks, frustrated as he glances at his watch for the second time. "You are late and quite frankly, I'm sick of your shit lately."

De Carlo nods in agreement. "So am I," he says, handing Curtis the envelope. "Here's the report from last night. I stayed up until four in the morning. Are you happy now?"

Curtis shakes his head in anger as he takes the envelope from De Carlo's shaking hands.

"Sit," Curtis orders.

Without objection, De Carlo sits into the plush chair facing his boss's desk. He feels like a five-year-old scolded by his mother.

At a time like this, De Carlo chuckles. He hasn't been scolded by his mother since he was sixteen years old. He remembers that day like it was yesterday.

He was caught sneaking out of the house to go to a party with his then girlfriend. He was grounded for getting an "E" on his math test and he wasn't allowed to go anywhere.

Of course, he liked to defy his mother at that time and do whatever he wanted at that age. Sixteen was when De Carlo began, "acting out," and misbehaving at school. His teachers were extremely concerned and wanted him to see the school counselor for a two-week session.

He was just tired of being the nice guy. He was tired of having good grades and nothing to show for it. He wanted to be a rebel. He wanted people to think that he had the balls to be bad. He wanted to impress his new girlfriend. She had no ambition and no plans for her future. She wanted to stay home and party every night.

She was a bad influence.

That influence didn't last long though. Three colleges that De Carlo applied to, had threatened to dismiss his application and they refused to acknowledge him if he didn't stop the nonsense. This lit a fire under his ass, and he finally realized that this girl was not worth it.

"You need to take a break," Curtis continues, opening the envelope as he stares at his agent with hurtful eyes. "You're not reaching for your full potential in this case."

De Carlo opens his mouth to disagree but then he stops, waiting for his boss to continue.

"You haven't reached your full potential in any case for the past year," Curtis accuses.

"That's bullshit," De Carlo says calmly.

His heart is beating a mile a minute. Anger rises through his neck and up into his face.

His cheeks flush with rage but he desperately tries to calm himself down by envisioning Jada running through the beach as the sand wraps around her pedicured toes.

He stares into space as Curtis continues his berating, "It's not bullshit. It's the truth. You know it. I know it. You haven't focused on the department's needs. You haven't focused on keeping yourself out of trouble."

De Carlo contemplates Curtis's accusations. *The department's needs? What in the hell is he talking about?*

"Do you mind explaining what the hell you're babbling about?"

Curtis laughs, "That's what I'm talking about right there, your rude and insensitive behavior. The department doesn't need nor want that any longer."

De Carlo nods with sarcasm. He smiles, laughing at Curtis as if he's telling a joke.

"I work my ass off," De Carlo says. "Day after day I put my life on the line for this ungrateful department. I've put my life on the line for thirty-seven years. And what do I get? An ungrateful boss who is deceptive himself... a boss who lies to protect his own ass! A boss who gave up years ago! A boss who doesn't give a shit about his agents!"

De Carlo stands up from his chair. It falls backward onto the floor with a loud thud.

"What happened last night De Carlo?" Curtis asks, ignoring De Carlo's outburst.

The agent smiles smugly, "The asshole attacked me inside of my own hotel room. I chased him out into the balcony and fired my gun at him in the alleyway as he ran from the scene."

Curtis tosses the envelope and the report onto his desk. He then smiles smugly as he sits onto the corner of his desk, loosening his tie.

"What were you doing at a hotel when you have your own place of residence?"

"I wanted to see if I could catch the killer in the act. He seems to be nesting at the same hotel over and over again. I wanted to try something new."

Curtis nods but continues to smile with a smug expression, "So, you didn't have Rosary Chime staying in your hotel room then?"

De Carlo's face flushes. He's not angry for lying to his boss, he's angry for getting caught.

"No sir. I was by myself," De Carlo continues to lie.

"We caught you two on surveillance... the hotel's cameras. Come on De Carlo, you work for the FBI. Do you really think that you wouldn't get caught? You know what we can find."

"Caught for what? Found what?" De Carlo asks, "I have nothing to do with Rosary Chime."

Curtis gets up from his desk and struts toward a file cabinet. As he opens it, he swiftly lifts a brown folder from the front of the cabinet. He then leisurely places his arm on the remaining files as he sifts through the paperwork inside of the folder.

Curtis laughs as he turns each page inside of the folder. He then glances at De Carlo's angry expression. He can't help but feel sorry for the man. He has been through a lot.

Curtis quietly closes the file cabinet and then slowly walks toward De Carlo. De Carlo picks up the fallen chair and then plops his butt back onto it, exhausted. He places his head into his hands as Curtis tosses the open folder onto his desk and in front of De Carlo's saddened eyes.

The top picture is of Rosary Chime and De Carlo entering the hotel room together. De Carlo gently picks up the stack of photos and looks through them. The second photo is of De Carlo exiting the hotel room on his cell phone.

The third photo is of Rosary knocking on the neighbor's hotel room. The fourth photo is of De Carlo returning to the room with a yellow envelope clutched in his hands.

"How did she escape detective?" Curtis asks, watching De Carlo's face fill with fear.

"I have no idea sir," De Carlo lies.

De Carlo now knows that he is in some serious trouble. This is worse than what he thought. He had no idea that they would look into the hotel's security cameras.

*Damn I should've thought of that. I should've let her stay at my house!*

He made a rookie mistake. After what seems like a lifetime as an FBI agent, he made the biggest mistake of his career.

He got caught.

"Do you want to answer that question again?" Curtis asks.

De Carlo is confused. He can't seem to concentrate on Curtis's question as he continues to look through the photos of him and Rosary Chime.

He knows that he's busted. He just doesn't want to admit it. His stubbornness is taking over his mind and he can't seem to escape it.

"I'm sorry sir. What was the question?"

De Carlo has honestly forgotten what his boss has asked of him. He doesn't have an answer.

Well, he has an answer. But consciously, it's not one that he wants to admit. He doesn't want to admit that he helped a serial killer escape prison. He doesn't want to admit that he hired this said serial killer to... KILL ANOTHER SERIAL KILLER.

Who in their right mind would do such a thing?

*I would,* De Carlo answers his own question. *I would do it again in a heartbeat.*

Curtis takes a deep breath. He's desperately trying to act calm, but his frustration might take over his whole entire body. He is completely done with trying to save De Carlo's ass. Curtis doesn't have any more say-so over De Carlo's future in the FBI. The department head, Shania Brown, just ended a morning phone call meeting with Curtis minutes before his agent stepped into his office.

Shania Brown is not happy with Detective Anthony De Carlo.

Curtis sighs. He must be blunt and say what the meeting with his boss was all about.

"How did Rosary Chime escape from prison?" Curtis asks one more time as he sits at the corner of his desk once again, watching De Carlo skim through each photo.

"I have no idea sir," De Carlo answers as he comes across the next photo.

It's at the prison. It's a photo of De Carlo entering the prison on his first visit. The next photo is of De Carlo sitting across the table from Rosary. The third photo is of De

Carlo squeezing Rosary's neck. The fourth photo is of De Carlo returning the second time as he holds Rosary's hand.

*That conniving bitch, Adeline Montana! The fucking warden did this!*

The last photo is of De Carlo and Rosary on the steps of the prison, leaving.

"That's not me," De Carlo denies.

Curtis is dumbfounded. His shocked expression doesn't even faze De Carlo as he tosses the photos to the floor like a child with a temper-tantrum.

"This isn't proof of anything! That could be any Black man!"

"Give me a break De Carlo!" Curtis yells.

"Is that what this is? Attacking a Black FBI agent for doing his job?!"

"What the hell?!" Curtis screams at the top of his lungs. The remaining officers inside of the building stop what they are doing and stare into the office with fear in their eyes.

"How dare you!" Curtis continues to scream. "It has nothing to do with your race! Don't play that bullshit with me! I'm a Latino FBI superior! You don't think that I deal with racist bullshit?" Curtis catches his breath. His breathing is rapid as he continues, "You helped a felon escape from prison for your own benefit! We haven't figured out yet why in the world you would do something like this, but we know damn well that that man is YOU!"

Curtis quickly pulls a cigarette out of a pack from inside of his jacket pocket. He lights it inside of the office, watching the shocked expressions of his fellow officers through the glass.

"There's no smoking in here," De Carlo says as he stares at a photo lying on the floor.

Curtis exhales the smoke up into the ceiling.

He then laughs, "And there's to be no helping of a convicted murderer of escape!"

De Carlo falls silent. He doesn't have anything left to say on the matter.

Curtis takes a deep breath and sighs. He then calmly continues after two minutes of smoking his cigarette, "I'm putting you on a two-month paid leave. Go relax. Enjoy yourself."

De Carlo continues to wallow in sadness.

*I seriously need to get my shit together.*

"And" Curtis says, smashing the embers into the ashtray, "You are permanently off this case. Tiara will continue without you. Someone else will be reassigned with her."

De Carlo feels as if Curtis just punched him in the face. He can't breathe and feels as if he's suffocating. He suddenly envisions Curtis stuffing a plastic bag over his mouth and nose. He struggles to breathe as Curtis pushes the bag down his throat. He's choking, dying.

"You can't do this to me. This case is all I have," De Carlo begs.

"You did this to yourself agent. Besides, it wasn't my call. I begged for this not to happen as well. I'm sorry De Carlo. This case is no longer yours."

"You didn't try hard enough," De Carlo accuses. "You don't give a shit about me."

Curtis shakes his head in shame, "You're lucky that's all you got. Shania wanted you fired and your ass sitting in a jail cell."

Since the death of his wife, De Carlo refuses to shed another tear in front of others. At this very moment, he can no longer hold them back in front of his boss.

"You leave me with no choice," Curtis whispers. "Detective Anthony De Carlo, I need your badge and your weapon that is clipped to the front of your belt."

After thirty seconds, De Carlo finally stands up. He slowly unclips his gun from his belt and calmly lays it onto the desk. He then reaches into his jacket pocket and pulls out his badge.

After a moment of staring at it like a prized possession, he tosses it next to his gun.

"You will get them back in two months. Take a trip. See the stars and the moon if you must. You need rest and you need time away from all of this."

De Carlo doesn't know what to say. He feels like bawling into his boss's chest. He wants to hug him and thank him for everything that he has done for him.

He wants to apologize for the things that he has said lately. He wants to shake his hand.

But he does none of that.

He turns toward the door and solemnly opens it like it's the last time that he will step foot inside of this office.

De Carlo suddenly thinks to himself, *I can't be taken off this case! I have other people to interrogate! I have a meeting with Emilio Delgado!*

He almost forgot about that. He spoke to the man this morning. Emilio was more than willing to give a statement. *To be honest, he sounded quite relieved to tell his story.*

"I'll see you in two months brother," Curtis says as De Carlo takes a step out into the hallway. "You are the best agent that I've ever had the pleasure of overseeing. I love you man, and I hope you get some much-needed relaxation."

De Carlo nods, quite shocked at Curtis's admittance of love.

"See you," is all that De Carlo manages to say.

The hotel room is becoming stuffy and uncomfortable. It's also become a nuisance in her life and right now, she is done with the feelings of boredom, tiredness and weakness. She needs to get some fresh air and stretch her legs. Being cooped up in this room has made her bones brittle and her mind crazy. She needs new scenery.

She needs to get into trouble if that's what it takes.

Rosary laughs as she quietly steps into the empty hallway. As she closes the door, she feels like she's being watched so she looks up and down the hallway as if someone is taking pictures of her. She then looks around, noticing a camera in the top corner as its red-light blinks.

"Shit," she whispers. She knew she was being watched. She had a weird feeling about this hotel along with the strange and unusual employees who are never around to help.

She readjusts the duffel bag over her right shoulder and then quickly makes her way toward the elevator doors.

She is wide awake and finally feels refreshed from a depressing couple of days. She has gotten enough sleep to last a week. She ate so much food this morning that her belly feels as though it's about to burst like a volcano. She imagines eggs and bacon spewing out of her intestines.

She laughs it off as she enters the elevator, pressing the button for the main lobby.

She has no idea how to manage this situation anymore. She doesn't know where to go from here. One thing is for sure, she must find out if there are other witnesses to the killer's escape.

She blames it on De Carlo. If he wasn't there to distract her, she would have been able to put a bullet in the killer's head. He would've been taken down and she would've been one hundred thousand dollars richer.

As the elevator climbs down to floor three, Rosary pauses, thinking of De Carlo once again. Speaking of her money, she should demand half of it right now. She has done everything that he has told her to do. She has risked her life with this mission. She deserves some kind of compensation right at this moment. She needs stability. She needs to know that he is serious about his offer.

She decides to bring this up to him the next time she sees him.

The elevator dings and the doors open to floor two. A gentleman built like a football player, steps into the elevator. As he stands beside Rosary, she takes in his scent of cologne.

*He smells good.*

As the elevator creeps to the main lobby, Rosary chuckles aloud. The man turns and looks at her like she's a crazy loon.

*Maybe I am.*

As she steps off the elevator with good-smelling-man, she looks toward the receptionist.

*She's finally at that damn desk.*

It's the same receptionist that De Carlo had a hard-on for. Her beautiful smile lights up the lobby as Rosary approaches her with a wide grin on her face.

She can see why De Carlo is infatuated with her. Her beauty is like none other. Her blonde hair tied back into a long ponytail with a pink hair tie. Her cheek bones are rosy from make-up and her bright green eyes stick out like a sore thumb.

Good-smelling-man is actually one of Shania Brown's FBI agents. He was supposed to be arresting Rosary inside

158 – ANGELA SANNER

of that elevator, but he decided against it. He wants to know what she has up her sleeve and he plans to follow her.

He'll arrest her when the time is right.

He sits on a plush chair and pulls out the latest newspaper. He watches Rosary as she approaches the receptionist. They giggle like schoolgirls as Rosary admits to the receptionist's beauty and charm.

"Are you flirting with me?" she asks Rosary.

"Maybe," Rosary answers as she glances at the receptionist's name tag. "Phoenix, is it? Beautiful name for a beautiful woman."

Rosary isn't lying. She would jump into bed with this woman if she had the chance.

Phoenix blushes as she clears her throat, "Can I help you with anything? New towels? New bed sheets? More soap or shampoo?"

Rosary chuckles, "Actually, I do want to ask you a question."

"I'm all ears sugar," Phoenix says, smiling.

It's Rosary's turn to blush.

She clears her throat, "Did you happen to witness anything last night?"

Phoenix's eyes quickly dart around the lobby. She looks frightened but she continues to smile as the corner of her eye crinkles.

Her eyeballs stop at the FBI agent with the newspaper. He's pretending to read the words to the comic page as he quietly laughs as if he's actually reading the words.

"Cop, isn't it?" Rosary whispers without turning to look.

"Why yes ma'am! I can help you with that!" Phoenix exclaims as she writes a message on her notepad for Rosary to meet her in the back alleyway.

After waiting thirty seconds, Rosary smiles and nods. She then leaves the hotel.

Once outside, she hurriedly picks up her pace down the sidewalk. She turns the corner into the alleyway and hides behind a dumpster.

Back inside, Phoenix blows her bubblegum into a huge bubble and then pops it on purpose. The gum stretches to her chin and saliva drips onto the front of her uniform.

The FBI agent watches her in silence.

Phoenix giggles, saying, "Excuse me, I must clean up. I'll be right back."

The agent watches her enter a side door that leads into the office portion of the hotel. Phoenix passes two maintenance workers who are sitting at a table drinking coffee. She waves at them as she laughs, spitting the gum into the trash can.

As Phoenix exits the hotel through another door that leads into the alleyway, she pulls out a pack of cigarettes and lights one up as she approaches Rosary behind the dumpster.

"Smoke break," Phoenix says, inhaling a long puff of the cigarette.

"Those will kill you," Rosary says.

"Same with being shot at by a convicted murderer," Phoenix answers, smiling.

Rosary's grin is wide and sly, "I knew it. You know who I am."

"Of course I do. I'm a huge fan of yours."

Rosary quietly laughs, "I didn't do much to have sacred fans. I am a killer."

Phoenix shrugs her shoulders, "Ahhh...so is everyone else. Anyone can have the ability to kill another human being."

The girl does have a point. But they need to move on with this conversation. Rosary needs answers and she's suddenly becoming impatient.

"I know, move on, right?" Phoenix asks as she exhales a puff of smoke.

*Damn does she read minds too?*

"Last night," Phoenix continues, "I was on my smoke break when I heard gunshots. That heffer prostitute was talking to me like we were best friends," Phoenix rolls her eyes.

Rosary watches her lips, painted in red lipstick, as they form an "O" ring around the butt of the cigarette. *This woman would blow my mind,* Rosary thinks, giggling.

She takes another hit of her cigarette, "I then saw someone climbing down the emergency ladder. The person had on green gloves, a black coat, and a ski-mask. I immediately hid behind my car that I parked in the alleyway. You were shooting like crazy. I didn't want to get hit."

Phoenix blows the smoke up into the air, "I saw you though. Plain as day...like an angel from up above. I couldn't believe it was you. I was kind of awestruck before I realized I had to look back at who was running from you."

Rosary contemplates this explanation as she nonchalantly looks up and down the alleyway. She doesn't want newspaper-good-smelling-cop to find them hiding behind the dumpster.

"So then what?" Rosary asks, impatiently.

Phoenix ignores her bluntness, "I felt like I was in a dream. I have been one of your biggest fans from the beginning. I truly admire your fierceness. You're beautiful and one of a kind," Phoenix dotes on her new best friend as she inhales another puff of smoke.

Rosary can just imagine the girl's lungs, black and destroyed.

Rosary snatches the cigarette from Phoenix's lips and tosses it to the ground, stomping on it with her combat boot.

"Feisty too," Phoenix says, grinning. "Any who, the person ran east," Phoenix continues while pointing her finger to the right of the building, "and then climbed into a red Saturn. Two doors, I think. It was a fartin' little thing."

Rosary chuckles as she looks around the alleyway once again. It will only be a matter of time before that agent finds out that they are in cahoots together.

That's the last thing that Rosary needs. She doesn't want Phoenix to get into any trouble.

"As a matter of fact, I took a picture of the license plate. Not sure if you can see it all but you can zoom in," Phoenix offers as she slips her cell phone out of her bra.

Rosary laughs, "Boob sweat. Thanks," she says as she scrolls through the pictures of the license plate of the red Saturn.

Phoenix then pulls out a pen from inside of her bra as well.

"You got anything else in there? Candy? Alcoholic drinks?" Rosary asks as Phoenix bursts into laughter. She then hands Rosary the pen.

"Not at the moment," Phoenix answers, "but I'm sure I could." She laughs.

Rosary writes the license plate number onto the front of her arm.

"Thank you," Rosary says as she hands the pen back to Phoenix. "You've been a big help."

"Do you have a phone?" Phoenix asks, seeing that Rosary is only carrying a duffel bag.

"No, I do not, and it's become a problem," Rosary says as Phoenix takes her cell phone out of Rosary's hand.

"I have a friend who can help with that problem. He owns a phone shop downtown. I can give you the address. I'll text him and tell him to hook you up."

Rosary looks awkward for a minute as Phoenix sends a text message to her friend. "Don't worry girl, I won't tell him who you are. I'll just say you're my new girlfriend."

Phoenix winks.

Rosary laughs, "Thank you for your time and help. I genuinely appreciate it."

"Not a problem. We should probably hurry up before agent man finds us," Phoenix says as she starts to put the pen back inside of her bra.

She stops for a moment, thinking.

"One more thing love," Phoenix says as Rosary checks the alleyway one last time. "Can I have your autograph?"

Rosary smiles a devilish grin. Phoenix hands her back the pen.

"Right here," Phoenix says, pointing to her boob.

Rosary shakes her head with laughter, signing her name on Phoenix's left breast.

# TWELVE

Rosary heads for downtown, but for some reason, she's feeling nervous and suspicious. Her investigation has become a little too easy. Phoenix was a little too helpful.

She wants to shrug off these thoughts, but she can't seem to get them off her mind. Phoenix was extremely helpful and gave her a lot of information that might actually crack this case.

Rosary thinks she knows who the killer is.

She realized it while looking at the blurry photos. They were tremendously blurry and that is why she must find out for the last time, if this killer is who she thinks it is.

*It can't be. I hope and pray that it isn't. I might be wrong.*

For the first time in her life, she WANTS to be wrong. Her suspicions have taken a nosedive and her body shakes with fear.

She's not normally scared out of her mind. She's strong and determined. Nothing scares her easily. But lately, she has become a soft marshmallow. She needs to get back into her "macho" persona so she can feel alive once again.

She misses being a hard ass so to speak. She misses being intimidating. She misses scaring people in general. It makes her feel like she's standing on top of the world, and no one can stop her. She's hungry for power. She's hungry to be the boss.

*Maybe I should start my own company in another country.*

*That's perfect. That's exactly what I'm going to do!*

But she needs her money first. Tony De Carlo must not back out on their deal.

*If he does, I know where to find him.*

But would he really stiff her like that? Would he have the balls to run and hide like Rosary did for several years? Would he take her money and run for his life?

That's what he would be doing. Rosary Chime is no fool. She would catch him. It might take months or even years, but she would find him, and she would kill him.

She WILL get her money somehow.

De Carlo doesn't quite understand that Rosary has put her life on the line. She is sacrificing her career and her escape from finishing out the prison sentence. She would've been released on good behavior. She spent most of her time alone. She didn't like to interact with anyone inside of those walls. She didn't want to. She refused to.

Most of those people in that prison are scum bags. Rosary Chime is not a scum bag. She's a beautiful woman with a strong head on her shoulders. She can take care of herself. She doesn't need nor want anyone to tell her what to do.

Not anymore.

She did that for many years. She hid behind strong-willed, corrupted, and egotistical men. She hid behind their ferociousness. They knew no fear and that's why she is the way she is.

They taught her to be strong. They taught her not to fail. Hell, they even taught her to not fear anyone on this Earth...including THEM.

She has refused time and time again to not fear anyone.

But right now, she fears this killer. For the first time, she is scared out of her mind. She's only scared because she wishes deep down in her heart that it's not that person.

She's begging to be wrong. She doesn't want this in her life.

She doesn't want to deal with what she might have to do.

This pains her to her core. She is becoming physically ill over this revelation, and she can't tell De Carlo quite yet. This information would mess up any chance of them catching the killer in the act. That's what De Carlo wants. He wants to be the hero.

Besides, he wouldn't believe her even if she told him right now. He would call her a liar.

Rosary chuckles as she struts down the sidewalk as if SHE is a model on the runway.

She knows that she's beautiful. It's no secret. She could've become a famous model and made lots of money that way. But no, she chose a life a crime.

And she wouldn't have it any other way.

Rosary smiles as she contemplates her life. Her strong-willed attitude and powerful abruptness are what she needs to bring back to the table. She needs people to fear HER. She needs to be that fierce woman again. She became her at sixteen-years-old.

She CAN become her again.

However, she knows that she's taking this daring chance by walking around downtown without covering her face. De Carlo told her not to, "Do anything stupid."

And this is stupid. She should cover herself from head to toe. She shouldn't be wearing her own clothes and boots. She should've worn Jada De Carlo's cashmere sweater.

But right now, she honestly doesn't care. She has enough faith in herself that she will get out of any mess that falls onto her lap.

Even if she has to look down or right in front of her eyes.

Rosary checks the address of the phone shop that's written on the inside of her hand.

She grips her mother's rosary in her other hand as she prays that this visit goes well. She just wants a phone, damn it. She needs one. She doesn't need any confrontations or any issues to arise. She wants to get in, get the phone and get out of dodge.

Phoenix promised her that she wouldn't tell her friend, Jake, who Rosary truly is. And for Rosary, promises are not just words coming out of a mouth. Promises flow deep into her heart. She doesn't trust easily so this girl had better be telling her the truth or she will be on her hit list as well.

That's right...Rosary has started making a mental hit list. She will fulfill the scratching off the names if those people betray her.

Rosary is very loyal and trustworthy to the people who are loyal and trustworthy to her. She doesn't like to portray herself as a hypocrite or a liar because she's none of those things.

And if Jake at the phone shop decides to betray her, well then, he will be on the top of the hit list and be dealt with, first and foremost.

Right inside his phone shop if she has to.

She isn't playing anymore games. Rosary Chime is back. No more feeling sorry for herself. No more moping around and making herself sick. No more destroying her body by not eating. No more sulking about every negative obstacle that has been thrown her way.

She can't do it anymore. She will not and that's a promise that she made to herself.

As Rosary crosses the street, she looks around for any sign of someone following her. She has gotten herself into a pickle and she doesn't like it. But she can't turn back now.

Not ever.

Besides, she doesn't want to turn back. This case has gotten more interesting, and she doesn't mind being involved. She likes dramatic scenes, twists and turns and raunchy vibes from unknown individuals. She kind of likes the fact that she escaped prison. It makes her feel like she can conquer the world. It makes her feel like she can take on anything, even sneaky FBI agents who think that they always have one point above her score.

She sees newspaper-good-smelling-cop perched inside of his black SUV that's parked across the street from the phone shop.

*Now, how the hell did that happen?*

*Oh... Phoenix from the hotel...you little devil you. You think you're so smart.*

*BUT I'm smarter bitch.*

Rosary is quite calm and relaxed as she enters the phone shop. Her heart pounds with excitement. People think that she's completely stupid and won't figure things out on her own.

She's far from stupid. She's generally smarter than the average population. She once took a genius test at the age of eight because her mother thought she was, "Too smart to be my child."

The doctor congratulated Sherry as if she gave birth to "Albert Einstein."

Sherry couldn't believe her ears. Her daughter has an I.Q. of 220. Sherry laughed in the doctor's face and asked, "Then why does Rosary act so stupid?"

The doctor couldn't believe HIS ears.

Rosary laughs at this memory as she approaches the counter. Jake, with long brown hair and a tattoo of a worm on the side of his temple, looks up from his cell phone that's gripped in his hand. He suddenly looks scared and awestruck at the same time.

Rosary gets that same look every time she meets someone for the first time in their life. It's quite precious actually. She watches their eyes light up like a cigarette. Then, the corners of their eyes twitch and their mouth curves into a sly grin. That's those nasty thoughts that they have in their mind. Their mind wonders to a place where they can make love to her.

She knows this and it makes her giggle inside.

Sometimes, she likes to pin-point in her own mind, the location of where she's making love to these people.

Rosary laughs as Jake freezes from her beauty. He's speechless. He's acting as if she's pointing one of her rifles at his head.

She just might if he tries to do anything slick.

*I'm sure he isn't very clean as his hair is oily and looks dirty. His blue jeans are dirty, and the front of his "Metallica" shirt is covered in some sort of stain. I'm sure he's making love to me on a crusty couch with dog piss smell that's wafting into our noses.*

*Or maybe...*

Rosary instantly snaps out of these images as Jake places his cell phone onto the counter. She was too involved with her nasty thoughts as well.

She cringes. This man is gross and clearly unstable.

He smiles with crooked and yellow teeth.

"Howdy! You must be Rosary," Jake says as he opens a glass container hidden inside of a secret compartment under the counter.

He takes a cell phone out of the glass container and then places it in front of Rosary.

She stares at it for a moment. *That was quick. No flirting. No questions. No small talk.*

Jake reaches for her hand to shake it, but she politely declines. She has no idea what that brown stuff is on the inside of his fingers.

*Probably wipes his ass with his fingers too.*

"Go ahead and check it out!" Jake urges.

Rosary is incredibly suspicious. She isn't sure if this man is a secret detective. He could've placed a tracking device inside of this phone. He could be playing her like an actor in a school play. He could be lying through those crusty, black teeth. She finally got a good look at them.

*Disgusting...*

*Well, the joke's on you, asshole.*

Rosary slowly picks up the cell phone as if it's about to explode like a firecracker. She doesn't even want to touch it. This guy is so incredibly disgusting. She isn't sure if ANY detective would stoop this low to look like such a douchebag.

"Can you tell me anything about it?" Rosary asks.

"It's a phone," Jake quickly replies.

*What a moron.*

"I know dip shit. What kind? What service? Do you have a tracking device on it?"

Jake's face flushes.

*Gotcha...*

"Ma'am, I didn't expect you to come here with a bad attitude. Phoenix said that you are amazing. I don't think you are. I think you're a miserable chump."

Rosary giggles, "Is that so Jakey?"

"It's Jake. And yes. You can shove that phone up your ass for all I care."

Rosary nods with laughter, "Wouldn't you like to see that huh?"

Jake picks up his cell phone and types a message to Phoenix.

"Oh no, are you tattling on me?" Rosary taunts.

Jake looks up from his phone, angry and annoyed. "It's a minute phone bitch. You don't have much time. Get the hell out of my store."

Well, that didn't go as planned. She didn't expect this, "monster of dirt," to kick her out. She didn't expect this whole conversation to go downhill so quickly.

*I was rude. BUT he basically just warned me. Phoenix knows that I'm here and that I crawled into her web of lies. I'm like a helpless bug inside of a spider web.*

*I have to get the hell out of here before newspaper-good-smelling-cop catches me.*

Rosary snatches the phone off the counter, shoving it inside of her back pocket of her tight jeans. She suddenly curses to herself. She should've worn more comfortable clothing for running. She should always be prepared for "fight or flight."

As she leaves the counter, Jake shouts back, "See you soon!"

As she opens the door to the shop, Rosary turns to smile at Jake. "No, you won't," she says, making Jake scowl in anger. "Thank you for the phone. I'll be sure to mention you to my FBI agent boyfriend."

Jake's eyes light up with a fiery glare.

*He's definitely not a cop but does he know that Phoenix is involved with one?*

Rosary nonchalantly glances across the street as she crosses it. The cop's SUV is gone.

Rosary feels perplexed. *What kind of game is this?*

She was preparing herself to run from newspaper-good-smelling-cop.

*I really have to find out his name.*

She feels confused and lost at the same time. They must be playing games with her. Why are they letting her go? Why didn't he arrest her while she was inside the store?

*Is Phoenix a police officer too?*

Rosary sure hopes not. If she finds out that she is, then, she will shoot Phoenix directly into the left breast where she signed her autograph.

*How is THAT for an autograph, bitch!*

Rosary picks up her pace as she suddenly feels as if someone is about to jump her from behind. She's feeling anxious and nervous about these new people that she's suddenly meeting.

She didn't expect this. She expected to be hidden the whole entire time at De Carlo's house. He promised to protect her. He promised that she wouldn't be seen.

She quickly realizes that this is her fault. He left her in the hotel room to lie low for a while. He told her not to do anything stupid.

And she did because she's stubborn and doesn't like to follow the rules.

Rosary reaches an alleyway and stops to catch her breath as she leans on a dingy wall of an apartment building. She feels like she's having an anxiety attack.

*Get your shit together Rosary Chime!*

As she takes a deep breath, she pulls out the cell phone from her back pocket.

She stares at it for a moment. She doesn't trust this whole situation and she sure as hell doesn't trust Jakey poo. This cell phone could be the devil in disguise.

She clenches her mother's rosary in between her fingers.

"Please forgive me Lord for I have sinned," she whispers, slamming the phone to the ground. Angrily, she stomps on it with both combat boots. The phone shatters into pieces, breaking the screen in half.

She stares at the phone as if she instantly regrets her decision. She desperately needs a phone. She might be able to persuade De Carlo into buying her one. He needs to have that communication with her. Besides, he should've had one for her before helping her escape.

Rosary leans forward as she spots a red chip inside of the back of the phone. Bending on her knees, she slowly picks up the phone and examines it as if it's poisoned. She then immediately slides the tracking chip out of its slot.

*Gotcha...*

De Carlo knows that he shouldn't be doing this behind Rosary's back. He knows damn well how upset she would be if she ever found out.

*Well...she will not. He promised to keep his mouth shut.*

This meeting is essential to this investigation. He doesn't care that he was just kicked off of it. This is HIS case. No one can solve it like he can. He's almost at the finish line, he can see it. He's reaching his arm outward as his fingers are gripping the award for best FBI agent.

He deserves that title. The FBI is going to miss him while he's gone.

De Carlo grunts. His cockiness is what got him into trouble. But he can't help it. He can't help having the confidence needed for this particular career move. He's the best of the best and Curtis is too stubborn to have that talk with Shania Brown. She doesn't know him like Curtis does. Curtis knows that De Carlo is an excellent agent, but he unfortunately couldn't beat that into Shania's head.

This is all HER fault.

But he isn't giving up and he sure as hell isn't allowing Tiara Mills to take over everything that he's accomplished with this case.

She isn't as good as he is.

De Carlo suddenly feels guilty for thinking this way about his partner. He stops his SUV at a red light as he contemplates on calling Tiara and apologizing to her for his rude thoughts.

He watches pedestrians cross the street as he laughs to himself. *On second thought, I'm not calling her. All she will do is gloat about having to take over my pride and joy.*

The light turns green, and De Carlo makes a left-hand turn onto a curved road.

He's been to this part of town plenty of times before...as a detective. This is out of the city's jurisdiction, but he does know this area quite well.

He grew up in it.

This is where the Mafia lives, crime bosses and young Italian punks who run to their Mafia daddies and cry into their mommy's titties.

And he will never tell Rosary Chime that he knows Emilio Delgado quite well.

In fact, he is family.

As De Carlo drives through a cul-de-sac, he waves at a group of small children as they jump rope and sing to the music blaring from someone's cell phone.

De Carlo suddenly misses normal things like listening to music from a radio. He remembers walking these streets with a boom box placed over his shoulder. His friends would make up lyrics to different songs and they would sing them for days on end.

*The good ole days.*

De Carlo pulls into the driveway to Emilio Delgado's house. As he places his SUV into park, he immediately notices that one of the front windows boarded up with lumber.

Emilio steps out of the doorway with his ten-year-old grandson looking up at him with fear in his eyes. The child looks shaken up and terrified to be outside of the house.

Emilio nods his head as De Carlo approaches them, reaching his hand out to shake the boy's hand. De Carlo has never seen him so frightened.

"Enzo...keep your head up kid. You always have to watch the person approaching you," De Carlo says as he places soft fingers underneath Enzo's chin, "Toughen up."

Emilio grunts, "That's easy for you to say."

De Carlo is puzzled as he steps into the house. They've been acting strange lately and De Carlo doesn't know how to react to their frightful behavior.

This isn't them.

The house smells of eggs and fried chicken, and it makes De Carlo's stomach growl. Emilio laughs, gesturing toward his cook in the kitchen to fix De Carlo a plate. The cook nods and then smiles at De Carlo. Her smile is warm and inviting.

"Let's go to my office," Emilio says to De Carlo. He then slowly bends down toward Enzo. He continues, "Go play with the kids outside. You will be fine. Robinson is out there and will keep you protected. There's nothing to worry about. No one will be stupid enough to do anything with an FBI agent present."

De Carlo peeks out of a window and spots one of Emilio's bodyguards, Robinson, jump roping with the kids.

Enzo nods, hurriedly putting on his shoes. He then runs outside to Robinson.

"Am I missing something?" De Carlo asks.

Emilio gestures for them to continue to his office. The cook hands him a plate of eggs, toast and two huge pieces of fried chicken. De Carlo's mouth waters as they make their way inside Emilio's office, quietly closing the door.

"Have a seat. I'll talk. You listen," Emilio orders as he sits into his plush office chair.

De Carlo crunches into a piece of chicken as he looks around the office. Framed picture of the smiling faces of the Delgado's puts a smile on De Carlo's face.

"I'm going to cut to the chase. I didn't ask you to come for peasantries," Emilio continues as he opens the top drawer to his cherry-wood desk. He pulls out a Cuban cigar and his father's ancient lighter.

As De Carlo continues to eat, Emilio lights the cigar and then takes a long puff. He blows the smoke up into the ceiling and then coughs as it sticks to his lungs.

"Sorry," he apologizes as De Carlo takes a bite of toast, "I think I'm getting too old for these," Emilio laughs.

De Carlo laughs with him, "You're never too old to have that wonderful taste in your mouth." He shoves a piece of egg down his throat.

"Damn boy," Emilio says, "You hungry?"

De Carlo bursts into laughter, "Starving."

Emilio inhales another hit of his cigar. He then clears his throat, "She was here."

De Carlo frowns, wiping his mouth with a napkin. His eyes dart from the stack of paperwork on Emilio's desk, to the framed pictures on the walls, to the bay window behind Emilio's head, and then back to Emilio's angry expression.

"When?" De Carlo asks.

"Last night. Had her little red dot pointed right at my forehead."

"I've tried to convince her that you're not the killer. She's still fixated on you."

"Well," Emilio says as he blows smoke up into the ceiling once again, "try harder next time. If not, she'll have a bullet slice through that pretty little brain of hers."

Emilio stares at the agent as he waits for a response. He's known Tony De Carlo since he was in diapers. If only Rosary Chime knew how close these men have truly been for fifty-five years. She would kill them all in a heartbeat. She always wondered why or how De Carlo knew where she was and what she was doing.

The only thing that Emilio didn't tell De Carlo was the fact that he hid Rosary inside of his basement, right under De Carlo's nose. Emilio has never fully trusted his adopted nephew. He is an FBI agent after all. Emilio enjoyed watching him play a cat and mouse game with Rosary.

And the family wasn't too happy about De Carlo's career decision.

He's surrounded by Mafia men and killers. He grew up shooting at targets with faces of police officers pinned to the bullseye.

Needless to say, Emilio's half-brother, also known as De Carlo's adoptive father, wasn't pleased to hear that his son moved over to the "dark side," as they called it.

Cops were their enemies; therefore, Tony De Carlo became their enemy.

De Carlo pushes his plate to the side as he runs his fingers through his hair, "I'll talk to her again and clear our family name."

"Good boy. Your father would be proud."

De Carlo nods as he suddenly becomes angry. Rosary failed to mention this little rendezvous that she had planned for his family.

He still can't hate her though. He's torn between protecting Rosary Chime and protecting his own family. He hired her into this mess and now he must take her out of it as he makes sure that she finds the asshole who murdered his wife. And she needs to do it now.

For some God-awful reason, Rosary feels extremely exhausted. She isn't sure why her mind feels like a water-filled balloon that could pop at any minute.

A migraine is forming at the base of her skull. She needs medication but she's too scared to go to the grocery store. Hell, she's too scared to go back to the hotel.

She imagines stepping into a store and walking up to the cashier, "Hello sir, I'm a convicted murderer who recently escaped prison with the help of an FBI agent. Could you help me locate the headache medicine? My head feels like it might explode."

Rosary laughs as she crosses the street. She looks up at the fancy hotel that she's been staying at for what feels like months.

178 – ANGELA SANNER

It hasn't been months, and she feels silly for this exaggeration.

She suddenly hears the screeching brakes of a vehicle behind her. She quickly turns her head, seeing Tony De Carlo's angry expression as he beeps the horn at her, drawing attention from pedestrians. Rosary looks around calmly and smiles at a couple walking their dog.

She immediately frowns at De Carlo as she then watches him park his vehicle across the street and inside of a parking lot.

Rosary quickly enters the hotel. She isn't in the mood for one of his lectures. She isn't ready for his berating in front of strangers either.

Her heart races as she jogs past the reception desk. A male receptionist stands behind the desk, smiling bright white teeth. Rosary smiles back as the worker immediately looks back down at his comic book that she rudely interrupted him from reading.

*Thank GOD! No Phoenix...*

She is not in the mood to deal with that woman. Rosary feels betrayed and quite honestly, stupid for putting forth an effort into finally making a loyal friend.

She knows that people can be deceiving, and she shouldn't let it bother her. She won't let it happen any longer though. People lie. They are manipulative and they are dirty scoundrels.

*And that's the way it is.*

Rosary enters the elevator just as De Carlo enters the hotel. She presses the number five button as she shouts, "Come on come on!"

She has no idea why she's running from De Carlo. He has nothing to do with what she didn't accomplish this morning. He has nothing to do with her ALMOST caught and arrested. She has no idea where that sneaky cop is or where Phoenix is hiding.

The elevator creeps to floor five with ease.

*Good, I don't want to be stopped by any asshole at the moment.*

She exits the elevator and hurriedly jogs toward her room. She spots a, "Sorry we missed you," tag from the housekeeper that's wrapped around the handle of the door.

"Miss this bitch," Rosary mumbles as she slips the key card inside of the slot, hurriedly opening the door and slamming it shut.

She knows that the cameras just caught her whereabouts. It's also going to catch De Carlo running through the hallway and pounding on her door.

She tosses the tag onto the floor and then drops her duffel bag next to it. She's trying to catch her breath as she listens to heavy footsteps running through the hallway.

De Carlo pounds on the door. He shouts, "Open it, Rosary!"

Rosary takes a deep breath and then exhales, gripping her mother's rosary in between her fingers. She doesn't know how she's managed to not lose it during all of this madness.

For some reason, her mother will always stay close to her heart.

To not draw any more attention, Rosary opens the door and grabs De Carlo's arm, pulling him inside of the room as if she suddenly gained a burst of energy.

She slams the door, glaring at De Carlo as if he had just shot at her.

Speaking of guns, Rosary looks him up and down, noticing that his gun is missing.

The man ALWAYS clips his gun to the front of his belt. There were plenty of times when she thought about gripping it into her fist and shooting him square in the eyes.

"Where the hell were you?!" De Carlo shouts, trying to catch his breath.

This is too much. He needs to retire. He needs to move on with his life and finally enjoy it.

"Will you keep your voice down?" Rosary whispers, "You're acting crazy!"

"Me?!!!" De Carlo shouts once again. "You're the one running from me, you psycho!"

Rosary has this sudden urge to laugh.

And she does. This is something she can't escape.

De Carlo unexpectedly laughs along with her. They howl with laughter for two minutes straight. Rosary's happy tears flow down her cheeks as if that water-filled balloon inside of her mind has popped.

"We are so crazy together," Rosary says. She smiles as she takes off her jacket.

De Carlo glances at her thin arms and pale skin. She needs a vacation at the beach. She is in desperate need of a tan. She looks like a ghost.

"You are one hundred percent correct," De Carlo replies as he watches her untie her combat boots. She slips them off and then lies down on the bed.

De Carlo watches the clock on the wall as it ticks each second. The sound vibrates through his brain like the beat of a drum.

He wants to scream and shout at her for leaving the hotel. He wants to choke her with his big hands for showing up at Emilio's house.

Only this time, he won't stop. Nothing will stop him now.

"So," he says, waiting a full minute for her reaction.

"I went for a walk," Rosary answers, interrupting his thoughts. "It is a beautiful morning."

"I can agree with that," De Carlo says. His mind is fuming right now. Smoke is pouring out from the inside of his ears. He's trying to stay calm. He doesn't want to fight or argue.

"Good," Rosary replies, smugly. She places her arms behind her head and then closes her eyes. She feels tired and achy.

"Well," De Carlo continues, "I'm here to take you to my house. This hotel exposes us too much. You can't stay here any longer."

Rosary nods, agreeing. "I could've told you that. Besides, I thought I was going to stay at your house the day I escaped."

De Carlo nods, "Yes, well, I thought we would be able to catch the killer red-handed so to speak. It didn't work out that way. He won't come back if you stay here."

Rosary sighs. She will miss her room here at this hotel. She seems attached to it, and she doesn't want to leave. She has freedom here. He will keep tabs on her at all times.

But she knows that she must leave. He is right. The killer will not return knowing that she's locked and loaded and ready to shoot fire from the balcony.

"Can I just rest my eyes for a minute?" Rosary asks as she begins to drift to sleep.

De Carlo doesn't answer as he sits in the plush chair. He watches her chest as it rises and falls with each quiet snore.

"Sounds like a good plan," De Carlo says, closing his eyes in relaxation.

# THIRTEEN

During the drive toward De Carlo's house, no one talked. The quiet atmosphere was incredibly peaceful, and Rosary felt relieved that she didn't have to strike up a conversation.

She played with her mother's jeweled necklace between her fingertips as she stared out of the rainy window. A cold chill made her shiver. De Carlo turned up the heat, not saying a word. He felt awkward. She seemed intimidating.

As they sit in his driveway, neither one of them acknowledges the fact that they can finally get out of the vehicle. They both stare into space as if they're placed into a trance by a magician.

De Carlo thinks about the past year and how his wife's case has affected his whole life. He hasn't been able to move on. He hasn't been able to get back to the way he used to be.

He misses his own personality. He doesn't like feeling sad and depressed every single day. He doesn't like missing out on dates with beautiful women. He misses hanging out with his fellow detective friends. They used to go bowling every Friday night and order pizza.

Those days seem so long ago.

He can no longer reach out to his friends. They ignore his calls. They ignore him at the station. They no longer invite him to their cookouts.

He feels isolated and alone. He has never felt like this before in his life.

He even feels abandoned by Rosary Chime.

He thought that they would become best friends, even lovers at some point. But she has done nothing but give him the cold shoulder lately.

She's mysterious and odd. Quite frankly, she terrifies De Carlo to his core. One minute she's a social butterfly and then the next minute she wants to put a bullet into his brain.

Sometimes, he wishes that she would. He misses his wife so much that he can't stop mourning the loss of her. He can't seem to move on.

He visits her grave every day. People do not know this information. They would probably think that he was crazy.

Maybe he is.

He's still trying to get over the fact that his wife cheated on him. After a year of pain and sorrow, he still can't wrap his brain around what he did wrong in their relationship. She ran to another man. She made love to another man. She fell in love with someone else.

His heart hurts when he thinks about this. He thinks about it every day of his life. It's a constant nag in the back of his mind. Her death is a reminder that she was the one who left the relationship. She was the one unfaithful.

And look where it got her...

*Six feet under.*

With a sideways glance, De Carlo tilts his head, glaring at Rosary. He waits for her to say something, ANYTHING. Her attitude just doesn't make any sense. He doesn't understand why she is being so nasty to him. He's done nothing but help her out.

Rosary can see in her peripherals, the look of anger in De Carlo's expression. She suddenly feels bad for treating him like a shark in the water. She doesn't even understand it herself.

Her passive-aggressive behavior has gotten the best of her, and she wants to apologize.

She's normally fun and happy. This case has put a damper on her life. Five minutes into sitting inside De Carlo's driveway, made her wish that she was still lying in her jail cell.

*That's a lie,* she says to herself. *You know damn well that you would rather be lying in Tony De Carlo's bed instead of lying on a dingy cot.*

Her heart suddenly skips a beat.

Lie down in De Carlo's bed? No such luck. *He probably hates me now...*

Rosary tilts her head and suspiciously looks at De Carlo as if he's hiding a secret. De Carlo cracks a smile, breaking the tension that has chiseled through their veins.

"Contemplating on sitting in here for the rest of the day?" he asks with a smirk.

Rosary chuckles as she loosens the necklace wrapped around her hand.

"Just watching the rain. Wondering why my life is so screwed up," Rosary answers, grinning. She looks at De Carlo's Easter decorations once again and giggles.

"Have you picked up Easter dinner yet?" she asks, making De Carlo laugh.

"I can later if you'd like. What would you like to eat for Easter?"

Rosary shrugs her shoulders, "Whatever you prefer."

This conversation is going nowhere. Rosary doesn't like to feel bossy. Whatever he wants to eat is fine with her. She's not picky.

"I want half of the money today," Rosary blurts out of her mouth.

De Carlo turns his body, glaring at her with darts shooting from his eyelids. Rosary is quite surprised by her own bluntness as well. She feels frozen in her seat. She's scared to look at his scowling face. She feels a sudden burning sensation on the side of her head.

It feels as though his glare is a fiery blaze. She might self-combust and fall to the floor in a pile of ashes. She had never seen him so angry with her.

*Well...money can do that to a person.*

Rosary waits patiently for his response. The look on his face is daunting.

She sincerely doesn't understand why he's so angry. What does he expect? She has been working her ass off trying to catch this killer. She deserves some credit. She deserves to receive half. She needs the money. She's relying too much on his control and power.

She wants nothing to do with his controlling behavior and she needs to take matters into her own hands. She needs to wake up and be herself again. She needs to be strong.

She's not taking any more of his shit.

"Today De Carlo. Fifty thousand dollars. You can give me the rest when I put a bullet in his brain," she demands as if he's a five-year-old-child listening to his parent discipline him. "I deserve this," she continues, "I deserve the currency. I've risked my life."

After a full minute, De Carlo nods, agreeing to her argument.

He then stares at his own Easter decorations. He suddenly realizes how ridiculous they must look. Life isn't about bunny rabbits and eating carrots.

*It's about sacrificing your life for the greater good.*

"Deal," De Carlo says, "You're absolutely right. You deserve it."

Rosary's heart skips a beat once again. She can't believe her ears. He's agreeing to her demands. She feels accomplished. She feels absolutely ecstatic.

She feels powerful.

She has taken the reigns and is fighting for her needs and wants for the first time in her life.

"Just like that? No argument?"

De Carlo shrugs his shoulders, "No argument here. Let's get inside and talk some more."

As they step inside of the house, Rosary suddenly feels like she belongs. She feels like a pivotal member of society. She is taking part into getting rid of a ruthless killer off the streets.

She knows her worth. She knows how successful she can be.

"Make yourself at home," De Carlo says as he makes his way into the kitchen. "Want some coffee?"

Rosary tosses her duffel bag and De Carlo's luggage bag filled with Jada's clothing, onto the freshly shampooed carpet. She smells fresh blueberries and pink lemonade.

A small candle sits on the kitchen counter. The flame shines as bright as the sun.

De Carlo's house is clean. It feels warm and inviting. It does still have a woman's touch with flower decorations and purple satin curtains hanging from the kitchen windows.

Rosary smiles as she wonders what it was like to have known Jada De Carlo. The woman was magnificent and beautiful.

Rosary did some research and found out that De Carlo's wife volunteered at the women's shelter every other weekend. She helped serve food at the soup kitchen.

She loved to help the community. She was well-loved and praised for her kindness.

Rosary looks at De Carlo with sadness. He lost a wonderful woman.

"Sure, I would love some," Rosary answers as De Carlo pours hot coffee into two mugs decorated with sunflowers.

He carries the mugs to the coffee table and sits down on the couch. He gestures for Rosary to have a seat next to him. She complies, sipping her coffee and eyeing him suspiciously.

"We need to talk about some things," De Carlo says.

Rosary suddenly feels as though SHE is the five-year-old waiting to be disciplined by a parent. His tone of voice isn't reassuring.

De Carlo pulls out a cell phone from his back pocket and hands it to her. She slowly takes it, confused.

"It's yours. Just for now. I added another line to my cell phone plan. When all this over, you can decide what to do with it," De Carlo says, taking a sip of his coffee.

He doesn't want his breath to smell bad, so he quickly pops a mint into his mouth.

Rosary remembers the red-chip-tracking-phone from Jake and politely smiles, accidentally pressing a button on the screen. It lights up like a lightning bolt.

"I don't even know how to use these fancy ones," Rosary says, laughing.

Breaking his silence, De Carlo burst into laughter. "I'll teach you," he replies.

Rosary nods, thinking about telling him about her morning.

She quickly shakes the thoughts out of her mind. She doesn't want him to know anything. He will completely break down. He might even kick her out.

He has been acting too jumpy and frightened at every move she makes. That would surely upset him, and she doesn't want to ruin this happy moment.

Rosary places the phone onto the coffee table.

"So," De Carlo continues after he swallows the mint, "I've officially been..."

He pauses. He's too embarrassed. He doesn't want to let her know that he failed.

He failed in his career. He failed this case. He failed Rosary and most of all... he failed his wife. He can't believe that Curtis would stoop this low.

*He had every right too.*

"I need to stop blaming everyone for my problems. I need to stop blaming everyone for my wife's death. My boss is right. I've spun completely out of control. This isn't who I am," De Carlo admits.

Rosary can understand the guilt and shame that he feels right now. She has felt it every day of her life since the age of sixteen. It's a dark place to live in. It's hard to survive.

"I'm here to help," Rosary says, taking De Carlo's hand into hers. "I completely understand. My behavior hasn't been the best. It's not who I am either."

De Carlo smiles as he squeezes her soft, pale hand.

He then lifts it, touching her soft skin. "You need a tan girl," De Carlo says, making Rosary burst into laughter.

"I've heard that all my life," she says, giggling like a schoolgirl.

*I sound like Phoenix;* she suddenly thinks at the back of her mind.

*Phoenix...that little bitch.*

"Well, "De Carlo says, placing Rosary's hand back onto her lap, "maybe someday we could go together."

Rosary is shy, nodding in agreement. She feels her face flushed with embarrassment.

"My meeting with my boss didn't go so well this morning."

Rosary's skin covers in goose bumps. She feels nervous as she waits for De Carlo to continue. His demeanor has changed. He is sick to his stomach to tell her what's next.

"I'm assuming he's unhappy with the investigation?"

De Carlo sighs, "You can say that. He's officially kicked me off the case."

Rosary is shocked. Her heart pounds with fear. She can't believe this. This can't be happening. How the hell will they move on with this roadblock?

"Who is taking over?" Rosary manages to ask. It's not what she wanted to say but it's the only thing that came to mind.

"My partner," he answers, popping another mint into his mouth.

"What the hell are we going to do?"

De Carlo looks around the living-room as he sighs, "Continue business as usual."

Rosary is speechless. This is not how things were supposed to go down. They were not supposed to avoid any incoming information.

"Don't worry," De Carlo says, "I've already spoken to Tiara. She promised to keep me updated. We must keep that on the down low or she will be in big trouble."

Rosary nods, sipping her coffee. She doesn't feel like drinking it now. She has lost her appetite. Hell, she has lost her will to live. This is too much for her. She should've stayed in prison like a good little girl. She was on her way to being released on good behavior.

"Do you want a tour of the house?" De Carlo asks, changing the subject.

Her knees feel weak, and her legs feel wobbly. She doesn't want to walk anywhere. She wants to stay on the couch and cry for a week straight.

"If I have to," Rosary answers. De Carlo's chuckle is nervous. He knows that she feels defeated but he will not let this slip-up keep them from catching the killer.

Or...killing him...

That is what he hired Rosary to do. He doesn't just want him caught; De Carlo wants him dead. He wants to see the man's worthless body buried six feet under.

"Let's go look at my charming beauty," De Carlo says, smirking.

Taking her hand, he shows her the open floor plan of the kitchen and dining room. His furniture is antique cherry-wood. She would do anything to have that type of furniture.

A sliding glass door leads out onto a deck. The rain splashes onto her face as she becomes awestruck at the size of his swimming pool. A Jacuzzi sits right next to it, covered over with a tarp for protection.

He shows her the rest of the downstairs. He has a game room and a finished basement. He shows her the newly painted bathroom next to the living room.

He then leads her upstairs.

Her heart pounds with excitement. She isn't sure if he's trying to lead her into his bedroom in order to do something that they both know they shouldn't do at the moment.

De Carlo smiles as he opens his bedroom door. Rosary looks around in awe. She can't believe how fancy the woodwork is and the pink lace curtains covering the windows. He didn't bother to change his wife's style at all. He's still clinging to her presence.

The sleigh bed is humongous, a California king painted black. The two dressers alongside the wall are black with gold trim. She has never seen such beauty in furniture before.

This is all new to her and she doesn't know how to respond.

"Let's check out my office. You might like it," he says excitedly.

They pass two more bedrooms as they hurry down the hallway toward De Carlo's office space. Rosary peeks into one of the bedrooms and smiles. The walls are painted yellow with pretty sunflowers drawn on the ceiling.

They enter the office. A cherry-wood desk sits in front of a bay window. The curtains are dark-green and satin. The plush chairs in front of the desk are also green.

Family photos align perfectly on the wall in the shape of a clock.

Rosary looks around as De Carlo sits in the computer chair, clicking the keyboard with his fat sausage fingers. He has stacks of paperwork piled at the corner of the desk. A pile of color-coded folders lies open for a robber to see.

Rosary notices the opened folders. De Carlo notices the direction of her eyeballs and quickly closes the folders as if he's hiding a secret...AGAIN.

"Secretive, aren't you?" Rosary playfully asks.

De Carlo shrugs without answering. His cell phone suddenly rings and he stands up from the desk. He looks nervous, maybe anxious.

Glancing at the caller, he quickly says, "Excuse me. I have to take this."

After excusing himself, he heads toward the downstairs. Rosary can hear muffled whispers. She forgot that she isn't supposed to be seen or heard. No one is to know that she is staying at his house. Hell, no one was supposed to know that she escaped from prison.

A string to a lightbulb inside of her mind is suddenly pulled.

She lifts her sleeve and glances at the license plate number that she had written on her arm this morning.

*Thank you, Phoenix. At least you did something right.*

Hurriedly, Rosary sits into the desk chair and nervously searches through De Carlo's folders on the computer screen. She finds a folder titled, "Websites," and double-clicks on it. The folder consists of lists pertaining to FBI websites that he uses frequently.

She can hear him talking downstairs much louder now. It sounds like he's pacing in the kitchen with his big, heavy feet. The tone of his voice frightens her as the perspiration sticks to her forehead like a piece of gum.

Her face flushes, and she feels like a burning volcano. She must hurry, or she will get caught in the line of fire.

She clicks on the words, "License plates." As it takes thirty seconds to load, she shouts, "Come on!" louder than she intended.

The website pops up just as she hears De Carlo shouting at the person on the phone. She quickly types the license plate number into the space bar and slams her finger onto the "enter" button.

While waiting for the results, she listens to De Carlo yelling and screaming. She hears him say, "Tiara! You've got to be kidding me! We had a deal!"

"Great," Rosary mumbles sarcastically as the blue circle on the screen twirls like a Hoola-Hoop. "Come on!" she shouts.

She can hear De Carlo slam his fist into something. The object shatters to the ground.

The blue circle twirls.

"Hurry up!" she shouts.

The sweat pours down the sides of her temples. The heat rises on her neck and down her spine. Her heart is pounding out of her chest. The hair on the back of her neck is standing up in salute. Her breathing is rapid, and she feels as if she's suffocating.

"Damn you!" she whispers.

She doesn't want De Carlo to know this information quite yet. She hates keeping secrets from him, but it's been apparent that he's hiding things from her as well.

*Two can play this game.*

She doesn't want to act childish, but this is something that SHE needs to take care of. This is her investigation, and this is something that she must keep to herself until she receives confirmation of who this killer is.

And she might know in about five seconds...

The blue circle stops twirling. De Carlo hangs up on Tiara.

Rosary stares at the name and address on the screen. She's puzzled and quite confused. She then hears De Carlo's boots stomping up the staircase.

"Shit," she whispers as she quickly writes the name and address down on a piece of paper with De Carlo's favorite pen decorated with paw prints.

She hurriedly clears the search and clicks the big red and white "X" at the top right corner of the website. De Carlo continues to stomp down the hallway.

Rosary then clicks back onto the website that De Carlo had previously pulled up.

She stuffs the piece of paper into the back pocket of her jeans and then quickly sits into one of the plush green chairs.

She's shaking with fear. She hates to hide anything from him, but she has to do this alone. She must follow her gut and intuition. De Carlo has to trust her. He doesn't have any other choice. She is all that he has because he can't even trust his own partner.

De Carlo is sluggish as he enters the office. He slips his cell phone into his pants pocket and lazily sits down into his desk chair.

He looks exhausted. He feels drained. He can't take much more bullshit.

And that's why Rosary has to keep this secret.

She's quiet as she watches him sigh with defeat. He runs his fingers through his hair and then rests the back of his head onto the back of his chair. He stares up at the ceiling.

"Are you alright?" Rosary asks after a minute of silence.

There goes their happy moment. There goes their laughter right out of the door. There goes that moment when they were on the right track to make this situation better.

"Um...not really. You?"

"Me either," she admits without hesitation.

She really isn't alright. She feels like her head is about to explode with a migraine forming at the back of her skull. Her headaches have been random at times and usually she can manage them, but lately, she's having more of them than usual.

De Carlo nods.

"Was that Tiara?" Rosary asks nonchalantly.

She's afraid to say something that might shoot his mouth off like a cannon. She's afraid of him for some reason. Maybe it's because of his build. Maybe it's because of his demeanor.

*Or maybe it's because he's a Goddamn FBI agent. I do not mix well with cops! I'm a hired hit woman for Christ Sake! Why am I even here? I must be nuts!*

"Yes, it was her. Not good news and I don't want to talk about it."

"Good because I'm going to lie down and rest. Mind if I sleep in one of those spare bedrooms? Preferably the one with the sunflowers. It's beautiful."

Before De Carlo has a chance to answer, Rosary stands up and stretches like she hasn't slept in days. Well, it sure feels like it.

"You want to get a late lunch?" De Carlo asks.

"No, I'm okay for now. Let's make dinner together later and we can talk about the case and where to go from here," Rosary replies, satisfied with her decision.

De Carlo nods as she leaves the office and heads for her new bedroom.

Once inside, she slips the piece of paper out of her pocket and reads the name two more times. She then looks out of the window. The rain has stopped.

She opens her duffel bag, making sure that all its contents are resting inside.

Rosary then turns toward her bedroom door, making sure that it's securely shut.

She locks it, turning toward the window once again.

# FOURTEEN

*That name sounds familiar. I've heard it plenty of times.*
It should be embedded inside of her brain. It should be tattooed on the front of her forehead. She feels as though she's received a message from a floating bottle out in the ocean.

She feels confused. Nothing makes any sense to her. She just wants to crawl inside of a hole and bury herself ten feet into the ground. No one would find her. No one would try to kill her or arrest her. She wouldn't even tell De Carlo.

It would be her little secret; a secret hidden in the depths of her heart.

*I know who...deep down I -*
Rosary's eyes suddenly light up like a firework on the Fourth of July. It's as if someone snapped their fingers inside of her confused brain.

*There must be some mistake.*
It's as if a fire has been lit under her ass. The anger pulsates throughout her body, and she suddenly feels numb. She feels dumb. She feels lost and she certainly feels confused.

As she reads the name of the owner of that license plate once again, she looks back at De Carlo's house one last time. She should tell him, but she won't at this moment.

She then leaves, sneakily running through the yard and then hopping the fence.

As Rosary Chime walks the streets of New York City, she watches the homeless beg for change, the anxious employees who are late for work, the young teenagers who should be in school, and a group of thieves planning a bank heist.

She hears their whispers as she sneaks past like a Ninja.

She giggles. They are out of touch with life, and they have no idea what they are getting themselves into. *People think it's so easy to rob a bank.*

As she thinks this, however, she minds her own business as she passes them. They are so entranced into their conversation that they don't even notice her.

If she didn't have anything better to do, she would wait in the shadows and burst their bubbles. She wouldn't allow them to steal. She would sit nicely perched inside one of the adjoining buildings and pluck them off one by one like the feathers of a bird.

But...she has more important things to do. Well, important things for HER.

She feels relieved to finally have some sort of clue as to who the killer may be. This address doesn't confirm anything. She has to see them with her own eyes. She has to catch this person in the act in order to believe that they could actually do something like this.

Rosary suddenly feels nervous. What if she's caught and goes back to jail? That can't happen just yet. She hasn't fulfilled her mission.

Her mission is to kill this son of a bitch. Her mission is to receive one hundred thousand dollars for her hard work and dedication.

As Rosary crosses the street, she curses to herself.

*I should've demanded more money. That amount was too easy. De Carlo is hiding something, and I will get to the bottom of it...maybe.*

She still doesn't fully trust De Carlo. This notion makes her feel awful inside. She isn't sure how he feels about her, but his behavior has become suspicious more and more every day.

*Maybe he doesn't fully trust me and that's okay...I wouldn't trust myself either.*

She can be ruthless. She can be menacing. She can be evil.

It's in the job description. Feeling bad for people and having a good heart will never get the job done. She knows that firsthand.

And if you don't get the job done, there are terrible consequences that have to be faced. That's the power that this job can hold over a person. *Anyone in their right mind should know that killing people for money faces all sorts of consequences.*

*But...it can also make someone rich and successful.*

She suddenly laughs deep inside her belly. She condoned those people for planning a robbery, but it is fine and dandy for her to snipe people just for the hell of it.

She slowly shakes her head as she continues down the sidewalk, keeping it low and steady so she isn't recognized by any fans of her sinful behavior.

The fan mail that she received in prison was absolutely out of control. She was well-loved and appreciated for, "taking out the bad guys," one fan wrote in a letter.

The thing is, not all her victims were "bad guys." They were well-loved by their families and friends. They were ordinary people living ordinary lives. Hell, most of them didn't do anything wrong. They were hated by one individual in their life who no longer wanted them around. They no longer wanted them to live because they were jealous or annoyed.

Some of the reasons were outrageous. Rosary would argue with Emilio every day leading up to their death. She would argue that these people didn't deserve what was coming to them.

She didn't want to murder Lilly Brown right in front of her son.

As a matter of fact, Rosary refused to complete the job. For three days straight, Emilio locked her inside of a dog cage and fed her moldy bread and Vodka.

That was when she had had enough. That was when she made the decision to give up. She knew that detective Anthony De Carlo was on her trail. He was good.

He was damn good.

He seemed to know where she was and with who. He knew where Emilio lived. He knew that Emilio participated in every single death that occurred from the hit woman.

He was smart and cunning.

But he wasn't smarter than her...

Rosary had a sacred place to hide but she decided against it. She was done with Emilio's abuse and neglect. She was done with his demands and controlling behavior.

*That was the only reason why Tony De Carlo was deemed a HERO!*

Rosary glances at the address one more time. She then looks around the street suspiciously. She grips her mother's rosary tighter between her fingers and whispers a small prayer, "Please GOD forgive me for my sins. Please watch over me during this trying time."

She sighs. She has a lot of nerve asking GOD to watch over her.

She turns the corner of a café and walks through an alleyway. She then follows a dirt path that suddenly leads farther away from downtown.

She has never been to this area before. She didn't even know that it existed. It's like a whole new world. She's in awe of all of the trees lined up on each side of her. The dirt path changes into gravel. There are no more businesses or houses surrounding the area.

As she walks through the gravel path, she suddenly gets this sinking feeling that something bad is about to happen. She doesn't know or understand why but she feels this eerie, dark feeling that resonates throughout her whole body.

She clutches the duffel bag and squeezes the jeweled necklace between her fingers. She stops for a moment, taking in the scenery.

There are daisies and rose bushes planted throughout the grass alongside the trees. She notices a, "DO NOT ENTER. PRIVATE PROPERTY," sign sitting in the middle of the gravel path about ten feet in front of her.

Her heart is racing.

She quickly turns around to see if anyone is following her. She sighs as her eyes fixate toward downtown that is now about a mile away from her.

She feels as though she's entering the depths of HELL. This gravel path continues into, "no man's land." She doesn't want to die here. No one will find her. De Carlo has no idea where she is. He probably doesn't even know that she's gone yet...unless he went to check on her in the last hour.

She feels bad for leaving the way she did. She feels bad for not leaving a note.

*I should've told him...or maybe I should've called my lawyer!*

Rosary takes a deep breath, continuing her journey through trees and flowers.

Twenty minutes later, she approaches a large warehouse with a purple, "GET OUT!" sign built onto the front of the double doors. She NEVER knew that this place existed.

She stares at it with bright eyes and a glowing face. *Yes, I should've called my lawyer.*

She can't believe that she found something so secretive to the rest of New York. *Does anyone else know that this exists or is it just me? Does De Carlo have any idea?*

Rosary is completely dumbfounded as she stops to look at her surroundings once again. She's surprised that the warehouse doesn't have a gate or some type of security system to enter the building. She's also surprised that NO ONE has approached her.

She has come so far. This warehouse must be at least fifteen to twenty miles away from downtown. She hasn't even realized how far she's walked. She's not even tired.

She suddenly hears voices talking. Without waiting another second, she runs, hiding behind a tree. She closes her eyes and whispers another prayer, "Please GOD, this will be the last thing that I ask of you. Please keep me safe."

She kisses her mother's rosary necklace.

Opening her eyes once again, she slowly peeks from behind the tree and watches a man and a woman trudge down the long gravel path.

They're wearing black suits and carrying purple drawstring bags. As she watches them, she suddenly realizes that there are no vehicles parked anywhere on the property.

The man and woman are wearing black boots as they walk hand in hand, complaining about having to walk so far into the city.

"This is so weird," Rosary says aloud.

She turns back to the gigantic warehouse and waits another full minute before she continues. This time, she walks in the grass alongside the trees, stepping on daisies.

She feels like someone is watching her.

She has no idea if there are cameras. If there are, she's already busted. Whoever is inside the warehouse may know that she has come for them.

*Maybe...*

She's suddenly having second thoughts. She knows that this was a bad idea to come alone. She knows that she should've warned De Carlo.

But she did it anyways because she's strong and independent. She doesn't need or want anyone's help. She suddenly realizes that she's back to her old self. She can handle this.

She continues forward, approaching with caution.

She doesn't want to enter by knocking on the door and expecting to be welcomed with open arms. She has to find another way in. She must sneak in without being seen.

She knows that she can do that. She is determined to prove to herself that she can solve this mystery without anyone else's help.

She has to.

Rosary quickly and quietly makes her way around the left side of the warehouse without being detected. She suddenly notices that the grass is high and that her legs feel itchy as if bugs are crawling into her butthole.

She scratches her pant leg as she sees a small window at the bottom of the building. She thinks it may lead to the basement if there is one.

She can't believe how easy it is to enter inside. She thought that there would surely be some sort of detection or alarm going off outside to notify the owner.

As Rosary hears voices once again, she quickly opens the window and climbs inside.

Her boot gets stuck onto the windowsill and her body twists, falling directly onto her back. She feels paralyzed for a moment. Her breathing is hard and fast.

She hears voices once again. She quickly glances around the area and realizes that she's lying on a cold cement floor. She doesn't have time to cry about her injuries.

She jumps up, kicking her legs as if she's fighting someone in Karate. She looks around inside of the room that she's in, seeing all sorts of weapons hanging from the walls by screws. She sees AK-41's, Sniper rifles, flare guns, knives, swords....

*Whoever these people are, they're ready for a battle.*

This thought makes Rosary's heart beat a mile a minute. She can feel it pulsating...*boom, boom, boom, boom, boom, boom.*

Her body is shaking. She's never felt so unprepared for a mission in her life. She didn't think this through. She left in a hurry without thinking about the repercussions.

She doesn't want to die here.

The voices are closer now. She can hear two people arguing about what to eat for lunch.

*I wish that were all I had to worry about.*

She hears the key enter the lock on the door and she watches the handle slowly turn...

Two men wearing a mask covering their nose and mouth, enter the room, looking around with confused expressions upon their faces.

Rosary is gone.

"I feel like there's a ghost in here Bobby," one man says.

His friend Bobby chuckles, "You are so stupid. There's no such thing as ghosts."

"You didn't feel that gust of wind?"

Bobby shakes his head, "Diego, the window is open dumb ass," he says, pointing his finger toward the window.

They howl with laughter.

Bobby then closes it as Diego picks through the selection of weapons. He grabs a flare gun, a pocketknife, and a sword.

Bobby laughs, "What are you gonna do with that homie? Slice her to death?"

Diego chuckles, "Dude, she has a sniper rifle."

Rosary hides behind a huge barrel of gas. The smell is making her nauseous as she covers her nose with her hand. She wishes she would've worn her own mask as well.

She looks down at her duffel bag and then back up at the men, peeking around the barrel as she watches Bobby grab his own sniper rifle.

*Are they talking about me? Do they know that I'm here?*

Rosary is baffled but feels accomplished at the same time. They must have been watching her, but they let her enter without a fight.

*So strange... why would anyone do that on purpose?*

*Well... maybe they're not talking about me. Maybe it's someone else...*

"Let's go," Bobby says, interrupting Rosary's thoughts. "They're waiting for us."

After the door closes, Rosary quickly unzips her duffel bag and takes out her red sniper rifle. She checks the ammo inside and then places the strap around her shoulders. She then shoves her bag underneath a shelf.

She stares at her mother's rosary necklace. The beads are worn, and the string has stretched out because of her continuous pulls and strong grips.

Rosary then untangles the necklace from her fingertips and wraps it around her whole entire hand. She normally places it around her neck when she's getting prepared for a snipe job, but she feels confident that this battle will turn out well. The necklace will help her to not lose control. She needs it to focus and stay calm.

Rosary takes a deep breath as she stands up and slowly moves toward the door. With her rifle set between both of her arms, she then gently places a hand on the handle of the door.

She waits to hear voices or for some sort of movement.

There aren't any.

She slowly opens the door...and it creeks like a haunted house.

Her heart skips a beat. She's perspiring and her breath is caught in her lungs.

She doesn't want to be bombarded with multiple people pointing weapons at her. She feels claustrophobic. She can't maneuver anywhere but out of the window.

She exhales her breath as she peeks through the open door. She doesn't see anyone marching toward her like soldiers. She doesn't hear anyone yelling, "Off with her head!" like the bad guys do in that one movie she saw a few years ago.

She can't remember the name of it.

"Damn it," she whispers as she opens the door fully. "What was the name...?"

Her mind is suddenly jolted as she hears the sound of something crashing to the floor.

"I said now!" she hears a woman shout about fifteen feet from her.

Rosary can hear footsteps leaving toward the direction of the double doors to the warehouse. She pauses for a moment, waiting for someone to jump out in front of her.

She hides behind boxes as she makes her way toward the woman's voice. Rosary can see pallets stacked sky high with items wrapped in plastic. She can't quite tell what is inside, but she has a feeling that it's illegal.

"Where the hell am I?" she whispers.

Sometimes, Rosary doesn't like to feel out of her comfort zone. That's why she hides inside of buildings, perched behind windows so she can't be seen. She feels exposed right now.

She looks around for somewhere to hide.

There isn't anywhere. The warehouse is wide open with pallets and boxes stacked neatly up against the wall. Rosary notices two vehicles parked in the middle of the warehouse.

*The fartin' little red car...*

Next to the car is a long table. It contains paperwork and folders stacked neatly into the corners. Boxes of opened donuts and water bottles wait patiently to be eaten and drank.

Rosary licks her lips. She's hungry AND thirsty.

As she creeps around a stack of boxes, she sees a woman speaking to Bobby and Diego. They nod their heads, dispersing toward the front doors with their weapons of choice.

The woman takes a gulp of wine from her glass and then angrily places it onto the table. She then grabs her purse, pulling out her powder compact. She dabs fresh powder onto her nose and cheeks and then replaces the compact back inside of her purse.

The woman seems nervous and anxious. She paces the floor as if she's waiting for someone.

Rosary exhales her breath that she had been holding.

*I knew that name was familiar.*

Rosary is angry as she recognizes the side of the woman's face. She has only caught a glimpse of her a few times but she's now sure of whom this is.

And a name...

Rosary grips her mother's necklace with such force that the jewels shatter from the weakened string, directly into her hand. She slowly begins to realize what she has done, looking down at the necklace with tears in her eyes.

She suddenly loosens her grip, letting the jewels fall loosely to the floor, bouncing like tennis balls.

She feels as if she's living in slow motion. Everything has caught her off guard. Is she really ONLY ten feet away from someone who is involved with these murders?

*What the hell does the warden have to do with anything?*

*Adeline Montana...* Rosary thought that was her while looking at those blurry photos.

Rosary steps out from behind the stack of boxes, pointing her rifle at Adeline.

The warden's hair flows like a waterfall as a gust of wind blows through an open window. Adeline smiles as she turns toward Rosary, winking.

Rosary stares at her through the scope of the rifle.

As she walks slowly, creeping closer toward Adeline, her face is immediately perplexed. She feels as though her heart has stopped beating. She can't breathe as she watches Adeline take another gulp of her wine.

*This can't be. I must be living in a dream.*

*Wake up Rosary! Wake the hell up!*

"I'm not surprised," Adeline says as she finishes the last of her wine, placing the glass back onto the table. Rosary watches her every move like a hawk watching from the sky.

Rosary slowly takes three more steps, staring into the scope.

She doesn't understand why she feels so emotional. This shouldn't be a surprise. Besides, this is something that this woman would do. She's ruthless. She's cunning. She's...

"Adeline Montana," Adeline says, holding out her hand, "Your warden."

Rosary can't believe her eyes. Tears flows down her cheeks as she watches Adeline smile an evil grin. She's evil and heartless. She hasn't seen this woman in ten years.

She knows that evil grin. She knows those crinkles in the corner of her eyes.

She has changed her looks, but Rosary will never forget someone so close to her heart.

Rosary steps closer, pointing the rifle directly into the warden's face. The warden reaches for Rosary's cheeks with the tips of her fingers, softly wiping the tears away.

"I wasn't expecting a reunion with my beloved sister," Rosary says, glaring.

The warden laughs, waving her hand, "Agatha Chime at your service."

Rosary has this sudden image of blowing her sister's brains to pieces. She pulls the trigger and aims it directly at her forehead. Her sister falls to the floor in a heap of her own blood.

"It didn't take you long. I'm not surprised," Agatha continues, "I knew you would figure it out eventually, you and that nosy FBI agent."

Rosary is completely baffled. *Yeah, I should've called my laywer.*

"You don't have to point that thing in my face. I knew you were coming silly," Agatha continues, pointing toward the cameras above the warehouse doors. "I've ordered my men to stand down. I told them not to harm the hair on your head. The least you could do is return the favor." Agatha laughs as if she was telling a joke.

Rosary stares at her sister in awe. She's suddenly jealous that this woman that she's known her whole life, can pull off something like this and get away with it. She never thought that Agatha had it in her.

Rosary suddenly chuckles. *I knew she had it I her! She killed our mother!*

Rosary is confused and speechless as she lowers her weapon. Her mind is so confused. Deep down, she knew that her sister had it in her, BUT she didn't think that she would act upon it.

Agatha used to talk about serial killers when they were growing up. She was fascinated with "Ted Bundy" and "Jeffrey Dahmer." Rosary thought it was just a phase and that she would snap out of it. Agatha loved the idea of people running around and killing others for the hell of it.

Agatha once drafted a paper for her psychology class. It scared the teacher so much that she called their mother to the school. Sherry Thomas was extremely frightened, reading the paper with her mouth covered with her hand. The teacher advised Sherry to send Agatha somewhere "safe." But where was SAFE?

"Oh," Agatha continues, "by the way, Jada De Carlo was delightful. I thought maybe my killing spree would end. I thought maybe that I finally found the one for me."

Agatha is suddenly sad as she stares at Rosary with tears in her eyes.

"She told me she loved me. She told me she was leaving Tony in the dust."

Rosary places the muzzle of her rifle onto the cement floor, still gripping the butt of the gun in case Agatha tries to pull something slick out of her ass.

Agatha continues rambling on, "She then proclaimed her love for her husband. She didn't want to end things with him. She just wanted to have me as her side piece. I wasn't good enough. She didn't want to marry me. She didn't love me like Tony."

Rosary suddenly feels bad for her sister. She sees the sadness in her eyes. She can feel the love that her sister felt for this woman.

"So, I killed her," Agatha admits, "Just like the rest of them. These women come to...ME! They come to me bitching about their dickless husbands. They tell me they want ME! And then they break my heart. They all say that it was their first time being with a woman. I'm always the guinea pig! The one they blow off after having their fun!"

Agatha cries as she wipes her tears with her fingers. Rosary suddenly has that same image of blowing her sister's brains to pieces. *Maybe I should just end this mission right now. That's what I was hired for...to end this bullshit.*

But how can she just kill her sister? How will Rosary live with herself?

She didn't sign up for this. She didn't know that the killer roaming the streets would be her flesh and blood. She

214 - ANGELA SANNER

had no idea that she was hired to put a bullet in her sister's brain.

*Does De Carlo know this? He can't possibly... he would've told me.*

Agatha watches as Rosary stares into space. It's as if she's been hypnotized and stuck inside of a trance.

"Don't worry," Agatha continues, "Your precious agent doesn't have a clue."

She read Rosary's mind. She's extremely smart and self-satisfied.

Agatha didn't have the greatest life. She didn't have the greatest mother or the greatest family, but, for the past ten years, she's taken good care of herself. She's happy with her life, besides the fact that women use and abuse her. But she moves on quickly and quietly. She's just looking for the right person to spend the rest of her life with.

And she doesn't want a man. She wants the love of a woman to protect her and guide her. She wants that bond between two women, a soft touch on her cheek.

She wants someone who will take her seriously. She wants someone who is SERIOUS.

Jada De Carlo wasn't serious. She was scared. She didn't want her husband to act out of jealousy. She didn't want De Carlo to kill anyone for her crazy actions.

He would have. He would've killed them in a heartbeat. Either way, Jada De Carlo would've been killed by the hands of detective Anthony De Carlo.

He would've done it in a fit of rage.

Rosary blinks, coming out of her trance.

"I was hired to kill you," Rosary blurts out, "That is why De Carlo bailed me out. It was all a ruse to kill the notorious, "woman hater." And I can't believe that it's you."

Agatha laughs, "I don't hate women. I love them. They just turn on me...just like you."

Rosary thinks for a moment, contemplating her sister's statement. "I didn't turn on you. You turned on our whole entire family."

Agatha nods in agreement but stays silent. Rosary is trying to think of something to say, but she can't. An awkward silence falls between them.

Time is running out. Rosary wants her money, but she can't decide if she is willing to kill her flesh and blood for one hundred thousand dollars.

"What was in it for you?" Rosary asks.

Agatha is confused as she looks at the time on her watch. She seems impatient now, scrambling to figure out how to get out of this mess.

"For what?" Agatha asks as she looks around for her men.

"You let me escape with De Carlo...why?"

Agatha laughs as she hears Bobby and Diego approaching the double doors.

"The same as you silly...MONEY."

As Bobby and Diego enter the warehouse, they immediately point their weapons at Rosary. Rosary does the same, glaring at them through the scope. Agatha gestures for the men to lower their weapons. They comply but Rosary continues to watch them with an image of blowing their brains out.

Agatha smirks, "So...um...can I have a head start?"

Rosary feels this sudden urge to burst into laughter. She hasn't laughed with her sister in ages, and it would be nice if they could do that for the last time.

Rosary has made her decision. She will kill her sister.

Agatha is a risk. She's evil. She will continue this madness if she isn't stopped.

Agatha Chime doesn't care about anyone but herself and Rosary must stop her.

Rosary thinks about Agatha's question for a full two minutes. Agatha is impatient as she taps her purple heel onto the cement floor.

Bobby and Diego begin collecting items around the warehouse and placing them into their vehicles. Bobby grabs Agatha's purse, all the paperwork and folders and even her wine glass. Diego grabs the donuts, removes his mask, and then shoves one into his mouth.

"I'll give you twenty-four hours," Rosary finally answers, watching Diego grabbing the bottles of water and tossing them into the back seat of the red car. "If you don't leave town," Rosary continues, "then I will put a bullet straight through your skull and into the back of your head."

Agatha laughs. Then, Rosary laughs.

They both burst into laughter as if Rosary told the funniest joke they've ever heard.

Rosary suddenly lifts her rifle and glares at her sister through the scope.

"Contact me in twenty-four hours and let me know where you are. If you don't do that sweet sister of mine...well...you know the repercussions."

Agatha slowly takes multiple steps toward Rosary, watching the tears in her eyes. Both women have had a soft spot for each other all their lives. They would never let anyone hurt the other, but they wouldn't care to hurt each other.

Agatha whispers in her sister's ear, "I could kill you like Sherry Thomas."

Rosary whispers back as she stares at Bobby and Diego pointing their rifles at her head, "Tell me why I shouldn't just kill you right here...right now?"

Agatha giggles, "Because we're sisters. We love each other." Rosary lowers her rifle.

She then laughs, trying to get the shock of this event out of her mind. She still can't believe she's been duped. Her sister is slicker than Rosary once thought.

Agatha takes a few steps back as she realizes that Bobby and Diego are pointing their rifles at Rosary. She shakes her head at them, "Get the hell inside of the car!" she yells at them.

They comply in a huff.

"You know Rosary," Agatha continues one last time, "I kill women who look like Sherry Thomas. I have this attraction toward women who look like her. Isn't that creepy? Our mother damned me for life. She turned me into a psychotic killer," Agatha pauses and thinks for another moment, "Hell, she turned us BOTH into psychotic killers..." Agatha trails off.

"Jada De Carlo didn't look like Sherry Thomas," Rosary points out.

"No, she didn't," Agatha says with a smile, "Jada De Carlo was to turn the tracks away from your trail. But it was too late. Jada was killed when you were arrested. You gave up too easily. I was waiting in the wings for you. I was there to save you."

Rosary is completely and utterly shocked. She stands like a mannequin in the window of a retail store. She doesn't know whether to laugh or cry. Her sister has released all these pent-up emotions that Rosary has been hiding for years.

Agatha places her soft fingertips onto Rosary's sweaty forehead. She then moves the hair out of Rosary's saddened eyes.

"I miss you my sweet little sister. Come join me. We can share De Carlo's money together."

Rosary quietly laughs, thinking for a moment, "Not this time. Maybe in another lifetime."

Agatha silently nods.

Rosary watches her sister climb into her little red car. Bobby and Diego are perched inside of the black truck that they have been patiently waiting inside of.

The attached garage door opens, and Agatha puts her car into reverse. Bobby is in the driver seat of the truck and does the same thing. Diego stares at Rosary and gives her the finger.

Rosary points her rifle at Diego, the red light shining in the middle of his forehead. He glares at her but immediately looks scared out of his mind.

*You'll get yours soon enough.*

As they leave, Agatha waves, pressing the button to her remote to close the garage doors.

The warehouse is eerily quiet. Rosary feels this sense of doom impeding her heart. She should've taken her only shot. She doesn't know if she will ever see her sister again.

De Carlo will kill her if he finds out what she has done...or didn't do.

All she had to do was pull that trigger...but her heart got into the way.

She knew that would happen. She has warned herself time and time again. She let Agatha Chime slip through her fingers like melting ice-cream on a sunny day.

The warden of the prison...of all the people in this world.

In a solemn mood, Rosary walks back toward the room where she left her duffel bag. In passing, she sees the jeweled beads of her precious necklace. The string is lying on the cement floor like a tethered string from an old rag doll.

She picks up the beads and the string, staring at them for a moment.

She closes her eyes.

Agatha Chime is in for a rude awakening.

# FIFTEEN

The evening sunshine has disappeared, and a cold wind blows through the trees. The spring air has suddenly changed back to winter, making De Carlo's flowers droop with sadness.

The weather here changes as much as he changes his underwear...every single day. One night the sun is shining and feels hot on his dark skin. Then, the next night, the heater is turned on to get rid of the crisp, cold air that blows through the cracks around his windows.

Every so often, De Carlo likes to feel the chilly air brush into his face like wildfire. On most days, he sweats tremendously and this cold air calms him down.

He has decided to keep the heat on for Rosary Chime.

If she ever comes back...

He thinks of her black hair entangled with his sausage fingers. He stares into her dazzling blue eyes as he feels his groin tighten with that tingly feeling.

He's thinking about her curves as he glances at his watch. It's almost five o'clock and she still isn't back from wherever she ran off to. It's not like he can call someone and report her missing. He can't call the police and tell them that a felon has run off into the sunset without his permission. He can't call Curtis or Tiara for help.

This scenario is mind-boggling, and he faces all sorts of emotions flowing through his mind like water in a faucet. He feels angry. He feels saddened. He feels betrayed.

Rosary doesn't trust him, he knows this. She's a delicate flower on the brink of destruction. She refuses to tear down her walls and sacrifice her feelings.

She likes De Carlo. He's funny, witty and they do get along extremely well.

But they only get along when all thoughts of serial killers and old snipe jobs are thrown out the window. Sometimes, Rosary refuses to hear any more of it. She wants to move on with her life and forget about the past. She wants to live happily and freely with her thousands of dollars.

She has never received that kind of money for any type of mission. Emilio Delgado degraded her and never believed that she was worth his time or money.

De Carlo is in the living room, sitting on a kitchen chair facing the front door to his house. His back slouches as he waits with a pistol in his hand.

He has no idea what he's going to do with it. He might shoot her, he might not. His mind is jumping in circles like a child jumping on their bed. His brain is bouncing up and down as he thinks of different scenarios in his mind.

She could walk right through that door as he shoots a bullet straight through her heart. That's exactly how he feels...as if a bullet has been pierced through his heart, exploding into thousands of pieces.

He didn't think that she would leave like this. She didn't even have the decency to tell him where she was going.

He saw her. She jumped the fence like a thief in the night. He saw something in her hand. It looked like a piece of paper, but he wasn't completely sure. She had been standing too far of a distance and his vision isn't the greatest.

He has been sitting here ever since she left.

He hasn't eaten. The coffee inside of his mug is ice cold. He hasn't been to the bathroom. He has to pee like a racehorse but he's afraid that she will come home while he's in there.

He doesn't want her running into her bedroom and locking the door again. He wants to see her expression as she lies to him about where she had been.

De Carlo knows that she will lie. She's a convicted felon with multiple murders in her back pocket. She could step in dog poop and convince someone that it came from a human.

She's good like that.

It doesn't make any sense to him. He truly doesn't understand her concept of hiding things from him. He's an FBI agent who was hot on her trail. That moment when she realized that she couldn't run anymore, she gave up. But he caught her. And now, she thinks she can hide things without him catching her again.

He shakes his head as he looks down at the pistol once again. Honestly, he wants to kill Rosary Chime. He wants to end this bullshit so that he doesn't get into any more trouble with Curtis and Shania Brown.

He should've never helped her to escape. He regrets this decision, and it has been eating at him since the day she left the prison.

But he was desperate. He knows this. He wanted the killer caught in the worst way and the only way was to hire a more "professional" individual for the job.

It had to be Rosary Chime. It MUST be Rosary Chime.

She can do it, and he has the upmost faith in her, more than she would ever believe. *She's sophisticated and so god-damn smart. We can pull this off if she stops acting like a child.*

Her behavior is beyond ridiculous. She doesn't seem herself. He misses that daring and funny personality the day he met her inside of that church.

He suddenly lifts his head as another thought comes to mind.

*The church...she has to be there!*

As he contemplates on leaving to head toward her mother's church, he hears the sound of the door handle twisting and turning.

De Carlo lifts his pistol with both hands, pointing it toward the intruder. The door slowly opens as Rosary quietly steps inside. Her duffel bag strapped to her shoulder and her broken necklace inside of her fist.

She looks tired and anxious. Her hair slicked back from sweat. Her thin physique looks fragile, and her back slouched into a hump.

She turns to close the door quietly, not realizing that De Carlo is sitting in her path. He continues to point the pistol at her head. He imagines pressing the trigger, watching her eyes explode with sadness. He imagines her look of despair, hurt and betrayal.

That's exactly how he feels but she doesn't seem to care. He has been the only friend to her. He has been the only one to help her and she doesn't appreciate it.

Rosary turns, facing the pistol. Her eyes light up with shock as she stares at him with a, "Go ahead, I dare you," look upon her face.

At this point, she wouldn't mind it. She's in deep trouble anyways so why not just end it all right here and right now?

"I'll bet that you have a good explanation," De Carlo says with a smirk.

"I went out for a bite to eat?" Rosary says in the form of a question.

"Try again," De Carlo replies, still pointing the pistol at her head.

"I went to take a walk?" she places her broken necklace onto an end table.

De Carlo shakes his head, disagreeing, eyeing the broken necklace.

"My dog ate my homework?" Rosary continues, taunting him.

"You think this shit is funny?" De Carlo asks.

Rosary thinks for a moment. She wants to say, "Yes, of course I do," but she decides against it. De Carlo is extremely angry, and she doesn't blame him. She would be angry too.

"If you're going to point that thing at me, you better make that move before I do," Rosary threatens. She feels the heat rise on the sides of her neck and up into her cheeks.

She never thought that he would be this upset enough to actually kill her.

*I don't really know him so it's not a surprise.*

"Are you threatening me Rosary Chime?"

Rosary shrugs her shoulders, "Sure, but you best pull that trigger. I'm not like your other criminals in custody. I'll put a bullet right through your brain."

De Carlo nods. Her statement is one hundred percent true.

"I'll put it away on one condition," De Carlo answers after staring at her for a full minute.

The silence is excruciating. He doesn't like these stare downs. She will not back down and neither will he. She's a criminal and she will not have the upper hand in this situation.

"And what's that detective De Carlo?"

"Tell me where you were. It's that simple."

De Carlo inhales a deep breath and then exhales as if he's blowing smoke from a cigarette. He feels nauseous and completely sick to his stomach. Her hidden agenda is sickening.

Rosary tosses her duffel bag onto the floor as she chuckles, "You see, it's not that simple. You haven't shown any trust in not only me, but in yourself. You don't even trust your gut instincts. You said that I was wonderful and someone you needed in your life. Now you're sitting there like a lonely duck in the pond for the simple fact that I didn't include you. You're pitiful, pointing a gun to my head without even knowing my intentions. You can go straight to hell."

De Carlo doesn't answer as he re-plays her statement over and over again inside of his mind. He suddenly feels foolish. She is right. He has no idea what she has been doing for the past eight hours and he's ready to end her life because of it.

He smirks, lowering the pistol. "I've been in hell since the day my wife died."

Rosary feels pity and sadness for the agent. She knows that he's been trying hard to catch the person who murdered his wife in cold blood.

And he has been way off.

"What if I told you that I have a lead? Would you believe me?" Rosary asks.

"Do you?" De Carlo fires back, angry. He just wants this son of a bitch caught. He doesn't care how they do it. He will put a bullet in the killer's brain himself if he has to.

Rosary slowly nods as she takes off her boots. Her feet hurt and she's hungry. She suddenly wants to cook a delicious meal for the two of them.

"I do," Rosary admits, "but I can't tell you at this moment."

De Carlo becomes puzzled, angry, and confused. He wants to give up but that's not what he does. He will not give her this accomplishment. She would love to see him fail. She would love to see him break down and fall to his knees at her command.

Rosary sees his expression and smiles, "You have to trust me."

De Carlo looks at her devilish grin. He suddenly laughs, standing up as he places his pistol inside of his back pocket. He glances at the broken necklace once again. She notices.

"Are you hungry?" Rosary asks as she walks past him with a sway in her hips.

"Starving," he answers as he follows her into the kitchen, watching her buttocks bounce with every step that she takes.

"Good," she replies, pulling out a pan from the cupboard. "I'm going to make us some chicken a la king. My mother has the best recipe."

De Carlo nods as he takes a seat at the kitchen table. He feels the barrel of the pistol digging into his skin. He removes it from his pocket and places it onto the kitchen table.

Rosary watches him but chooses to ignore it. She doesn't want to ruffle his feathers any more than what she already has. He then excuses himself to the bathroom.

After she cooks their meal, she sits down across from him, eyeing the pistol. It sits quietly next to his left hand. She isn't sure why she feels nervous about it lying there like a napkin.

"So," Rosary says as she cuts a piece of chicken, "my older sister murdered my mother inside of the mental institution she was living at."

De Carlo is quiet as he chews on a piece of chicken. He has been waiting for her to tell this story because he knows that it's juicy, just like their dinner.

Rosary swallows, taking a sip of her wine. "She snuck inside of the building through an opened window. She wore a black ski-mask with a clown mask over top of it."

Rosary laughs as she imagines this notion.

"The thing is," Rosary continues, taking a bite of rice and peas, "she went there to help my mother escape. Sherry didn't remember the conversation they had had the night before. That's how crazy my mother was." Rosary swallows her food, watching De Carlo cut his chicken into tiny pieces. "She didn't remember so when my sister entered her room, Sherry screamed like a banshee." Rosary shakes her head.

De Carlo is silent. He doesn't want to be rude and interrupt the story. He chews a forkful of rice and peas as he watches Rosary gulp her wine.

"A travesty I tell you, "She says, shaking her head again. "My sister freaked out. She didn't understand why Sherry was screaming. My mother ripped off Agatha's clown mask. Then, Agatha took off the ski-mask and held her finger to her lips, shushing the old bat."

Rosary laughs, drinking the rest of the wine. She then grabs the bottle, pouring more of it to the rim of her glass. She loves red wine. It has been her favorite since she was old enough to drink. The bottle is almost empty.

"Needless to say, my mother decided to stay. She didn't want to escape. She then called Agatha nasty names and told her she was useless. My sister didn't like that one bit. She hated my mother with a passion. She later admitted to me that she didn't know why she was going to help her in the first place. Agatha wanted Sherry to rot in there," Rosary shakes her head once again. She sighs, thinking of the tragic loss.

"Sherry was placed into that mental institution because she was our pimp," Rosary continues, eating more chicken.

"What?" De Carlo asks, stunned.

"Yes," Rosary answers, "my mother was our pimp and kept the money for herself. She threatened our lives if we didn't do what we were told. Agatha became fed up with it. I mean," Rosary continues as she watches De Carlo take a sip of his wine. "I was fed up with it too, but I didn't want to kill her for it. I wanted her to get help. I was the one who signed her into that place. Agatha was so upset with me. She wanted our mother to die."

De Carlo thinks for a moment, "Do you have any idea why Agatha would help her escape? She hated her. I'm sure she didn't want to be around Sherry for the rest of her life."

Rosary shrugs, "After some time, I think Agatha started to feel bad for Sherry. My mother was good at making people feel bad for her. She would cry on the phone and beg for release. However, Agatha did call the institution and requested Sherry to be released into Agatha's care within a month. The institution denied her request."

De Carlo nods, "Why?"

"They claimed that Sherry wasn't ready to be released. She hadn't completed the required six months stay and she was still acting loony I guess."

De Carlo takes another gulp of his wine, finishing off the glass. He pours more, smiling at Rosary. They're sure to be drunk by the time this conversation ends.

"Anyways," Rosary continues, "Agatha killed my mother for what she did to us, plain and simple. The institution called the police, and my sister escaped, never to be heard from again."

"I think I remember that case. I wasn't assigned to it, but I find it familiar now that you talk about it. The agent involved had mentioned the situation," De Carlo admits.

Rosary nods, thinking about her altercation with Agatha just hours beforehand.

"I don't miss either one of them," Rosary lies.

She does miss them tremendously. She misses her sister's laugh and her goofy sense of humor. She misses her mother's talks that they used to have about life in general. At one point, they were all incredibly happy with one another.

Her mother's greed and cowardly behavior is what caused friction between them all. Agatha hated doing what Sherry made her do with men. But she learned to live with it after Sherry threatened to take Agatha's life because her daughter wanted out. She didn't want to do it anymore. She didn't like feeling dirty and disgusted every night.

Sherry decided not to share the proceeds from her daughter's shameful behavior. Agatha was ashamed, and so was Rosary. They were both terrified as well. Every day they wondered if they would live through another night. Every man was different. They asked for inappropriate favors that both girls hated doing.

"Are you sure of that statement?" De Carlo asks as he pushes his plate to the side. He's stuffed like a lobster and can't eat any more. His stomach feels like it's about to burst open.

"I'm really not sure of anything," Rosary admits.

She stares at the leftover chicken on her plate. She can't eat any more either. She would rather drink the rest of the bottle of wine and go to bed.

Talking about her mother and sister suddenly made her feel depressed. Even though she had a surprise visit with Agatha not too long ago, she still feels like she hasn't seen her sister in years. That wasn't her. It had to have been a demon taking over her body.

Rosary wishes that she could've at least said goodbye to her mother.

Agatha ruined her plans. She was going to visit Sherry the very next day. She couldn't believe her ears when the institution called her and told her what happened.

"Your mother was murdered. We're so deeply sorry for your loss," the manager said to Rosary. The woman hung up without waiting for a response.

The police contacted Rosary the very next morning and asked if she had heard from her sister. Rosary was baffled. She had not. Her sister was wanted for murder. Rosary was told to contact them if Agatha reached out at any time.

She did once, just to explain what happened. Agatha hung up after a three-minute call.

Rosary's heart had broken into two the day Sherry died. One piece left with Sherry and the other piece left with Agatha. Rosary had no family, no one to run to, and no one to comfort her.

She was alone in a world full of lost souls and demented human beings.

"You look lost," De Carlo says, watching Rosary stare into space.

"Just a lost soul in a demented world," Rosary answers as she gulps the rest of her wine.

"I hope you will continue to move forward with our deal," De Carlo suddenly says, pouring the rest of the wine into both of their glasses.

Rosary is puzzled, taken aback by his statement. Confusion written all over her face as her cheeks flush with heat. She isn't sure if it's from the wine or from his stupid comment. He completely changed the subject on her.

She takes another gulp of wine.

"Are you?" De Carlo continues.

"Of course!" Rosary snaps.

She isn't sure why he's asking her this. She hasn't done anything to make him think that she wouldn't. She needs closure. She needs to end her sister's wrath.

"I know you won't back out. I just wanted to hear it," De Carlo says as he reaches into the back pocket of his jeans, "I have something for you."

He hands Rosary a folded yellow envelope. She takes it, drunk and smiling.

She opens the envelope and pulls out her fifty thousand dollars in cash.

"There's half, just like you requested."

Rosary smiles, placing the cash back inside of the envelope. She doesn't count it. She does trust him. *Maybe this will give me more motivation to have the balls to kill my sister.*

Rosary laughs at her own thoughts.

De Carlo smiles as he takes her hand. He has surely missed that laugh of hers.

"Thank you, De Carlo. Now, I think it's time for bed."

De Carlo checks his watch, "It's only six-thirty."

"Exactly," Rosary answers, clutching De Carlo's hand. She raises her eyebrows, flirting.

*Flirting with disaster...*

De Carlo smiles that devilish grin.

# SIXTEEN

De Carlo is awestruck by Rosary's naked body. He can't believe that he's finally gotten a beautiful woman in his bed. Seeing Rosary in this kind of vulnerable state has become a dream come true. He never thought that he would put himself in this type of position with Rosary Chime. It has become a blessing in disguise.

Or an unforgettable regret...

He doesn't want to regret this moment. This is what he has been waiting for since the day he met her. Her beautiful figure spins his mind in circles. It's as though they're making love inside of a tornado. It's crazy and wild. It's passionate and true.

De Carlo kisses her lips as she moves her hips. He plunges his erection inside of her, making her cry out. He wants her to enjoy this moment. He wants her to never forget how loved he can make her feel. He wants her to know how serious he can be with her in the future.

He isn't sure of her plans for the future; she seems to keep that to herself. But he secretly hopes and prays that it includes him.

He wants all of her, every single inch. He wants to make love to her every day and come home to her every night, like husband and wife.

Rosary digs her sharp nails into De Carlo's back, making him moan in ecstasy. Her soft skin glows with happiness. Her beauty is radiant and her smile lights up his heart.

This is the Rosary Chime that he has fallen in love with. Not the depressed and solemn Rosary Chime. He loves to see her happy and smiling. He loves her daring personality and that sway of her hips when she walks.

It drives him crazy.

They passionately kiss, sending chills down De Carlo's spine. Rosary giggles as she softly touches the goose bumps rising all over his arms.

He pushes harder and harder, making her moan with such force that he lets loose. The pressure has erupted and somehow, he feels like a new man. He isn't quite sure why. Maybe it's because Rosary is much younger than him, but age doesn't matter to him. She's beautiful and successful. She's smart and wonderful all at the same time.

And she's a convicted murderer.

De Carlo's body shakes as he hurriedly pulls out. He suddenly yearns for her love. He wants to be with her for the rest of his life and he doesn't understand why these thoughts suddenly flow through his mind. It sounds completely crazy, and he knows it.

De Carlo is dizzy, seeing stars as he gazes into Rosary's eyes. She smiles at him, grabbing his hand with comfort. Sweat pours down the sides of her temples.

De Carlo then lies down next to her, thinking that he has disappointed her. He's old and fragile. He doesn't last as long as he used to as a young stallion.

He doesn't want her to ever leave him. He has fallen in love with her, and he can't get her off his mind most days. He loves being around her when she's happy and compassionate.

Even when she isn't in the best of moods, he still wants to protect her and love her. Most days, he's not in the best of moods. It's a match made in heaven.

Rosary stares up at the ceiling as she feels relaxed and happy. She hasn't felt relaxed in such a long time that she isn't sure HOW to feel this way.

Tony De Carlo has turned her life upside down. She isn't sure if it's been in a good way or a bad way. Some days she's grateful to have him in her life. But then, some days she regrets ever meeting him. Ever since she spoke to her sister, she has regretted giving herself up to De Carlo.

He wouldn't have arrested her that day. She knows this for a fact.

She regrets not going into hiding. Pastor Nicholas has always been there for her. He promised to be, "waiting in the wings," just like Agatha claimed to be doing.

Rosary thinks about the pastor, her sister and even her mother. She wonders who would've saved her first had she not given up like a coward. Her mother has been long gone but she wonders if her mother's influence could've helped her to snap out of her, "I'm done. I'm giving up," thoughts that ultimately caused her to spend a year in prison.

It was hell and she doesn't ever want to go back.

Rosary suddenly thinks about her sister as the warden. That bitch made her life a living hell inside of those walls. *And why?* She claimed to have been waiting to help her, but then treated her like garbage only a month after she stepped foot into that prison.

It doesn't make sense.

*Well...Agatha is just as crazy as Sherry Thomas.*

Rosary understands that she may never find the answers to her questions. She plans to kill the sibling that she's loved and known her whole life.

She can't believe that she's made that decision. But Agatha Chime is a coward, a killer, and a danger to society. She's crazy and delusional. She would never make it as a "normal" human being out in the streets. She would have to fight off the urge to kill someone walking past her.

Rosary is sad by this notion, but she tries to hide her emotions. She doesn't want De Carlo to think that she's disappointed with their five-minute lovemaking.

Rosary giggles as De Carlo kisses her hand with his sweaty mouth. He looks tired but handsome. His brown eyes sparkle with happiness and she knows how he feels about her. She can see the love in his eyes.

Rosary likes De Carlo, but she isn't sure if she LOVES him. She does have feelings for him, but they aren't as strong as his. She senses his vulnerability, and it certainly scares her quite a bit.

He has fallen for her too fast and she doesn't want to hurt his feelings. She needs time to think things through. She isn't sure if she wants to spend the rest of her life with this man.

He's too dominating and bossy. He would have to work on that issue but deep down, Rosary knows that he will not change just for her. He is who he is. If he likes to take the reins, so be it. He will just have to do it with someone else.

De Carlo is smiling from ear to ear as he gently places his finger on Rosary's cheek. She smiles back as he kisses the top of her nose.

It was such a loving gesture that Rosary suddenly feels guilty. She doesn't want to break his heart. She just wants more time to dig deep into her own heart and see where their paths lead them. If they are meant to be, then they're meant to be.

*Life works in mysterious ways,* she thinks.

De Carlo clears his throat.

*Uh-oh...he's going to profess his love for me...*

"I just want to say," De Carlo begins. Rosary places her finger on his lips.

"Let's save that for another time, shall we?" Rosary says, kissing him long and hard.

De Carlo laughs, "Of course, your highness."

Rosary bursts into laughter as she shakes her head, "I wish I was a queen."

"You're my queen," De Carlo blurts out.

Rosary frowns as she places a strand of her hair behind her ear. De Carlo's eyes are full of love and lust. He doesn't know who she truly is. He has no idea what kind of person she can become. She's truly ruthless and not his type of woman. He thinks that she is, but Rosary knows deep down in her heart that he wouldn't agree with or try to stop the things that she likes to do.

That would make him into another controlling man in her life. She doesn't want or need that type of negative energy. She wants to live freely. She doesn't want tied down, especially by an FBI agent. She would always feel like she's doing something wrong.

*Maybe that's how Jada felt. De Carlo is very domineering.*

De Carlo sees the sadness in Rosary's eyes. He decides to let the subject go. He doesn't want to upset her more than he already has.

"So, um..." De Carlo continues, "What happened to your mother's necklace?"

He twirls Rosary's hair in between his fingers, imagining Rosary twirling the jeweled necklace around her hand.

Rosary thinks for a full minute before answering, "I squeezed a little too hard."

De Carlo laughs but immediately regrets it when he sees the look on Rosary's face. That necklace was sacred. It was a momentum of her mother's past. It was who her mother was.

"I'm so sorry," De Carlo apologizes.

Rosary nods but smiles in anguish, "You are forgiven," she says, kissing De Carlo's cheek.

"Maybe I can take a look at it and try to fix it," De Carlo urges.

Rosary shrugs her shoulders, "Can't fix something that's broken. It will never be the same."

De Carlo then kisses Rosary passionately. He wants to prove how good of a man he is and can be for her. He wants her to change her mind about their relationship. He wants her to be with him. He feels sad when he thinks about her leaving.

"We're broken. We can be fixed," De Carlo begs.

Rosary kisses De Carlo's forehead and then climbs out of bed. She wraps Jada's robe around her naked body just as they hear a knock at the front door.

Rosary's heart skips a beat.

"Expecting company?" she asks.

De Carlo glares at her as he jumps up from the bed, slipping on a pair of jeans and a white T-shirt. "Of course not," he snaps. He immediately feels guilty for answering like a jerk.

He then grabs the pistol off the end table and shoves it into his back pocket.

They hear pounding and then a key entering the lock.

"Tony? Are you home!?" His partner, Tiara Mills, steps inside of the living room, closing the front door behind her. She looks around, suspicious.

"Why the hell does she have a key?!" Rosary asks, frantic.

"In case of emergencies. Go hide in the bathroom!"

Rosary grabs her stranded clothes and boots lying on the floor. She runs inside of the adjacent bathroom and throws her belongings inside of the shower tub.

She then climbs into the tub herself and shoves the curtain closed. Her heart is racing as she thinks about what will happen next. Tiara absolutely cannot see that Rosary is staying here. They will be in so much trouble. De Carlo will be fired, and Rosary will be sent back to prison.

She can't let that happen.

Rosary suddenly feels as though her hiding spot isn't good enough. She starts to panic, unsure of where to turn.

She peeks around the shower curtain and eyes the door to a closet. She then looks up at the small window above the shower.

De Carlo jogs down the staircase just as Tiara places her fingers onto the zipper of Rosary's duffel bag.

"What are you doing here?" De Carlo growls, startling Tiara.

She lets go of the zipper, embarrassed.

"You haven't been answering my calls."

"There's a reason for that," De Carlo fires back.

"Listen," Tiara says, looking around the kitchen. She notices two glasses of wine, an empty wine bottle and two plates filled with half-eaten chicken. "I know you're still upset with me. Curtis told me not to tell you anything. What am I supposed to do?"

"Oh...that's right, blame it on our boss. Oh wait...YOUR boss!"

"De Carlo, you're acting like a child. You did this to yourself. There's no one to blame but you. I don't understand you sometimes."

Tiara walks over to the kitchen table and notices a lipstick mark on the rim of Rosary's wine glass. For a split second, Tiara has the inclination to pick it up and bag it for evidence.

De Carlo watches in silence. He has this sudden urge to shoot Tiara in the head. His imagination is running wild as he watches himself lift his pistol into the air. She needs to be silenced, or she needs to mind her own damn business. *She's becoming too suspicious as she stands here with that dumb look on her face.*

"Have I interrupted?" she asks, eyeing De Carlo suspiciously.

"Yes, you have," De Carlo answers, glancing at the duffel bag sitting on the floor.

"Is it her?" Tiara asks as she exits the kitchen. She seems frantic as she charges toward De Carlo like a bull.

"Who?" De Carlo asks. He knows damn well who she's implying.

"You know who! Is she here?!" Tiara shouts as she pushes De Carlo in his chest. He takes a step back as Tiara jumps into the air, trying to smack him across the face.

De Carlo grabs both of her wrists, stopping her from attacking him a second time.

"You're out of your mind Tiara!"

She struggles, trying to release her wrists from De Carlo's fists. She cries out in pain.

De Carlo suddenly lets go of her, frightened of what he wants to do to her.

He blinks, shocked about his own thoughts. He wants to kill her. He had never envisioned hurting Tiara ever in his life. She has been his lifeline, his shoulder to cry on, his inspiration and his partner for too many years.

Tiara stares at him with tears in her eyes as she rubs the soreness from her wrists.

Without another word, Tiara quickly turns, running up the staircase toward the second floor.

She's fast as she makes it to the top of the stairs before De Carlo even places his foot on the first step. He looks up at her, angry and disoriented. He feels as though he's about to pass out. She can't see Rosary. She can't find her hiding inside of this house. De Carlo knows that his life would be over, and it would be his fault.

As he climbs the steps, he hears Tiara shout, "Rosary Chime! Come out with your hands up!"

As De Carlo reaches the top of the stairs, Tiara runs out of his bedroom, gripping her gun.

De Carlo is frantic, pulling out his pistol from his back pocket. He grips it in between both hands as he slowly walks down the hallway toward the bathroom.

Tiara enters the bathroom as she shouts again, "Rosary Chime! Come out now!"

De Carlo's heart is beating fast. The hair on the back of his neck stands up straight like a soldier in combat. His body shakes with fear as he slowly makes his way down the hallway.

He can't believe that this is happening. This night went from making love to a gorgeous woman to his partner trying to kill this said woman or arrest her. Tiara has no problem doing either one. Tiara has wanted to shoot Rosary since she found out that she escaped from prison.

Tiara doesn't care about her. As a matter of fact, she wants Rosary Chime dead. Tiara feels as though Rosary killed way too many people and deserves to receive the same outcome.

DEATH.

De Carlo can't let that happen. There's too much at stake here. If he must stop Tiara, he will, no matter what he has to do to do it.

Even if it means shooting his partner to death.

"Come out come out wherever you are!" Tiara shouts as she opens the closet door inside of the bathroom. The window above the tub is open and the chilly night air blows inside.

It feels good on Tiara's sweaty, hot skin. She's perspiring and she doesn't know if it's from running around like a chicken with its head cut off or because she's completely angry.

She's pissed.

As Tiara places her hand on the shower curtain, De Carlo steps into the bathroom, shouting, "Get the hell out of my house or I will shoot you down!"

Tiara slowly turns to De Carlo, shock and utter disgust plastered on her face.

"Oh really?" Tiara asks, "You would shoot me over some dumb bitch who murders people for a living? She's trash and you know it!"

"Go home," De Carlo responds.

Tiara turns toward the shower curtain, ripping it open and then pointing her gun at an empty tub. She's puzzled, staring at it as if it's filled with blood and guts.

Tiara suddenly nods, agreeing to her outrageous behavior, "I'm leaving."

As she walks out of the bathroom door, she places her gun inside of the back pocket of her jeans. Turning to De Carlo one last time, she says, "I'm requesting a new partner.

Don't bother talking me out of it. We were supposed to be there for each other. You're not..." she trails off.

"You're not either," De Carlo fires back, "the boss fried your brain like an egg."

Tiara shakes her head, defeated. She looks worn out and completely exhausted.

"Do what you want De Carlo. But don't come crawling back to me."

As Tiara leaves, De Carlo is frantic as he searches upstairs for any sign of Rosary.

"De Carlo!" He hears her say, frightened.

He follows the sound of her voice back inside of the bathroom. He looks around, puzzled. He checks the closet but she's not in there. He then looks out of the open window, tilting his head downward, seeing Rosary hanging from the windowsill with her fingertips gripping on for dear life.

He grabs both of her forearms and pulls her body upward, "I've got you," he encourages, gripping one of her armpits and lifting her through the window.

His foot slips and he falls backward, Rosary landing on top of his stomach.

They burst into laughter.

Then, they passionately kiss one more time. De Carlo stares at Rosary with that love in his eyes. He desperately wants her to feel the same way that he feels about her. He isn't sure how their lives will intertwine in the near future, but he hopes and prays that he gets a chance to make her fully happy. She deserves it.

"I'm going to get cleaned up. We need to get some sleep," Rosary says, smiling.

De Carlo nods in agreement. They help each other up off the floor. Then, De Carlo places a soft finger on Rosary's cheek and smiles from ear to ear. He has fallen hard for this woman.

As he leaves the bathroom to give her privacy, Rosary frowns as the door quietly closes. Her heart aches for this man. She feels incredibly guilty and saddened.

De Carlo's heart will snap into two once he finds out what she has been hiding about the investigation. He might even go crazy once she tells him that she doesn't feel love for this man.

She loves him like a friend. End of story. He has been, "friend zoned." She doesn't want a romantic relationship with not only him, but not anyone else at this moment. She needs to be alone for a while. She needs room to breathe.

She only wants her damn cat.

Rosary opens the closet and pulls out her hidden belongings of clothes and her cell phone shoved inside of her jeans pocket. She can hear the vibration of the cell phone, acknowledging that she has received a message.

Her heart skips a beat once again.

She frantically digs the phone out of the pocket and looks at a text message sent from an unknown number.

The message reads:
*Meet me at the hotel in a half hour. We need to discuss a few things.*

*Adeline Montana*

Rosary sighs. She thought that she would have one more night with De Carlo before everything would change into a hectic fiasco. His temper has frightened the hell out of her and she's afraid of his reaction to what's been going on behind his back.

Rosary places the phone back inside of her pocket. She then takes off the robe, slipping on her own clothes and combat boots. She then quickly brushes her knotty hair as she stares at herself in the vanity mirror.

She's trying to understand how her life has twirled upside-down. One minute she was a hired hit woman, to the next minute, dying inside of a jail cell, to another minute of answering to an FBI agent who needs anger management. She wants to run and hide. That's what she's done for many years. She wants to crawl inside of a hole and hide for the rest of her life.

She suddenly realizes that she does want left alone.... with her cat. She wants to live in a cabin in the mountains. She wants to hunt animals and cook them over a fire.

She is completely different from De Carlo. He lives this life of luxury inside of a beautiful home. This isn't her lifestyle. This isn't what she wants, it's not what she likes and it's not who she is. Deep down, Rosary has a feeling that De Carlo would try to change her into something she's not. He wants what she's not.

The sudden vibrating sound of her cell phone interrupts her thoughts once again.

The message reads:
*And hurry up. I will not wait long. Don't be late. Your funeral.*

Rosary shakes her head. Her sister has a lot of nerve threatening her in any type of way. *I will not have a funeral for an exceptionally long time...*

Taking a deep breath, Rosary opens the bathroom door, trying to think of something to tell De Carlo. She's going for a walk. She's running to the grocery store. She needs feminine hygiene products. Her stomach hurts, she needs medication.

She needs time to think...

Rosary steps into the bedroom and sees De Carlo lying on his back on the bed. He's snoring ferociously like a chainsaw cutting a tree down.

She exhales her breath. *Thank GOD!*

Tiptoeing, she exits the bedroom, looking over her shoulder at De Carlo as he peacefully sleeps. Her heart aches and she suddenly feels like crying. She will not though, she's stronger than that. It's time to get back to normal. She doesn't cry. She's not a sentimental person. She never, "feels bad," for hurting people's feelings.

She's a bad ass. No one can take away her self-image or personality traits.

Rosary quietly closes the bedroom door and heads toward the staircase. She sees her duffel bag still lying on the floor.

Tony De Carlo opens his eyes, gazing at his bedroom door.

Glaring; his heart pounds with anger.

Rosary steps through the revolving doors of the hotel that she has grown to know and love. She misses her room and the peace and quiet. She misses being alone and able to fart on her own accord. She misses being able to clean her weapons without judgment. She even misses the complementary meats and cheeses that she liked to stuff down her throat.

She suddenly pauses for a moment, glancing over at the receptionist. Phoenix is at the desk, talking to someone on the phone.

Rosary then searches for the newspaper-good-smelling-cop but doesn't spot him anywhere. However, she does spot a familiar detective sitting in a plush chair.

*Tiara Mills...damn it.*

Is this some sort of ruse? Is Agatha Chime playing games with her? If so, Rosary will have no problem with shooting her beloved sister right in front of the detective.

Adeline Montana would no longer be the warden of that hell hole.

Rosary pulls out a pair of sunglasses from her back pocket that she stole from De Carlo's personal items on the coffee table. She then quickly places them on her face as another detective approaches Tiara.

While talking, Tiara turns away, facing the opposite wall.

Rosary quickly glances at Phoenix as she continues her phone call, laughing as her nose snorts like a pig. She then closes her eyes, oblivious to Rosary running inside of an open elevator. She thanks another patron as she enters, pressing the number five button.

Rosary watches through the dark sunglasses as the detective walks away and heads toward the reception desk. She sighs a breath of relief. She thought for a split second that she was toast.

The elevator stops on floor five. The doors slowly open. Rosary peeks out of the doors before she exits, unsure if her sister is waiting in the hallway to attack her.

She has no trust in Agatha Chime.

She never truly did.

Rosary creeps through the hallway until she reaches room number 504. She checks the empty hallway before she knocks, hoping to not draw attention from other hotel guests.

She waits in silence.

After five minutes, she checks the time on her phone. She's not late. She's on time.

*What the hell?* She thinks to herself.

She knocks again, quietly this time.

After waiting another minute, the door slightly opens. The room is completely black.

Rosary kicks the door open and steps inside, flicking the light-switch mounted on the wall.

The room is immaculate as if no one has been inside. There are no suitcases, no complementary silver plates filled with goodies, nothing.

No Agatha Chime.

*How the hell did the door open?*

From behind, a green suede, gloved hand covers Rosary's mouth. The hand squeezes her face, trying to stop her breathing.

Rosary is smarter than this. She understands her I.Q. What she doesn't understand, is why her sister is trying to kill her. She should've known that Agatha would pull some bullshit like this. She knew not to trust her and that's why she doesn't.

She knew something was wrong as soon as she stepped foot into the hotel. She should've just turned around and headed back to De Carlo.

*I shouldn't have left in the first place.*

Rosary lifts her elbow, slamming it into Agatha's upper arm. She then drops her duffel bag as Agatha wraps her other arm around Rosary's neck, squeezing tighter.

Rosary struggles to get out of Agatha's grip.

She then punctures her elbow into Agatha's stomach, making her cry out. Rosary then grabs her sister's head and slams it into her knee.

Agatha falls backward onto the floor, holding her forehead. She isn't wearing her black ski-mask this time. She suddenly wishes that she had because that blow wouldn't have hurt so much.

Rosary lifts her boot to stomp it onto her sister's chest, but Agatha is quick, grabbing Rosary's leg and twisting it like a screw.

"Ahhhh!" Rosary shouts as her body turns, falling onto her left knee.

She kicks her foot, trying to get it out of Agatha's grip, but Agatha is quick on her feet, pulling out a pocketknife from her back pocket.

"That's all you got?" Rosary taunts.

"It's time to see mother," Agatha replies, taking the time to open the pocketknife.

Rosary takes this chance to kick her foot once again, slipping out of Agatha's grasp. Rosary quickly kicks out both of her legs like a Ninja, taking out both of Agatha's legs.

Her sister falls to the floor, dropping the knife.

"It is time for YOU to see her. You have some apologizing to do," Rosary says as they both dive for the dropped knife.

Agatha somehow takes the lead, gripping onto the knife like it's her lifeline. Rosary quickly glances at her duffel bag, contemplating if she has enough time to open it.

She dives for it, placing her fingers onto the zipper. Agatha is fast, wrapping her arm around Rosary's neck once again. She places the knife onto her sister's throat.

"See, I am faster than you," Agatha taunts.

She leads Rosary toward the bed as she continues to squeeze her throat from behind. When they reach the foot of the bed, Agatha pushes her, making her fall onto the mattress.

"I'm going to tie you up and strangle your throat just like the rest of them. You all deserve to die," Agatha threatens. She then makes her way to a bag sitting on a plush chair.

She opens it, pulling out a rope and red lipstick.

"You're going to look like another poor victim, a cheating wife."

Rosary thinks for a moment.

"And you don't?" Rosary asks, acting as if she's confused.

"Don't what?" Agatha asks as she returns to the bed.

"Deserve to die?" Rosary asks as she watches Agatha tie the rope into a noose.

Agatha chuckles as she looks up at her sister with bright eyes. "We all deserve to die, don't we? We all need to pay for our sins!" Agatha yells as she lifts both arms up into the air.

"You don't have to preach to me. I just want to know why you're doing this. I thought we were going to talk things through. You wanted me to join your crusade."

"Well," Agatha says, lowering her arms, "I had a change of heart. I just don't trust you at all. I know your line of work. I'm sure you had other plans as well."

Rosary chuckles as she glances at her dropped duffel bag.

"You think you're slick, don't you?" Rosary asks as she sits up from the bed.

Agatha pushes her back down, howling with laughter. "I don't think. I know."

"Alright," Rosary continues, "Let me ask you something. How do you know that I didn't mention this rendezvous to De Carlo?"

Agatha thinks for a moment. She smiles, "Because we all know that you're smarter than that. You wouldn't want him to ruin this happy reunion."

Rosary nods, "And did you know that there are plenty of cops downstairs in the lobby?"

Agatha stops messing with the tangled rope for a moment, glaring into Rosary's eyes.

"I call you bluff," she says, strutting toward the bed post, trying to tie the rope around Rosary's right wrist. Rosary puts up a fight, moving her wrist into circles.

Suddenly and without another thought, Rosary screams at the top of her lungs.

She isn't sure why. She knows damn well that Detective Mills is downstairs, waiting for another murder to take place right under her nose.

She then screams, "HELP ME!" as Agatha covers her mouth with her gloved hand.

Rosary is erratic, slamming her body onto the mattress as if she's possessed by a demon. She then shoves the bed against the wall, making it sound as if she was having rough sex.

The bed pounds against the wall... BOOM, BOOM, BOOM...

"Stop it!" Agatha shouts as she increasingly tries to tie the rope around Rosary's other wrist.

Rosary suddenly punches Agatha right into her nose, making it bleed. She then hurriedly punches her a second time, right into her mouth.

Agatha stumbles backward then falls to the floor onto her buttocks. Rosary quickly jumps up from the bed, rushing toward her duffel bag. She hurriedly opens it as Agatha holds her bloody nose and mouth with her gloved hand.

As Rosary reaches for her rifle, Agatha asks, "Is that all you can do?"

Rosary chuckles as she checks the rifle for ammo. Quickly, she then points it at Agatha, watching her through the scope.

Agatha leans her back against a wall, holding her broken nose in her hand.

She watches Rosary through the scope of the rifle, pain in her eyes.

"You won't do it," Agatha taunts, "You're too big of a bitch!" she spits blood.

Rosary's body is shaking with tears in her eyes. She wants to shoot and kill her sister once for all. She deserves to die. She hurt innocent people.

*So did you,* her mind is taunting her brain.

They can hear hotel security running down the hallway. They pound on the door as they shout, "Open the door!"

Agatha smiles with bloody teeth. Shakily, she stands up from the floor and makes her way toward the balcony, looking over her shoulder at her confused-looking sister.

*Do not let her get away Rosary.*

Security pounds on the door once again. Rosary watches as Agatha opens the sliding glass door leading out to the balcony. Rosary continues to point the rifle at her sister's head.

Rosary's breathing is hard and fast. She's sweating profusely as she hears a key enter the lock out in the hallway. Everything feels like she's living in slow motion.

Agatha disappears. Rosary can no longer view her from the scope of the rifle.

She feels as if she let herself down. She feels like a complete failure once again. She couldn't do it. Agatha was right. She's nothing but a soft bitch.

Her sister knew that she would get away once again. Rosary can't handle that type of pressure. She had her right in the palm of her hand, but she couldn't make the move.

She couldn't shoot her sister.

Emilio was right. Her heart is too soft.

Rosary snaps out of her dream of running down the emergency exit and escaping with her sister. She has done nothing but contemplate on taking her sister's offer of them, "riding into the sunset." It would be amazing to have a sister duo of hit women.

Rosary jumps from the floor, grabs her duffel bag and slides underneath the bed like a baseball player sliding toward home base. She closes her eyes, panting like a thirsty dog.

The door bursts open. Security guards and FBI agents pour into the room like sugar inside of a juice pitcher.

Detective Anthony De Carlo steps inside of the empty hotel room. He gestures toward his fellow officers, pointing toward the balcony doors.

He looks at the unkempt bed and the rope tied into a noose. He's puzzled, slowly taking steps toward the bathroom as he glances around the cleaned and unused room.

He checks the bathroom, searching inside of the closet, the tub, opening the window and looking out into the night air. He looks down, seeing streetlamps and pedestrians walking past with confused expressions upon their faces.

He returns to the room, glancing toward the bed as his officers come in from the balcony. They shake their heads "no" as they close the sliding glass door.

De Carlo saw her peeking. She thinks she's slick.

"I'll take over from here," De Carlo tells the officers.

"No, you're not," one of the officers' replies, standing his ground, "You're suspended until further notice. I'm not sure why you're here or what you're up to."

De Carlo glares at the officer, unsure of how to proceed. He doesn't want to be caught.

"I was requested to be brought in," De Carlo lies.

There was a sense of untrustworthiness that brought him here in the first place. Rosary was acting skittishly, and De Carlo knew that something was up. She was in a hurry. He had to follow her. He had to find out what she was hiding.

"So," he continues, "I would appreciate it if you would follow my orders and get the hell out of here before I call your superior."

The officers shake their heads, obviously unfathomed by his threats. They laugh as they exit the room, looking over their shoulders as De Carlo steps toward the bed once again.

"It looks like we've missed our mark again," De Carlo says to the remaining officers, "Let's go to the main lobby and discuss things with Detective Mills."

The officers disperse, leaving De Carlo alone in the room.

His heart pounds as he thinks of something sophisticated to say. He doesn't want to sound stupid. He doesn't even want to sound rude. Rosary Chime is a smart cookie and knows how to handle a smart-ass mouth.

As he continues to stand above the bed, he glances at his watch. "We have about one minute before Tiara Mills steps inside of this room. I suggest we move it along."

Rosary climbs out from underneath the bed, gripping her duffel bag over her shoulder. De Carlo grabs her arm, and they hurriedly run out onto the balcony.

They climb down the emergency exit in silence.

Rosary never imagined that she would be escaping from a hotel room with a suspended FBI agent. If someone would've told her this a year ago, she would've laughed in their face.

They run through the alleyway. Then, De Carlo leads Rosary around the building, turning left and bolting down the sidewalk toward his vehicle.

They hurry inside, slamming their doors in silence.

De Carlo peels off toward the direction of his house.

He sacrificed his career to help save her once again. Quite frankly, he's tired of saving her and not receiving anything in return. He knew she was hiding something, but he never imagined it had something to do with the killer.

He feels betrayed. He feels lost and alone.

"I was able to distract Tiara with a phone call at the desk," De Carlo offers to start the conversation. Rosary is silent, looking ahead as the light turns green.

De Carlo is angry. He feels the heat rise into his cheeks. He can no longer hold his frustration inside of his enraged body. It feels as if it's about to erupt like a volcano.

Suddenly, De Carlo pulls over onto the side of the road. He gets out and slams his fist onto the driver side door. His heart is raging with fire. Rosary sits there staring into space.

De Carlo stomps around the vehicle to the passenger side door. He swings it open, gripping Rosary's right arm, angrily pulling her out. He then slams the door shut, pushing her body up against it. He grips her throat into his bulky fist and squeezes hard.

258 – ANGELA SANNER

"I could kill you right now and no one would know. I could throw you into the trunk and dump your body into a lake, or river, whichever you prefer."

How nice of him to give her an option.

Rosary continues to be silent. She lets him choke her to death.

Tears are quietly spilling out of her eyes. She doesn't care anymore. She's worthless anyways. She couldn't take the shot.

*I couldn't take the damn shot!*

It's eating her alive. Her body has given up this fight. Her depression has taken over and she can't even speak a word to De Carlo. Nothing comes out. It's as if her lips have been glued shut.

Her brain is frozen in time. She doesn't even know what she's doing or where she's at. She can't focus on De Carlo's angry face. He's a ball of blur.

De Carlo continues to choke her as spit flies from his mouth, landing onto her nose and cheeks. He sees the sadness in her eyes and suddenly loosens his grip. But he then grabs her jaw into his fist and makes her stare into his eyes.

"I trusted you. I've taken care of you. I love you," De Carlo says. Rosary is quiet as she stares into De Carlo's angry eyes.

He continues, "You betrayed me. You've hurt me. You've lied to me."

Rosary doesn't know how to respond. De Carlo is right. She did all those things, and she doesn't know how to apologize. She doesn't know what to do to make it right.

"You've kept pertinent information from me," De Carlo continues. He's expecting a reaction from her, but she doesn't give him one.

"So, I have a new plan Rosary Chime," he says, loosening his grip on her jaw. Rosary continues to stare into his eyes. She wants him to see the hurt and pain. She wants it embedded inside of his brain.

She doesn't want him to forget this moment.

She wants him to know how much he's hurting her, physically. Her neck is throbbing, and her jaw feels like it's about to explode. But she doesn't want to give him satisfaction. She doesn't want to admit the pain by complaining.

"You will contact the killer and make arrangements to meet at the church," De Carlo orders, letting go of her jaw. "After that, you will go there and hide in a secure location. You will then shoot him. I don't care where, as long it kills him."

De Carlo is waiting for a response. Rosary stares into space.

"Do I make myself clear?" he asks, watching her blink back tears.

After a painful minute, Rosary nods, agreeing to this ridiculous "plan" of his. He thinks it will happen, "just like that," as in a snap of a finger.

It will not...but whatever makes him feel happy. She will do it.

"Good," De Carlo says, tapping the top of her head like she's a five-year-old child. "Now, get in before we're caught out in the open."

They both climb back into his vehicle.

He speeds off in silence. He has nothing more to say to her. He isn't sure how to feel about her anymore. The love is still there, but he's starting to realize that it may be lust and attraction that's pulling him toward her like gravity.

He knew this from the beginning, but he hoped and prayed for something more.

Rosary looks up; she moves her fingers as if the rosary necklace were still there, intertwining it with her hand.

"It's my sister," she simply whispers.

# SEVENTEEN

De Carlo is somber, reluctant to speak another word to Rosary Chime. A bomb had blown in his direction, and he let it blow up in his face. A flame has ignited inside of his skull and he's trying to blow it out. He's trying to end this madness once and for all.

He watches Rosary as she rocks back and forth on a rocking chair outside on the deck. The backyard is peaceful and tranquil as she grips her sniper rifle in between her fingers. The chilly air outside and the warmth inside makes the window foggy from De Carlo's hot breath.

She has been sitting there in that position for about an hour. It's getting extremely late, and De Carlo is having a hard time keeping his eyes open.

But now is not the time for sleep.

It's time to forgive and forget. It's time to finally end this war with Adeline Montana.

*Agatha Chime...whatever the hell her name is...*

De Carlo isn't sure if he's more upset about chasing a woman killer or the fact that his wife cheated on him with a woman. This scenario has completely blown his mind, and he isn't sure how to move forward. He may have trust issues with any woman that he encounters.

*Especially Rosary Chime...*

He thought they were partners. He thought she would become his lover, his friend, his woman to show off.

*Who am I kidding? She's out of my league.*

He's out in left field while Rosary is playing first base. She's better at making people feel like crap. She's better at hiding secrets and keeping important information to herself.

She's better at hurting people's feelings, whether she knows it or not.

His heart is crushed, wasted, and smashed into pieces like a broken mirror. He imagines taking one of those pieces of broken glass and...

He stops. That isn't him. Rosary Chime isn't worth his life. He has come to that conclusion as soon as he heard her whispered words.

*It's my sister...*

The warden of the prison is her sister, and she didn't know it. That in itself is crazy. It was a shock to find out that he had paid two siblings with two different agendas.

De Carlo is still trying to put together the pieces of the puzzle about Agatha Chime. He doesn't understand why she treated Rosary the way she did inside of those prison walls. She wanted to help her escape the wrath of De Carlo. She didn't want her caught and arrested.

*Maybe she was jealous of Rosary's fame. She was well-loved by fans and supported by many. It could be a triangle of jealousy, love and picking up the pieces of a broken family.*

De Carlo knows at this point, he will never find out the answers to his questions. And quite frankly, he doesn't care to get them. These two women deserve each other. They both deserve to rot in hell. His feelings for Rosary have subsided. There's a pinch of love there but he doesn't want to sprinkle it on top of any more thoughts or actions.

He wants left alone when this is all over. He needs a break. Maybe he will take Curtis up on that offer and take a long vacation.

*I might not come back...*

He wants to buy a boat and sail on the sea. It's a lifetime commitment and he's ready for it.

He wants crystal blue waters and the sun beating on his head. He wants to drink cocktails with pretty ladies. He doesn't want to worry about drama and cheating. He could rotate women and do whatever he wants. He would have that power and luxury.

His bubbles of fine ladies suddenly pop as he watches Rosary pick up her cell phone from a small drink table next to the chair. The screen lights up but De Carlo can't see what she's doing.

He knows it's time. De Carlo told Rosary what she had to do. She agreed but he still doesn't believe her. All the trust that he had for this woman is now thrown out of a window.

She places the phone up to her ear.

Rosary waits for her sister to answer her call. She isn't sure if she will at this point. Everything has gone to shit. Agatha had the nerve to try and kill her.

Rosary still can't process this issue. She never expected Agatha to turn on her, EVER. They didn't have the best childhood, but they were always there for each other. They both went through the same bullshit with their mother. Agatha promised to always be there for Rosary. She is the older one, she was the protector.

Rosary tries to ignore the sadness and pain as the phone continues to ring.

*Pick up dammit!*

Rosary knows that she must follow De Carlo's orders because if not, he threatened to put her back into prison. He threatened to lie and say she escaped with the help of her sister, and only her sister. He threatened to deny being involved in anything. He said that he would make it look like they forced him and threatened his life if he didn't do what they both said.

He's good...damn good.

Rosary isn't one hundred percent sure if his boss would believe that bullshit, but De Carlo is willing to try anything at this point. He's only looking out for himself.

And Rosary doesn't blame him.

That's all she's done her whole entire life. It's time to make a change. She needs to end this battle with Agatha Chime. Rosary knows deep down in her heart that she's the only one who can stop her. She's the only one who can pick up the pieces of a broken family.

Agatha may be older, but she isn't wiser. She isn't smarter. She isn't more powerful.

The line stops ringing and Agatha's voice interrupts Rosary's thoughts, "Why am I not surprised? Miss me already?"

Rosary smiles a devilish grin.

"Of course, that's why I would like to meet up with you again," Rosary replies.

"And why in the world would I do that?"

"We need to discuss some things, and you know it."

There's silence at the other end of the line. Rosary looks at the screen to make sure that Agatha hasn't hung up on her. She can hear Agatha's soft breathing and then a quiet giggle.

"You're right but that doesn't mean that we should. I don't think there's any more left to say to each other. How about we go our separate ways?"

Rosary thinks about her offer for a moment. The idea is delightful, but it isn't customary to ignore a serial killer on the loose.

"Separate ways? And let you continue to kill innocent women?"

Agatha laughs, "Innocent? Hardly..."

This conversation is going nowhere. Rosary is sick of her sister's bad attitude and bossiness. She has always gotten the upper hand growing up and Rosary will not let it happen again.

She can't. Agatha is a menace to society. She needs squashed like a deadly spider.

"Meet me at the church in thirty minutes," Rosary demands, "We need to end this once and for all."

Agatha laughs once again. This makes Rosary's blood boil. Agatha thinks that everything is a joke. She laughs at serious situations. She always has.

She laughed when she killed their mother.

"Once and for all...for who? This will never end my sweet little sister."

Rosary shakes her head in frustration, "Let's talk about what CAN end."

Silence at the other end of the line once again. Rosary takes a deep breath as she closes her eyes. The exhaustion has hit her like a ton of bricks. She can barely keep her eyes open any longer. She wishes that De Carlo would wait one more night.

Rosary checks the time on her phone. It's three o'clock in the morning.

Agatha exhales her breath, "Fine. Thirty minutes. If you're late even one minute, I'm leaving and that would be the end of our communication."

Rosary nods in agreement. She would rather lose all contact with this bitch. She wishes that Agatha would pack her stuff and leave the country for good.

"Mom's church," Rosary reminds her.

Agatha laughs again before she hangs up the phone.

In anger, Rosary throws her phone out into the yard. It lands with a thud in the wet grass.

De Carlo watches Rosary as she breaks down in tears. He never thought that such a strong and powerful woman could cry this much in her life. This situation has taken its toll on her mind and body. She's ready to be done with it all.

She's ready to give up once again.

But she knows that she can't right at this moment. People's lives are at stake. As long as Rosary keeps Agatha occupied, she will not be killing anyone else.

Rosary suddenly turns to look at De Carlo through the window. She knew he had been standing there, watching her like a hawk. Somehow, she could feel his hot breath on the back of her neck.

He looks at her with sadness in his eyes as she gives him a thumbs up. De Carlo nods, closing the curtain and giving her some privacy.

He then fills the ammo to his pistol, checking the time on his watch.

Twenty-eight minutes...

Thirteen minutes later, Rosary and De Carlo climb out of his vehicle as the frosty night air slaps them in the face. Rosary feels the burning sensation under her eyelids. Her eyes are fighting to stay open. She can't afford to lose this next shot and miss her only opportunity.

They both search around the church for any signs of Agatha. They were hoping to get there before she did to give Rosary enough time to set up her rifle.

De Carlo walks ahead of Rosary with his pistol pointing into the night air. He walks around the building as Rosary climbs the emergency ladder leading up to the roof of the church.

She hides behind the chimney and sets up the rifle stand. She then watches De Carlo make his way behind a tree in the woods next to the church.

As Rosary places her rifle onto the stand, she spots headlights coming about fifteen feet away from the church.

She turns toward the direction of De Carlo and clicks her fingers to get his attention. He's still gripping onto his pistol, his eye squinted and ready to pull the trigger.

He looks up at Rosary and she points her finger toward the road. She then places her finger onto her lips, shushing him.

De Carlo has waited for this moment. If he has a clear shot, he has every intention of taking it. He doesn't trust Rosary at all and if he has to take matters into his own hands, he will in a heartbeat. Rosary is too sentimental with this case.

He doesn't blame her though. After all, it is her sister that she was hired to kill in cold blood.

The headlights turn off as Rosary peeks through the scope of her rifle. She can see the driver's side door to Agatha's red Saturn quietly close. Agatha's long, brown hair pulled up into a ponytail.

She's ready for a fight.

She's wearing a pair of gray sweatpants, a black sweatshirt and a pair of old tennis shoes. She quietly tiptoes toward the church. She's prepared to run as well.

Agatha's heart pounds as she spots De Carlo's vehicle hidden under trees on the edge of the woods. She knew it would be a trap, that's why she planned her clothing accordingly.

Agatha honestly thought that her sister wanted to talk and make amends.

She feels stupid. She feels betrayed and confused. She heard the urgency in her sister's voice just thirty minutes ago. She was begging for unity.

Agatha realizes that it was all a ruse in order to end her life, right here and right now. She never imagined dying in front of her mother's church. She absolutely hates this place. She grew up coming to this dump Sunday after Sunday after Sunday.

The only thing Sherry Thomas did was beg for forgiveness her sins. Pastor Nicholas would take their mother into his arms and give her a big hug. He always told her that everything would be okay. He told her that he would always be there for her and her daughters.

Agatha grunts as she spots a shadow on the roof.

"Not tonight, Rosary," Agatha says as she spots De Carlo stepping out from behind a tree.

As she turns to run back to her car, Rosary fires the rifle, purposely missing Agatha's head. The bullet pierces through the windshield of Agatha's car.

Agatha then jumps into her red Saturn, screaming obscenities. She knew she shouldn't have come. She knew De Carlo would be behind this as well. Her sister can't fight her own battles.

She speeds off down the street, watching De Carlo as he points his pistol at her. Rosary stands up from behind the chimney, pointing the barrel of the rifle at the car's front tire.

Rosary knows she can stop her but she's waiting to see if De Carlo pulls his trigger first.

*Stop her, you coward! Shoot her tires out! Do it now Rosary Chime!*

She watches the car through the scope as it drives further away. When it's out of sight, she can hear De Carlo's anger. He's screaming obscenities and cursing Rosary for her betrayal.

Her heart pounds with fear. She has never seen him this angry.

She quietly collects her items and then climbs down the emergency ladder toward the side of the building. When her feet hit the grass, she feels strong hands grip around her waist.

*This is it; this is my time to die.*

De Carlo slams her back up against the building. As he lifts her up into the air, he squeezes her neck, choking the life out of her. Rosary sees stars as De Carlo's face has become blurry. She can't keep her eyes open. The exhaustion has hit her like a ton of bricks, and she has given up.

As she chokes, she tries to grab onto De Carlo's wrist. She digs her nails into it, but it doesn't faze him. It doesn't stop him from squeezing tighter.

"I knew I couldn't trust you. Filthy bitch!" De Carlo shouts, "I want her dead! Do you hear me? I realized it wasn't supposed to be me! YOU are the one to kill her!"

Right at this moment, Rosary would rather be back in prison. As much as she hated it, she hates De Carlo more. She has lost all hope for their friendship. She has lost every feeling that she has had for the man. He thinks that he can just threaten her life and get away with it.

"If not, I will kill you myself!" De Carlo shouts as he squeezes harder.

De Carlo didn't have a good shot. He thinks of this as he imagines killing Rosary Chime.

She can't breathe and she's losing oxygen. She struggles, kicking her feet against the building and trying to loosen the grip from De Carlo's fingers.

As she swallows what seems like her last breath, she sees a blurry figure come up from behind De Carlo. The agent is immediately struck in the head with an object, falling to the ground as his hand lets go of Rosary's neck.

Rosary falls to the ground next to De Carlo. He's knocked out cold as blood pours from the back of his head.

Pastor Nicholas bends down on his knees, placing a soft hand on Rosary's forehead.

"It will be okay my child. You're safe now."

Rosary's blue eyes slowly open. She sees cream-colored walls and a gigantic fan on the ceiling. She sees paintings of crosses and a picture of Jesus above a fireplace.

She recognizes this room. It's Pastor Nicholas's sanctuary, the church's office.

She's lying on a black leather couch with a pink crochet blanket covering her frigid body. The fireplace crackles but there are only two logs burning for warmth.

Rosary spots Pastor Nicholas kneeling in front of the fireplace, praying for his sins. She wants to thank him for saving her life. De Carlo would have killed her.

*De Carlo....*

His head had been smashed with a two-by-four. She remembers now. Pastor Nicholas could have possibly killed De Carlo.

Rosary quickly sits up, searching the room for the agent. Her sudden headache hits her as if she suddenly ran into a wall. She cries out, placing a hand onto her sweaty forehead.

The pastor turns, frowning.

"You need to rest dear," he says, helping her to lie back down on the couch. He's calm and quiet as he looks at Rosary with love in his eyes. He so desperately wanted her for a daughter. He tried to make the Chime family feel happy and secure. Sherry Thomas was a stubborn devil.

"Where's De Carlo?" Rosary asks as Pastor Nicholas places a cold, wet rag onto her forehead. She's burning up, feeling drowsy and weak. Her body shivers from the cold. She feels sick to her stomach.

"I drove him to the hospital. I pray that he overcomes his injuries," the pastor replies.

He then pours water from a pitcher into a wine glass. He opens a bottle of headache medicine and picks out two pills.

As he hands them to her, he smiles.

"Thank you," Rosary says, swallowing the pills as she drinks the water.

The pastor takes a deep breath, "Forgive me father for I have sinned." He glances at Rosary and sadly smiles, "As a man of GOD, I apologize for hurting your friend."

Rosary nods, she isn't sure what to say. De Carlo deserved it. She was on the brink of being choked to death. The pastor saved her life, and she doesn't know how to ever repay him.

"I just couldn't bear to watch my little girl die by the hands of a beast from hell."

Rosary smiles as she feels a love of warmth cradle her heart. Pastor Nicholas has always been her father-figure for as long as she has known him.

"He's actually on my side, pastor. I've hurt him badly, lost his trust. I don't blame him for feeling such anger."

She feels ashamed and embarrassed at the same time. She doesn't want the pastor to know every detail but she's sure that he would listen if she tried.

"Agatha and I are in trouble," Rosary continues, "We don't see eye to eye."

Pastor Nicholas nods, "I feared that this would happen someday. I prayed that it wouldn't."

"Well, sometimes praying doesn't help a situation," Rosary says. She immediately regrets it as she looks at the pastor's saddened eyes.

"That is correct, but it doesn't hurt to try," the pastor answers, smiling.

His cheerful outlook has always stamped her heart with love.

The man is charismatic, loyal, caring, and undoubtedly honest to the core. Rosary has never understood why her mother pushed him away. She could've lived a meaningful and pleasant life with him. All of them could have. Maybe they wouldn't have turned out to be so crazy and wild.

"There's always a solution to a problem. You just have to figure out what that solution is... even if the LORD doesn't agree. GOD loves you no matter what. He will be there to guide you and support you. And so will I, you've always known that."

The pastor takes Rosary's hand into his, "Remember, you have to make a choice that saves your life and the lives of others. If something negative is impacting your quality of life, you have to remove it, whether you want to or not."

Rosary thinks about his statement for three minutes as silence fills the air. Then, the pastor stands up and pours himself a glass of water. As he takes a sip, he watches her mind twirl with endless possibilities and questions that will never be answered.

*Is he giving me permission to KILL Agatha? He must know what's going on, or at least have a sense of it. He has always known what's best for me. But I never listened to him...*

"It's about time that I took your advice. You must remove the old in order to move on with the new," Rosary says, smiling from ear to ear.

Pastor Nicholas nods, smiling a devilish smile, "That's a good girl."

# EIGHTEEN

Rosary feels refreshed and quite happy after leaving Pastor Nicholas's church. Talking with him truly opened her eyes to a better life. He's prepared to let her go if it means she lives in a sea full of happiness and relaxation.

"It's not goodbye, it's see you later," the pastor had said before Rosary stepped out into the sunshine. The warm, morning wind blew her hair out from behind her ears.

She decided to bury her duffel bag, the rifle stand, and her old rifle she received from Emilio, into the ground as a precaution in case she's caught once again. Pastor Nicholas promised to keep her belongings safe. He also promised not to say a word about her visit to the church.

He will keep his word. He always has. He will never in his life rat her out. She's leaving with a piece of his heart...which was crushed as he watched her leave with her red rifle strapped over her shoulder. She's ready for combat. She's ready to fight like a soldier.

Pastor Nicholas will pray for her. He will pray for her sins.

The almighty GOD will protect her and heal her heart.

Rosary smiles as she walks through downtown New York. The city is bustling with workers heading toward their useless jobs, homeless people begging for money, kids running the streets like they have nowhere to go.

Rosary, on the other hand, knows where to go. She knows who to deal with. For the moment, she doesn't have Tony De Carlo breathing down her neck.

She called the hospital before she left the church. He's in stable condition and should be released tomorrow.

Rosary sighed relief. She wouldn't be able to explain his death to his boss or his partner. Well, EX partner. Tiara Mills received a new partner this morning while he's lying in a hospital bed due to negligence on his part. He assumed that no one else had been there at the church.

Rosary had silently prayed for guidance. She had hoped that Pastor Nicholas was, "waiting in the wings," for her. He knows she comes back to him for safety and security. She can always count on him. As long as he's alive, he will always be there for her.

Rosary smiles as she turns the corner of the café. She pauses for a moment to take a deep breath. The warm air sucks through her nose and into her brain.

She feels alive once again. She feels like her old self. She feels strong and committed to completing her last mission.

This WILL be the last one. She no longer wants to be killer. She no longer wants to take innocent lives like Agatha Chime does.

Rosary feels at peace for once in her life. She has come to terms with the loss of her mother, the loss of Daryl, the loss of friendship with De Carlo and the soon-to-be loss of her beloved sister. She knows this is the end of this chapter in her life.

She needs to move on.

Rosary continues down the dirt path which then changes into gravel. Her heart pounds for the unknown. She envisions a scenario happening inside of her mind.

She takes a clean shot.

She has to. This is the moment they have been waiting for. Agatha knows that her sister will not stop until her mission is complete.

Rosary Chime doesn't back down. She stands her ground and kicks her fear in the butt. The only thing she's worried about is Agatha's henchmen. Rosary doesn't want to kill anyone else. Her purpose for arriving is for one individual only.

As she envisions kicking these henchmen like a Ninja, she moves into the tall grass alongside the daisies so as not to step on them. She plans to take her time and try to stay hidden behind trees. She wants to be sure that she creeps into this warehouse without being seen on camera. The only thing is, Rosary isn't sure how many cameras are placed inside and where they are facing.

Agatha has always lived inside of a treasure box filled with secrets by the devil.

The grass is wet by the morning dew and Rosary's combat boots are turning into wet mush. She hopes and prays that this doesn't slow her down. She doesn't want to slip and fall if she has to make a run from death.

Rosary isn't sure who is inside. She's not even sure if Agatha is home.

If she isn't, Rosary will be, "waiting in the wings," until she is.

When Rosary reaches the half-way point, her forehead starts to perspire. The warm spring air has finally arrived once again. The heat is making her sweat under her breasts.

She wants to take a small break, but she knows that will not be a clever idea. Agatha's men could potentially be watching her, waiting to take their clean shot.

She must move forward in order to end this war, a sibling war.

Rosary kind of likes the sound of that; a war between two sisters who haven't seen each other in ten years. The love is still there but power has taken over their ability to move on.

Good versus evil, devil versus angel...well...neither one of them are an angel.

Rosary laughs as she thinks of them floating in the clouds with wings on their backs. It would never happen. They know damn well that they're both going to hell when they die.

Then, they would be fighting about who would take over the throne.

It's quite impossible to be in the same vicinity or area as Agatha Chime. Her powers are reckless, and they would never see eye-to-eye with any given situation. Agatha believes that she is always right. Rosary believes that SHE is always right.

They could never meet in the middle...so one of them must go.

Rosary prays that it's not her.

She squeezes her hand as if her mother's necklace intertwined within her fingers. She's needed that to calm herself down. It was her treasure and now it's gone, breaking her heart.

Rosary closes her eyes as she continues down the path of destruction and mayhem. Agatha's world is about to be flipped upside-down.

Her world is about to end.

Rosary can feel the wetness sinking into the bottom of her socks. Maybe walking through the grass wasn't such a good idea. But it doesn't leave her vulnerable to an open area with cameras staring into her face.

"Forgive me father for I have sinned," Rosary whispers as her eyes continue to stay closed. She walks alongside the trees, almost running into one.

She stops to catch her breath, opening her eyes. The warehouse is about twenty feet in front of her. She hides behind a tree, peeking around the corner, waiting for someone to come out.

She pauses for what seems like an eternity. Her heart is pounding through her chest.

She wants to see the look on her sister's face when she pierces a bullet through her brain.

Sherry Thomas would be ashamed of them both, fighting this way. Their mother never wanted this to happen. When the girls were young, Sherry had them promise that they would always be there for each other. They were to respect one another and help each other when times were tough. Sherry knew that there would be conflicting issues between the two, but she wouldn't have wanted this. She wouldn't have wanted one of them or possibly both of them to die over their differences. They are the complete opposite to say the least, but they promised never to hurt each other or turn their backs on one another.

They both lied to their mother's face.

They were young. They were stupid. They were full of ideas and neither one of them agreed with the other. They knew how different they were from each other.

They knew that there would be a war. It was only a matter of time.

As Rosary approaches the side of the warehouse, she draws her rifle, peeking through the scope, breathing hard and rapidly. Her chest quickly rises and falls as if she's about to have a panic attack. That would be the worst thing that could happen at this very moment.

She searches the area through the scope and tries to listen for any movement or voices.

She hears nothing but birds chirping and a plane flying in the distance.

She then checks the window that she had crawled inside of the last time she was there. It is still unlocked and unsecured, enabling her to crawl through.

Rosary slowly climbs through it, the rifle still gripped into her fist.

She wants to be prepared in case someone jumps out from behind those huge barrels of gas.

Once inside, she creeps through the room, pointing the rifle in every direction. She moves behind the barrels and sees that the area is empty.

She sighs, nodding.

Closing her eyes, she whispers, "You can do this Rosary Chime. It's time to fight the beast."

The warehouse is too quiet. *Where the hell is everyone?*

Rosary suddenly pictures Agatha's henchmen waiting for her by the front doors with guns drawn. She pictures herself surrounded by hundreds of men, pointing their weapons at her head.

Rosary shakes the thoughts from her mind as she takes a deep breath. She slowly places her hand on the door handle and turns the knob.

The click of the door opening sounds like a drum to her ears. It seems extremely loud inside of this quiet warehouse. She feels like a rat sneaking for a piece of cheese.

Stepping out of the hidden room filled with guns and knives, she quietly walks through the warehouse, taking each step with ease. She searches the area through the scope of her rifle, her anxiety jumping through the roof.

As she turns the corner, she passes stacked boxes and pallets once again.

Agatha Chime feels a draft on the back of her neck. She's sipping a glass of wine as she holds her cell phone up to her ear.

She pauses in mid-drink, then slowly places the glass onto a table. She then hangs up the phone, slipping it into her pants pocket.

Rosary watches her through the scope, hoping and praying that Agatha doesn't hear her.

*Take the damn shot!*

Agatha suddenly raises her arms into the air, surrendering. She cries fake tears, slowly turning to face her sister.

But Rosary jumps behind a stack of boxes, breathing hard and calling herself a "bitch." The area is empty, and Agatha looks puzzled. She keeps her arms raised as she smiles, hearing the panting sound of Rosary trying to catch her breath.

Agatha continues her fake crying, hoping for Rosary to change her mind. She knew her sister was coming for her. It was a no-brainer. She prepared for this. She told her men to leave because she wanted to face Rosary alone. It is their battle and no one else's.

Her men begged for at least two men to stay but Agatha refused.

"I can take care of myself," she told them as she kicked them out.

Agatha looks around the empty warehouse. Rosary could be hiding behind the boxes to her right or the stack of pallets to the left of her. She can be hiding behind the dresser that's about fifteen feet away or underneath the bed that's about ten feet away.

Agatha turns slightly to the left, looking into the direction of her red Saturn. She could be hiding behind her car for all she knows.

Agatha doesn't want to feel defeated. She wants Rosary to think that she has the upper hand for now. Agatha has every intention of biting her like a venomous snake; letting the poison enter her veins and flow into her heart.

*It's time for Rosary Chime to go straight to hell.*

Rosary holds her breath as she peeks around the stack of boxes. She feels like a wuss.

She can't believe she's hiding this way. This is not what she came here for. She had every intention of TAKING A CLEAN SHOT!

*It's time for Agatha Chime to go straight to hell.*

"Go ahead and do it," Agatha pleads as she searches the warehouse for any signs of where her sister may be, "Just know...that I love you."

Her words are like a stab in the heart. Of course she would make Rosary feel awful for this decision. She has to make her feel guilty to get the upper hand.

Well...not anymore. Rosary will not let her make her feel this way. She has come to complete her final mission. She will make Tony De Carlo proud.

She will make herself proud. She has to.

Agatha's heart pounds as she immediately regrets not keeping a weapon strapped to her body. Her henchmen told her it would be a clever idea. Of course, she didn't listen to them.

She's the boss, not THEM.

That's where her stubbornness kicks in. Everyone thinks that they have the right to tell her what to do.

Sherry Thomas thought that she had the right too as well. Agatha proved her wrong.

Agatha giggles, "Remember that time when mom caught me sneaking out of the house that night of the slumber party to which I was invited? She grabbed my butt and pulled me like a rag doll. I'll never forget the look on her face. She was mad but she wanted to laugh at the same time," Agatha pauses, waiting for a response. When she doesn't receive one, she continues, "It was the first time I called her a 'bitch' for making me late to the party. She slapped me across the face while laughing. I couldn't believe it. That was the moment that I realized that our mother was genuinely insane."

Agatha waits for Rosary to respond but Rosary is smarter than that. If she replies, then Agatha will know her exact hiding spot.

"She laughed with tears in her eyes. She then told me to go and never come back," Agatha continues, "But she did let me come back in order to pimp me out. She had to make that money. She couldn't afford to lose me. I was her best client."

Rosary shakes her head. She desperately wants to call her sister a fool. She can hear Agatha laugh; the sound reminds her of their mother. It's a cackling witch sound that vibrates throughout Rosary's brain. That laugh used to haunt her mind day after day.

Rosary used to call it, "the crazy laugh."

"The good ole days," Agatha continues as she keeps her arms raised in surrender, "Come out come out wherever you arrreeee."

Rosary has had enough. She's done hiding.

As she steps out from behind the stack of boxes, Agatha smiles, nodding.

"I should've known you were that close. You're like a Ninja in the night."

Rosary nods, laughing as she slowly takes two steps toward her sister, pointing the rifle at her head. She watches Agatha through the scope.

"You want me to beg for my life?" Agatha asks, laughing again.

Rosary doesn't respond. She isn't sure if Agatha is playing another one of her tricks. She knows that her sister can be quite slick.

"Okay I will," Agatha replies after she stares at Rosary for two minutes. Her sister continues to creep toward her as the barrel of the rifle creeps closer to Agatha's forehead.

The red dot is blinding Agatha, and she raises her hand in front of her eyes.

"You don't have to point that in my eyes. Give me a break. I don't have any weapons on me. Go ahead and check if you don't believe me."

Rosary takes another step, reaching her hand out to pat Agatha's side pockets. They're empty. Rosary then pats the pockets on her sister's buttocks. She feels her cell phone.

Agatha keeps her arms raised even though they're starting to feel sore.

"I knew you never trusted me," Agatha says.

"Do you blame me?" Rosary asks, breaking her silence.

Agatha giggles as she shrugs her shoulders, "I guess not."

"Always thinking that everything is a joke," Rosary replies.

"Everything is a joke...especially you," Agatha says as she cackles once again. "You've always been a joke, hiding like a little bitch. I've been standing here out in the open, waiting for you to shoot me. You can't even do that right."

Rosary closes her eyes for a moment. She imagines pulling the trigger and watching Agatha's henchmen enter the building, shooting bullets. She imagines a bullet shot directly in her forehead...BULLSEYE.

As she shakes her head, tears fill her eyes.

"Oh...you're gonna cry now? Wipe those tears bitch and finish this war!"

Rosary blinks back her tears. They spill down her cheeks and into the corners of her mouth.

She wants to scream in her sister's face. She wants to call her names and tell her what a horrible person she has become. She has become a murderer, or the devil.

*So have you Rosary Chime.*

"You won't do it," Agatha continues to taunt Rosary, "You can't. Why do you think I stand here weaponless? You don't have the BALLS to shoot me. I'm very precious to you. I'm..."

The sniper rifle's barrel blows a bullet, piercing through Agatha Chime's heart.

It takes her by surprise, shattering her chest and making her fall to the ground. Blood pours over her breasts and onto her purple blouse. Her body shakes from shock and her eyes stare into Rosary's unforgettable look of pain.

Rosary places her knees onto the ground as she takes her sister's hand.

"I missed my target. You're the first person for that," Rosary says as her tears pour down her cheeks.

Agatha's tears spill down the sides of her temples. She slowly smiles, quietly giggling as blood pours out of her mouth, "Liar," she manages to whisper.

Rosary laughs and cries at the same time as she takes Agatha in her arms. Rosary looks up at the ceiling and screams at the top of her lungs.

"I'm ready to retire anyways," Agatha whispers, "Time to say sorry to mom."

As Agatha dies in Rosary's arms, Rosary rocks back and forth like her mother used to do in the institution.

She leans into Agatha's ear, "I love you."

# NINETEEN

Regret has settled in.
Feeling guilty flows through her veins like an infection in an opened wound.

Her heart is wounded with pain. Her mind spins in circles as she stares at her sister's dead eyes. One last tear trickles down the side of her temple.

"I finally made that clean shot," Rosary says to herself, "I did it! I did it you bitch!" she yells in Agatha's face, "Torturing me! That's what you get!"

Agatha's phone chimes a whistle, notifying Rosary that someone has texted her. Rosary checks the message. It's Benny from the prison.

The message reads:
*Where the HELL are you, Adeline? You're late!"*

Rosary suddenly becomes anxious and frightened. She needs to get out of here fast before Agatha's henchmen come looking for her.

But she doesn't want to leave her sister here alone.

Rosary stares into space, imagining the bullet slipping backward out of Agatha's chest and her sister standing back up with her arms in the air.

Everything is a blur with tears in her eyes. She can't concentrate. She can't think of what to do next. She's scared of the repercussions of her behavior. Agatha's men will come after her. She knows this for a fact. They might even come for Tony De Carlo.

She has put the agent in harm's way. They might even kill him at the hospital.

Rosary is frantic. She shouldn't have killed her. They should've talked things through. Their anger always keeps them from moving on with their lives.

Rosary snaps out of her trance and hurriedly texts Benny back, "I'm on my way. Don't you worry sweetie pie."

She then slips the phone into her back pocket, strapping her rifle over her shoulder.

For the first time in her life, Agatha looks peaceful. Rosary stares at her, unsure of what to do. She truly doesn't want to leave her here alone. She wants people to think that she's still alive.

Quickly, Rosary pulls the cell phone back out of her pocket and looks up a map. She finds directions for leaving the building without having to walk through the city.

It takes her a few minutes to study the map.

Another message pops up:
*Hurry love. We miss you.*

Rosary slips the phone back into her pocket and then bends down on her knees. She then places her hands under Agatha's body and lifts her up over her shoulder, struggling and grunting.

Only weighing one hundred pounds, this should be a piece of cake.

Rosary can't believe that she's doing this. She also can't believe that she had enough energy to lift her. It's crazy and fascinating at the same time. She feels this burst of adrenaline. She feels like she can run a marathon.

Leaving the warehouse, she carries her sister over her shoulder as she walks through a meadow filled with dandelions.

After walking for only ten minutes, the weight of her sister's dead body starts to take its toll and Rosary suddenly walks like a zombie, tears filling her eyes.

She isn't sure if she's crying because she killed her sister or because she made this awful decision to take her dead body with her.

*I'm too precious to you...*

Of course, Agatha is too precious to Rosary. They made a promise to their mother. Rosary will take care of Agatha and help her sister get through her own death.

Rosary laughs. That sounds absolutely insane.

An hour later, Rosary is slow and tired as she takes each step toward the church. She's carrying her sister in her arms, whispering a silent prayer that her soreness will end soon.

When Rosary spots the church in the distance, she cries happy tears.

She's almost there...

She must look like a crazy loon carrying a dead body to a church. But she doesn't care at the moment. She promised herself that she would give Agatha a proper burial and a candlelit vigil. She's not that big of a monster.

However, she would disagree with herself at this moment. She feels like a monster for shooting her sister. She feels like the bad guy.

*There's that guilt again...she can make me feel this way even in death.*

As Rosary slowly approaches the church steps, dragging Agatha's lifeless body, Pastor Nicholas peeks out of the window from behind a curtain. He looks absolutely terrified.

*I didn't expect Rosary TO BRING HER HERE!*

Pastor Nicholas quickly opens the church doors and takes Agatha's dead body into his arms.

It's like a weight has been lifted off of Rosary's shoulders...literally. Her arms and neck are aching with pain and her legs are sore. She has developed a migraine at the base of her skull as it crawls into her brain like a spider.

*I need a vacation...*

Pastor Nicholas places Agatha on the couch inside of his office. He then heads toward the adjacent bathroom to retrieve a wet wash rag. He cleans up the blood from her face and chest.

"What have you done?" the pastor asks frantically as he rips off Agatha's blouse.

As he waits for an answer from Rosary, he wraps a blanket around Agatha's naked chest.

Confused, Rosary says, "I didn't want her to be alone."

The pastor whirls around, "You brought her here!" he yells.

Rosary is taken aback. This has been the first time in her life that Pastor Nicholas has yelled at her. She hasn't been sure if he had that kind of voice in his throat.

"I...I didn't know what else to...to do," Rosary stutters.

She doesn't like angry Pastor Nicholas. He's a completely different person. It's as if the devil has taken over his body. He is truly upset with her, and it is breaking her heart.

The pastor's eyes are sad as he watches Rosary shake with fright. He immediately feels guilty for yelling at her.

He feels ashamed but also terrified of what she might do to him.

He stands up, grabbing Rosary and pulling her into his arms, hugging her tightly. Rosary cries out for the death of her sister. She cries loud and hard into the pastor's chest.

"Sshhhhh...my dear child. It will be okay," the pastor promises, "I will take care of everything. You don't need to worry."

Rosary lets out a long and exhausted cry. The pastor pats her on the back as he gives her another hug, "You need some rest. I'll take care of this mess."

He slowly picks up Agatha into his arms and gestures for Rosary to lie down on the couch. She follows his directions, watching him leave the office without saying another word.

Rosary lies awake as she tries to listen to the sound of a shovel hitting the ground out in the back yard. The bay window to the office faces the back yard, a convenience for the pastor to watch what is going on behind his church.

The pastor digs into his flower bed, destroying the dirt and flowers that he had placed there to cover Rosary's belongings. The duffel bag sits next to Agatha's dead body.

The pastor stops digging, looking over at Agatha as if she'll jump up and yell, "April Fools!" He waits another full minute, imagining her laughing about being shot.

As he shakes his thoughts out of his mind, he falls to his knees, crying out. He then grabs Agatha one last time and cradles her in his lap.

"It had to be you," the pastor whispers, "It was time to end this war."

Rosary watches the pastor from the bay window. Tears spill down her cheeks. He must feel the same pain that she feels right now.

"I'm so sorry," she says aloud, turning from the window and lying back down on the couch. She covers herself with a wool blanket.

Closing her eyes, she falls asleep.

Agatha is inside of her warehouse, standing by the front doors, reaching her bloody hands toward Rosary. She's begging for help as she's covered from head to toe with her own blood.

"Help me," she begs, crying.

Rosary points her rifle at her sister's head.

"You deserve it bitch," Rosary answers as she can hear someone creeping behind her.

As she turns to look, she suddenly hears the piercing sound of a gunshot. She feels excruciating pain and sudden pressure through her chest.

Rosary looks down as she watches the blood pour out of the bullet wound.

There's another shot, sending Agatha's lifeless body to the ground.

There's a third shot, sending Rosary forward, landing on top of her sister. She's completely immersed in Agatha's blood. She can't breathe as her face is stuck between Agatha's breasts.

Rosary tries to lift her head, but she doesn't have the energy or the ability to do so.

She begins choking on her sister's blood that continues to pour inside of her mouth. She becomes frantic as she can no longer speak or ask for help.

She wants to know who shot her. She needs to turn around and face her killer.

But she can't. Her attacker stands behind her, laughing at what he has done.

She knows that laugh...

Rosary chokes to death, exhaling her last breath...

Her eyes pop open like the cork of a champagne bottle. She hurriedly sits up, checking the wound on her chest.

There's no blood, no bullet hole, nothing.

She sighs, looking around the quiet office. She's exhausted, wishing that she could move on from this nightmare. She must move on with her life.

Rosary lies back down, closing her eyes, drifting off back to sleep.

Pastor Nicholas places Agatha's body inside of the four feet hole that he has dug up. This will have to do until he has more time later.

He quickly looks around the area to make sure that no one is watching him or creeping around his church. He can't be too careful. There are too many "bad people" that both women have come into contact with. Someone might have a hidden agenda.

He then covers Agatha's body with the dirt, spreading it with the shovel as if he's spreading icing on a pan of brownies. He replaces the flowers in their proper spots and then picks up Rosary's duffel bag. He then gestures the symbol of a cross with his hand across his chest.

He searches around the area one last time before going inside to check on Rosary.

Rosary awakens two hours later to the smell of fresh-brewed coffee. Her mouth is dry and her stomach growls from starvation. She can't even remember the last time she had something to eat or drink. It hasn't occurred to her that she might be dehydrated.

She feels sick to her stomach.

As she sits up, she spots Pastor Nicholas pouring coffee into two mugs. He then slips cream and sugar into both mugs before looking over his shoulder at Rosary.

His smile is sad, but he seems cheerful than he was when she first arrived.

"The beast has awakened," he teases.

Rosary chuckles as she takes the hot mug from his fingertips, "Thank you."

As she blows the coffee to cool it down, she watches the pastor sit down next to her. He looks tired and weak. He looks like he hasn't slept for days.

Dealing with Rosary and Agatha would make anyone exhausted.

Rosary clears her throat, "I've also come here to tell you goodbye," she blurts out.

The pastor slowly sips his coffee as he stares into Rosary's eyes, "I'm not surprised. I didn't expect you to stay here after what you've done."

Rosary looks down, feeling ashamed. It's hard to look into his painful eyes.

"I'll pray for my sins."

"I've already done that for you," the pastor answers as he places his mug onto the coffee table. "I've also prayed for your safety. You're going to need it."

Rosary nods in agreement. She does need all the help she can get. She knows that she's in big trouble and there's nothing she can do about it.

"You might want to secure that fifty grand that you carry around inside of that duffel bag. It fell out of the yellow envelope. Here," he says, lifting a green satchel bag from the floor. "Use this." He smiles as she takes the bag from his grasp.

Rosary doesn't want to leave her comfort zone. This is all she has ever known. She doesn't have anyone else to help protect her and guide her along the way.

*Maybe you need to stop relying on other people...*

The pastor suddenly looks uncomfortable. He takes another sip of his coffee before taking in a deep breath. He then exhales, taking a moment to tell her the news.

"And also," he continues, "Detective Anthony De Carlo called you here a little while ago. He stated that it's time for you two to meet up. He gave me an address."

His statement sends shivers down her spine.

"Yes, we do need to meet," Rosary agrees, chugging the rest of her coffee.

"Then I guess you better get going," the pastor says sadly.

His heart is breaking into pieces. He can't lose Rosary too. He doesn't want to let her go. It's bad enough that he's lost Sherry and Agatha. He can't lose the last Chime.

They both stand up, giving each other a long hug.

"I love you my dear. I will always be here for you."

Rosary cries in his arms. She doesn't want to leave but she knows that it's the best thing for her to do. She needs to not only save herself but save Pastor Nicholas as well. She has brought him into this mess, and she must get them both out.

She has to steer clear of the pastor, so Agatha's henchmen leave him alone. She doesn't want them anywhere near this church. She must think about other people's lives.

"I love you," Rosary replies, kissing the pastor on his cheek. "I'll keep you updated of my whereabouts...always."

Rosary collects her belongings and heads out of the office. She then walks down the aisle like a snail, turning around to wave goodbye to the pastor one last time.

Pastor Nicholas waves back with tears in his eyes.

Rosary still feels sick to her stomach as she slowly walks toward a deserted and run-down neighborhood. She isn't sure why De Carlo would want to meet here. She would've felt more comfortable at his house. He's acting strange and she doesn't like it one bit.

And how did he know that she was at the church? Did he call around to find out information? *Well...he is an FBI AGENT!*

Rosary shakes her head, one of the many mysteries of Anthony De Carlo. He always seems to be one step ahead of her, even if he has no clue as to what is going on in her life.

There's no way that he knew about the warehouse. He has been at the hospital. He doesn't have anyone to follow her. None of his fellow officers are speaking to him. Curtis and Tiara want nothing to do with him anymore.

This thought makes Rosary quite sad. The man has lost everyone in just a year. He's better off sailing the seas like he wishes to do.

But he had been wishing to do it with HER.

As Rosary thinks about sailing on a boat with Tony De Carlo, she approaches another warehouse located about six miles from his house.

*Maybe he's meeting me here to kill me...*

That is quite a possibility. He has been angry with her for GOD knows how long.

He has lost all trust within their relationship. He still has love for her but it's not as deep as it used to be. He has had some time to think about things. He has had time to create different scenarios in his mind that would benefit his life in a drastic way.

Some of these scenarios don't include Rosary Chime.

And he's okay with that. He has come to terms with the fact that she's not his type. She's right. She doesn't want to be a "rebound" and quite frankly, she doesn't deserve it. She deserves someone who genuinely loves her and would do anything for her.

De Carlo stands at a gate that is attached to a fence in front of the warehouse. He watches Rosary approach him with a green satchel on her back and the duffel bag strapped to her shoulder.

He smiles, some things will never change.

Rosary smiles back as soon as she sees his bright white teeth.

She laughs as De Carlo pulls her into his arms, lifting her up into the air and hugging her tightly. He doesn't want to let go but he knows that he has to.

Their relationship would never work out. He has come to terms with this information that has been brewing inside of his brain for days.

He sets her back onto the ground, fixing the front of his belt. Rosary notices that he still doesn't have his gun attached to the front of it. His badge still isn't inside of his front pocket.

He looks as though he lost a couple pounds. He looks refreshed and full of life.

He looks happy.

"I was ordered to bring you into the station by Curtis Garcia," De Carlo admits.

Rosary's heart flips, sinking into the bottom of her stomach. She knew that something was up. She knew that she couldn't trust him! It's a trap! *I should've called my lawyer!*

Rosary quickly looks around the deserted area. She will kill whoever she has to kill in order to escape. This is not how she planned their meeting. She wasn't prepared for this.

"BUT" De Carlo continues, seeing her frightened expression, "I will not honor that request." He smiles.

Rosary takes a deep breath and exhales as De Carlo laughs. She suddenly laughs with him, feeling like a fool. She doesn't understand why she can't trust this man.

"Besides," he continues, "I'm a retired FBI agent as of..." he checks his watch, "one hour ago. I no longer have to follow orders."

Rosary smiles as she nods, "Finally did it huh? Time to go sailing," she says, looking around the area once again. She notices a blue vehicle parked inside of the fence and next to De Carlo's SUV. She's puzzled, wondering if someone is hiding inside of the blue car.

De Carlo watches her eyes set on both vehicles.

"You have got to trust me Rosary Chime," he says, turning toward the direction of the vehicles, "The blue one is yours. I brought it here this morning. I figured you needed a getaway car," he laughs loudly.

Rosary laughs with him. That car is Jada De Carlo's. It was her pride and joy, a brand-new Honda Civic. It was something that his wife always wanted.

De Carlo shrugs his shoulders, "I don't need it anymore. She's no longer with me. It's just been sitting in my garage collecting dust. It can be more useful for someone else."

He then places a finger on her cheek and softly rubs it, "I'm going to miss you Rosary Chime. Are you sure that I can't convince you to stay with me? We don't have to be husband and wife, just friends enjoying each other's company."

His offer does sound appetizing, but she knows it's not something she wants to do at the moment. She wants to live off the grid in some far away land surrounded by forests and mountains. She wants a cabin out in the middle of nowhere.

She has explained this to him, but he keeps trying to persuade her otherwise.

Rosary chuckles, "Thank you for the offer...again...but I need time alone."

De Carlo nods, "I know. I figured that I would try again," he says, pulling out a yellow envelope from his back pocket. "Here's the rest...fifty thousand. I spoke to Pastor Nicholas. And before you think negative," he pushes as he watches Rosary's eyes become suspicious, "I figured that I would call the church first because he's your mentor. And..." he continues, "he apologized for hitting me over the head."

They both burst into laughter.

"I understand that he's very protective of you," De Carlo continues.

Rosary nods, "He certainly is."

"I also have this..." De Carlo replies as he digs into his front pocket of his jeans. He pulls out Sherry Thomas's rosary bead necklace, "I was able to fix it my love."

Rosary bursts into tears as she takes the necklace from De Carlo's grasp. She feels the jewels between her fingers as she places them around her neck.

"I can't believe you did this for me," she says.

"Why wouldn't I?" De Carlo asks, "You are very special to me. I want you to know that I am always here for you."

Rosary smiles as she kisses her mother's necklace.

"Don't squeeze too hard. I won't be around to fix it again," De Carlo teases.

Rosary bursts into laughter once again, "Oh I won't. Not this time."

De Carlo grabs her and pulls her into his arms, squeezing her with a long hug. His heart hurts with sadness. He desperately wants her to come with him.

Rosary's whole entire body aches with sadness. Her legs feel shaky, and her arms feel numb. She has to say goodbye and move on with her life. Maybe someday they can meet again.

De Carlo kisses her lips, long and hard.

"A couple other things to mention," De Carlo continues as he takes a step backward, "I spoke to your lawyer this morning. Expect a phone call from him. He's apparently been trying to find you. I gave him your number if you don't mind." De Carlo chuckles.

"I have been meaning to call him," Rosary says.

"He's been very worried."

"I'm sure he is. He probably had no idea that I left prison."

De Carlo laughs, "Oh yes, he did. Your sister had a big mouth."

Rosary shakes her head in sadness. *Of course, that bitch would rat me out.*

"Last thing," De Carlo says, clearing his throat, "Detective Shawn Cobbler was told to play a little, 'cat and mouse,' game with you. He was also very intimidating toward Phoenix Weatherby. He held her at gunpoint. She told him about your whereabouts. He was told by my superior,

Shania Brown, to follow you in order to figure out your plans. They basically used you in order to find the killer. Shania Brown wanted to be the hero, but it didn't work. You were too fast and too sneaky for them to keep up with you apparently."

*Detective   Shawn   Cobbler...newspaper-good-smelling-cop...*

"Peach cobbler or cherry cobbler?" Rosary asks.

They both burst into laughter.

As they stare into each other's eyes, a sudden awkwardness looms inside of their silent thoughts. They both know that this situation isn't funny, but they have to make the best of it.

"I had a suspicion that the killer was Adeline Montana weeks ago," De Carlo admits.

Rosary watches his eyes look around the area. He's too embarrassed to see her reaction.

"But I didn't want to believe it. I couldn't," he continues as he reaches inside of his jacket pocket. He pulls out a glass bottle of perfume.

Rosary is puzzled, staring at the bottle as if it's been possessed by a demon.

"This was left behind from victim...Amelia Dickinson. I smelled this same scent the day I met your sister at the prison. It's the smell of poison. It's what made the attraction that I had for her that very moment. Her scent was tantalizing."

Rosary's heart crumbles into tiny pieces. This man had the suspicions of Adeline Montana this whole time and he never told her.

*Who's the ruthless one now?*

This completely blows her mind. She kept this same information from him because SHE was afraid that he would either feel embarrassed or scream in a burning rage.

Rosary takes the perfume bottle from De Carlo's grip. She imagines herself splashing the poison directly into his eyeballs, making them burn. She watches him fall to his knees and beg for forgiveness. She watches his eyelids burn off as the smell of burnt flesh flows into her nose.

Rosary's silence continues. She really doesn't know what to say. Maybe she's better off not saying anything so she doesn't leave with regret chiseled into her mind.

De Carlo then takes her hand as he turns toward the vehicles. Rosary's heart is racing. For some reason, she still thinks that someone is going to jump out of the car and shoot her to death.

"Oh…and uh…" Rosary says when they approach the vehicles, trying to ignore what he just confessed. Her silence must be killing his insides. "I promise I won't kill another living soul ever again." She's trying to believe her own words of encouragement.

They both burst into laughter once again, breaking the awkwardness. "I'll hold you to that."

Rosary still feels some sort of tension and awkwardness between them. He seems to be stalling all of a sudden and she isn't sure for what. She must get going before they're caught.

She isn't sure by who but there's always a possibility that someone is lurking around every corner of the Earth…waiting to squash them like a bug.

"I have one more thing for you," De Carlo says, seeing her uneasiness.

Rosary is trying not to feel like she's ungrateful for his help, but she really needs to go.

She feels antsy and anxious. She suddenly feels as though the world is about to come crashing down on her. She feels terrified and angry that De Carlo would set her in a trap like a poor fly stuck inside of a spider web.

She doesn't know where to turn or where to hide.

She wants to pull the webs away from her shoulders and face. She wants to scream at the top of her lungs. She wants to lunge at De Carlo and beat him to a pulp with her angry fists.

"Rosary," De Carlo shouts, snapping her out of her awful thoughts, "Take a look."

De Carlo lifts a small-sized carrier up into the air. He then opens the caged door.

Rosary hears her cat, Berry, meowing. "My baby!" she shouts, snapping out of her trance.

She then pulls her cat out of the carrier and hugs him for what seems like an eternity. She kisses the top of his head and then pets his whiskers, whimpering.

He purrs, rubbing his head under her chin, licking her cheeks.

"How did you...?" she begins to ask but De Carlo holds up his hand.

"I had to fight to get him, but Tiara eventually let him go. She said she didn't have time for a pet anyways."

Rosary gives De Carlo one last hug and then places her cat back inside of the carrier. She then places the carrier onto the passenger seat, climbing into the driver's seat of Jada De Carlo's Honda Civic. She's ready to go and get the hell out of this city.

As she pulls away, she blows De Carlo a kiss.

His cell phone rings, Curtis Garcia is calling him.

De Carlo answers with a smirk, "Bye my sweet Rosary Chime!" he yells, waving.

He then hears Curtis screaming at the other end of the line.

De Carlo hangs up, smiling a devilish grin.

# IMMERSED BY BLOOD

Angela Sanner is a full-time writer with many written works such as books, novels, poetry and film scripts. "Gwyneth" and "Clinophobia" were her first and second published novels. Her fourth novel, "Play Me A Song," is coming soon! She has directed three short films of her own which include: "A Dash of Charlie," "Her Seething Hollow," and "Leaving the Dead Rose." Thank you for your support!

Milton Keynes UK
Ingram Content Group UK Ltd.
UKHW021932281024
450365UK00017B/1045